M000196574

BOOKS BY TINA FOLSOM

Guardian Undone is a work of fiction. Names, characters, places, and incidents are the products of the author's imagination and are used fictitiously. Any resemblance to actual events, locales, or persons, living or dead, is entirely coincidental.

Published in the United States

Cover design: damonza
Author Photo: © Marti Corn Photography

Printed in the United States of America

GUARDIAN UNDONE

STEALTH GUARDIANS #4

TINA FOLSOM

1

Zoltan slammed his fist onto the armrest of his throne and rose to his feet.

"Imbeciles!" he yelled.

Only a dozen demons were assembled in the throne room, messengers who brought news from up top—the human world. Months, hell, two years, had gone by since they'd brought him any decent intelligence on the Stealth Guardians, the protectors of humankind, who so far had thwarted every single one of Zoltan's attempts to expand his power and reach his goal of world domination.

Frustration charged through every cell of his body, bringing his green demon blood to a boil. With it, he could sense something else approaching: a migraine-like attack that would cripple him for minutes, if not longer. These painful episodes had started long before he'd become the leader of the demons, the Great One. He'd always managed to keep them hidden from his underlings. Still, he'd had some close calls, and if his subjects ever found out that he wasn't the picture of strength and power he portrayed, well, he wouldn't be the Great One for long.

He descended from his throne, eager to leave the vast cavern where flames shot through crevices in the rocks, throwing eerie shadows onto the jagged walls and uneven ceiling. Without a word, he motioned to his right-hand man, Vintoq, to release the assembly, and headed for one of the four exits.

A voice stopped him. "Oh Great One, you haven't heard my report yet."

Zoltan spun around and glared at the demon who'd dared to speak. His eyes fell on a stout blond man. He appeared nervous, but when Zoltan charged toward him, he didn't shrink back.

"Oh Great One," Vintoq interrupted. "Why don't I handle this for you?"

Anger already boiling over, Zoltan now directed his glower at his second-in-command. Had it been another time—or had Vintoq been more discreet—he would have acquiesced, but he couldn't allow his subjects to get the impression that Vintoq could make him do anything he hadn't thought of himself.

"I'm fully capable of listening to another useless report," he snapped, dismissing Vintoq's suggestion with an angry swipe of his hand. "And if his report is as disappointing as all the others', then I'm also fully capable of taking his head off."

Vintoq immediately bowed in deference.

"Good." Zoltan turned back to the blond demon. "Make it quick. My patience wears thin." And the painful attack was impatiently waiting in the wings.

Bowing, the demon said, "Oh Great One, I bring good news. I have discovered a psychic."

"A psychic?"

Zoltan wasn't the only one who echoed the word in disbelief. A rumbling of low voices traveled through the throne room, amplified by the rock walls.

"There hasn't been a confirmed report of a real psychic in twenty years! True psychics are rarer than a needle in a haystack." Or a demon with a brain.

Zoltan grunted in displeasure. "You're wasting my time!" He reached for his dagger, drawing it from its sheath.

"I have proof!" the demon quickly added and pulled a folded sheet of paper from his coat pocket.

Zoltan snatched it and unfolded it. He stared at the drawing, then waved it in the air. "What is this supposed to be?"

"She draws the things she sees in her visions. That"—the demon pointed to the piece of paper—"is one of the things she saw: a Stealth Guardian portal."

Zoltan looked back at the drawing and focused his eyes on the hastily scribbled lines and blotches. This psychic was no artist, but she was able to convey the essential idea. Zoltan recognized the distinctive dagger that the Stealth

Guardians carried and noticed that it was engraved in a door that looked like it was part of a stone wall. Could it really be a portal? Could this person truly be a psychic?

"Are there more drawings like this one?"

The demon nodded. "Many more. Different ones of portals, buildings, weapons. But I didn't want to arouse her suspicion, so I only took one that I thought she might not miss."

Zoltan raised an eyebrow. One of his underlings had a brain and knew how to use it? Definitely a novelty. But he stopped short of praising his subject. It was too early for that.

"What's your name?"

"Colton."

Zoltan nodded at the demon, then addressed the assembled messengers. "Colton will pick three of you to follow his lead and check out this psychic to make sure she's real. If she is, we have to bring her to our side. She's valuable beyond all else. A true psychic can provide us with information and insight on the Stealth Guardians that will enable us to destroy them. This is our key to winning the war."

The demons nodded dutifully.

A memory of what had happened two decades earlier when he'd last had a psychic in his grasp was suddenly all too vivid again.

He'd brought her to their side. She'd succumbed. But then the Stealth Guardians had swooped in and killed her. Zoltan's gut knotted, while his temples began to throb with the first waves of his migraine. "I'm warning you all. If she slips through your fingers, your blood will paint this cave green. I hope we understand each other."

"Yes, oh Great One," they said in unison, whether out of loyalty or fear, Zoltan didn't care. As long as they obeyed him and executed his orders faithfully.

With a nod, Zoltan rushed past his subjects and hurried into the corridor leading to his private quarters, his temples throbbing from the horrible pain. This attack was worse than the previous ones. He'd tried everything to make them stop, even human medication, but nothing halted the attacks or lessened the pain. As if he was cursed. He could only hope he would make it to the privacy of his rooms before he collapsed.

2

Winter Collins handed the tarot deck to her client. The woman had introduced herself as Jessica when she'd breezed into the tiny one-room shop just as Winter had been preparing to close for the day. Since it had been a quiet day and she'd barely made any money, she'd decided to invite the woman in.

"Please shuffle the cards," she instructed her now.

While Jessica followed her instructions, Winter noticed her glancing around the room. Most clients did the same, as if the décor might help them figure out whether she really could tell the future. She couldn't. But she was an excellent judge of character and could read people. Not only that, she knew what they wanted to hear. So she'd made it her profession to read fortunes.

The crystals that adorned every surface in her little shop, the incense that burned and infused the air with a mystical scent, as well as the pictures of occult artefacts and supernatural symbols that hung on the walls were mere accessories. Just as her gypsy-inspired outfit was all pretense. Yet Winter didn't feel bad about what she was doing. In today's world, people needed hope. So what if she provided it by telling her clients that they would get the job they wanted, meet the love of their lives, and overcome their current troubles, no matter what those might be? She wasn't hurting anybody. Besides, many of her clients came to her because they'd received a gag gift from a friend—particularly since she'd started offering gift cards online—and others because they had nobody to talk to. The same way people went to their family doctor to talk about their problems, they came to her for a glimmer of hope to brighten their dull lives.

"What now?" Jessica interrupted her thoughts.

"Cut the deck," Winter demanded, speaking slowly and quietly. She'd learned that speaking in a low voice caused the clients to instinctively draw closer. It created an atmosphere of intimacy, as if big secrets were about to be revealed.

When Jessica placed the deck on the purple velvet cloth that covered the small round table between them, Winter took the deck and closed her eyes for a moment, humming a few notes. Then she laid ten cards out in a Celtic Cross pattern, placing them facedown on the table, while the bangles on her wrists jingled.

Just because she didn't believe in tarot readings, didn't mean she hadn't learned the rudimentary rules of her craft. She was familiar with the meaning of all the cards in the deck, whether they displayed upright or upside down, not wanting to be tripped up by a client who might know enough to call her out as the fraud she was.

"What's your question, Jessica?" Winter asked her customer.

"My question?" There was a look of confusion on Jessica's face. This was her first reading.

"Yes, the reason you came here today."

Because there was always a reason. Maybe the man she was in love with wasn't making a declaration of love as quickly as she'd hoped, or perhaps she'd applied for a job and had still not heard back for an interview. Though, oddly enough, Winter couldn't put her finger on what concern Jessica had. Normally she got an inkling of her clients' desires pretty quickly. A lovelorn look, an anxious twitch; there were so many tells that gave away a person's internal state.

"Uh, yeah, I, uh, wanted to know if my boyfriend is cheating on me," she finally said.

"Hmm." Winter nodded. She wouldn't have guessed that this was what the woman was concerned about. Jessica didn't appear to be worried about an unfaithful boyfriend. Winter did a mental shrug. Maybe she was just tired and therefore not attuned to the woman's emotional state.

"Well, then, let's see," she said instead and turned over the first card of the Celtic Cross. It was the moon card, a card that suggested that unusual, supernatural events might occur. Though it was also a sign of lunacy. Not something she wanted to tell her client. So she started with a vague comment. "Unusual events brought you here."

The woman's eyes widened in surprise.

Winter suppressed a sigh of relief. Even a broken clock was right twice a day. She turned the second card over and followed her intuition in interpreting the High Priestess card, telling her client that she was strong and could weather any storm. She was on autopilot now. Once a client was hooked with a few correct assumptions, they would gobble up anything Winter offered.

By the time Winter had turned over the last card, she'd told Jessica that her boyfriend was true to her, but that she needed to be in charge of her own happiness and not let it be dependent upon another person. Always good advice, no matter the circumstances.

"Thank you, thank you so much," Jessica said and reached into her purse.

Winter collected the cards from the table and put them back into the stack, setting them neatly to one side, ready for the next day, while Jessica retrieved some cash.

"Is that the right amount?"

Winter glanced at the banknotes and nodded. "Thank you. Please come again."

Once the door closed behind Jessica, Winter flipped the deadbolt and turned the sign in the door to the side that read *Sorry, we're closed*. Then she pulled down the shade on the glass door and turned around.

She didn't get any further. Blinding pain shot through her forehead, making her knees buckle. She reached for the closest thing to steady herself, the windowsill, and gripped it for support.

"Shit!" she cursed.

This wasn't the first time this had happened to her. And somehow she knew it wasn't going to be the last time either. And the pain wasn't even the worst part. It was only a precursor of the terrible mental assault that would follow. It was much like a nightmare—a nightmare while awake.

She held onto the windowsill, squeezing her eyes shut, hoping against all odds that by closing her eyes she could block out the awful images that pounded down on her like relentless rain.

Poison-green was the first thing she saw. Two dots of a poison-green color that almost blinded her before the dots retreated and a face became visible. The face of a man. An angry man. A violent man. A man who wasn't human. She knew that much, because no human had eyes like that. Poison-green eyes that seemed to spew pure evil. And those evil eyes were glaring at her.

As her field of vision widened, she was able to make out more. The terrifying man was tall with broad shoulders and a muscular torso clad in what looked like army fatigues. A guerilla fighter? She looked for an ammunition belt slung across the creature's upper body, but there was none. No gun or rifle either. Instead, in his hand, he clasped a dagger. A dagger that was now veering toward her.

She tried to scream, but no sound issued from her throat, just a helpless gurgle. Fear paralyzed her. This was how she was going to die. She'd seen it before. Seen too many times how the knife plunged into her heart and robbed her of her life.

She braced herself for the inevitable, steeled herself for the pain, because death wasn't painless, wasn't instant like people wanted to believe. But the green-eyed man stopped in mid-motion. It took her brain almost a second to realize what was happening. A sword sliced through the creature's neck, separating the head from the body.

While the head dropped to the ground, rolling somewhere out of sight, green liquid spurted from the wound. Blood? Green blood! She had no time to move, to get out of the way, and was doused in it immediately. Some of it splashed into her eyes, blurring her vision. She could make out a man behind the falling monster, but couldn't truly see him through the horrible green blood.

Before she could thank her rescuer, she saw more poison-green dots appear in the distance. More green-eyed monsters?

Frantic, Winter stretched out her arm in their direction, pointing at them, while she tried unsuccessfully to form words, realizing only now that she was chained to a wall. The man who'd killed the creature whirled around toward the approaching green-eyed attackers. She wiped her eyes with her hand, managing to regain some of her vision.

They were in a cave with flames licking along the rock walls. All of a sudden, the smell of rotten eggs assaulted her. Grunts and curses reached her ears. And more poison-green lights flashed. More monsters. Too many.

She cried out in desperation.

This was hell. There was no escape from this.

This was her end.

Winter collapsed. And just as quickly as the nightmare had begun, it stopped. She forced open her eyes and looked around. Touched her torso, her thighs, her face. No blood, no green stains on her clothing, no wounds. No monsters in her little shop.

She was alone. For now.

She managed to get up, shaky at first, but with every step she gained more of her strength. Breathing heavily, she walked to the other end of the shop, where a door with a sign saying *Private* led to her apartment. She opened it and walked through a small hallway into the large live-in kitchen.

On the counter next to the coffee machine stood a tray with several small, orange plastic bottles containing prescription drugs. She hated taking them, but when she went without them for too long, the daytime nightmares came more frequently. At least the pills dulled her senses and calmed her somewhat. Right now, she needed one, because she was shaking.

The things she was seeing had become more vivid in the last few months. More real, even though she knew none of it could be real. Monsters like that couldn't exist. Poison-green eyes, green blood? Not even Hollywood could invent such ridiculous creatures, monsters that looked perfectly human apart from those two features. Yet whenever she saw them, whenever she saw the poison-green eyes, she was more terrified than she'd ever been in her life. Because she knew they were coming for her.

She felt them calling to her. Heard their voices in her head. And every time she heard them, she felt her blood turn to ice, because she felt the evil physically. Every cell in her body revolted. She knew she couldn't succumb to them. Couldn't give in to their calls. Or she would end up like her grandmother. She would spend the rest of her days in a mental hospital, clawing at the walls, claiming to hear voices in her head and see things that weren't real.

Tears shot to Winter's eyes, when she recalled the last few visits she'd had with her grandmother. The nurses had restrained her with leather straps bound to her bed for fear she would hurt herself or others. She'd had a crazed look on her face, and the things she'd said had made no sense. Two days later she was gone. Dead.

Winter swallowed two of the pills and closed her eyes. She was determined not to end up like her grandmother. That's why she'd gone to a psychiatrist shortly after she'd had her first daytime nightmare, hoping he could arrest the progression of the disease she'd inherited. He'd diagnosed her with PTSD caused by the trauma of losing her grandmother, the last member of her family, even though that event had occurred two decades earlier. He'd prescribed anti-psychotic medication and suggested drawing the images that assaulted her as a way to deal with what she saw, as a way to make them less scary. He'd promised it would help her deal with the episodes, as he called them.

But she knew he was wrong. Deep down she knew it, knew that she was going crazy, that she was succumbing to the same mental illness that had taken her grandmother.

And no amount of art therapy, counseling sessions, or pills could cure her.

3

Logan could hear the giggling of the children as he approached the great room. Life in the Stealth Guardian compound in Baltimore had changed dramatically two and a half years earlier, when Leila, Aiden's mate, had given birth to twins.

At first, everybody had thought that Aiden would retire from his duties as warrior, and the couple would move out of the compound and into their own secure residence. But Aiden and Leila had surprised everybody by staying. They wanted their children to grow up among the warriors of their race, teaching them from an early age what it meant to be a protector of mankind.

Besides, there was strength in numbers. The compound was still one of the safest places for any Stealth Guardian. Particularly Stealth Guardian children, who were more vulnerable than their immortal parents and needed to be protected to assure the continuation of their race. Danger was everywhere—because the demons were everywhere.

Over the past two years, the demons had killed a number of Stealth Guardians, though fortunately they hadn't been able to find and destroy another compound, as they'd done in Scotland several years earlier. That compound, which had belonged to their ruling body, the Council of Nine, had been relocated to another secure location.

Logan hesitated at the door to the kitchen and great room. He had nothing against children, but the twins were a handful. He missed the peace and quiet the compound had afforded him and his brethren before their arrival. But he would never voice that thought to Aiden, knowing that to his old friend the birth of his twins meant more than just becoming a father—it meant that he was finally getting over the death of his own twin, Julia.

Logan opened the door and stepped into the room. The smell of food wafted toward him, while laughter alerted him to the twins' whereabouts. To his surprise they weren't running around the vast room with their parents chasing after them. Leila and Aiden were sitting at the kitchen island, enjoying a leisurely breakfast.

The reason for the rather civilized scene in the great room was a visitor: the children's grandfather, Barclay, known to everybody else as Primus, the head of the Council of Nine.

"Morning," Logan said.

"Hey, Logan," Aiden replied, while Leila said, "There's an omelet in the oven if you want it."

"Thanks, Leila."

Then he looked over to Barclay, who was now getting up from the couch where the twins had been using him as a jungle gym. "Primus, guess you can't stay away, huh? Didn't those two monsters visit you just three days ago?"

Barclay grabbed both kids, tucked one under each of his arms, and walked toward Logan. "As much as I love these two, I didn't come to see them. Though I must admit, I relish every opportunity that presents itself to spend time with them."

"They adore you," Aiden threw in. "Leila and I wouldn't mind if you took them with you for a couple of days." He winked at his wife, who smiled in agreement.

Barclay chuckled. "Nice try, but I'm not a young man anymore. I don't have the kind of energy it takes to run after Xander and Julia all day long. Neither does your mother. So thanks for the offer, but no thanks."

Aiden exchanged a look with Leila and shrugged. "I tried."

Barclay dropped the two kids back on their feet.

Xander immediately ran toward Logan. Logan lifted him up into his arms and ruffled his black mane. He'd never seen a kid with such thick hair, except for the boy's sister, whose hair was just as thick and only a fraction longer. "Hey, buddy." Then he looked back at Barclay. "So what brings you to us?"

"I have an assignment for you and Manus. A very delicate one."

Logan lifted an eyebrow. In most cases, assignments were delivered electronically to the command center, then handed to the warrior who was either best suited for the specific task, or, as in many cases, didn't already have too many other missions on his plate.

"Shall we go to the command center?" Barclay suggested.

Logan nodded and handed Xander over to his mother.

While they walked along the corridors of the vast building, Barclay was silent. Logan wasn't one to press his superior for information, especially when said superior was clearly not ready to talk, and therefore walked in silence too.

Only two people were in the command center. Pearce sat in front of the computer console, where he monitored several large screens, one with data rapidly scrolling across the black surface like raindrops, another one showing images from several cameras, and a third one with various open windows for emails and other messaging applications.

Manus was sitting at a desk nearby, leafing through a stack of folders. Both looked over their shoulder when the door opened, a casual greeting on their lips. But the moment they spotted Barclay entering with Logan, they turned around fully and sat up straighter in their chairs. A sign of respect for the older statesman.

"Primus," both said.

"Pearce, Manus, good to see you." Barclay nodded at Pearce. "Would you give us the room please, Pearce?"

Surprised at the request, Pearce stood up. "Uh, sure." He pointed to the door. "I'll be right outside then."

"There's breakfast waiting in the kitchen. Why don't you take a break?" Barclay suggested.

"As you wish," Pearce said tightly, clearly a bit miffed about being expelled from his domain. After all, he was the resident geek, in charge of electronic communication and security devices.

"Thank you," Barclay said, turning to watch Pearce leave and close the door behind him.

During this short unguarded moment, Manus mouthed a silent question to Logan. But Logan could only shrug. He didn't know why Barclay was being so secretive. In general, assignments were discussed openly between compound mates. There was no need for secrecy among them. After all, they were all working toward the same goal: destroying the Demons of Fear, their mortal enemies, and saving humankind from their destructive influence.

"I'm sure you're wondering what this is about," Barclay started, his look bouncing between Manus and Logan.

Logan met his superior's gaze, but didn't respond. He knew he wasn't expected to.

"Let me make this short. The mission you'll be tasked with is to remain entirely confidential. Only a few people outside the council are privy to what I have to share with you." He cleared his throat. "We've been made aware of the existence of a psychic."

Logan sucked in a breath.

"A psychic? A real one?" Manus asked excitedly.

Barclay nodded.

"You've gotta be kidding me," Manus continued. "There hasn't been one in years, decades even. True psychics are rarer than a virg—"

Logan rammed his elbow into Manus's side to stop him from finishing his crude remark. Neither Barclay nor Logan needed a reminder of how rare psychics were. And how valuable they could be to the Stealth Guardians. Though psychics were supernatural creatures, they had no telltale aura, no special scent, making it impossible to identify them amongst a crowd. They could hide in plain sight.

"Where did you find him?" Logan asked.

"Her. An emissarius came across her in Wilmington, Delaware. She runs a small tarot shop."

"She's a tarot reader? That's not exactly what I'd call a true psychic." Logan shook his head. "Are you sure your emissarius got it right? Every town has a few tarot shops, and just because it says psychic in a sign in the window, doesn't mean the proprietor's the real deal."

Barclay tossed him a stern look. "I'm aware of that. That's why I sent a second agent to bring us more information."

"And?" Manus asked curiously.

"She confirmed the findings of the first. The woman is a true psychic, though we have reason to believe that she's unaware of her gift. Which makes the situation even more difficult than it already is."

There was a short pause, during which only the sounds of breathing cut through the silence.

"If she's not aware that she's a psychic, how can your emissarii be certain?" Logan interjected into the quiet of the room.

"Because she draws what she sees in her visions."

"Excuse me?" Logan asked.

Barclay let out a breath. "She's been seeing a psychiatrist." He shrugged. "Mentally unstable. He prescribed anti-psychotic medication and suggested art therapy as a way for her to deal with her so-called nightmares, her visions. Our agent took photos of the drawings that she displays openly in her shop."

He pulled out his cell phone and tapped his finger on it. A moment later he turned it so Logan and Manus could see the display. Both stepped closer. Logan focused his eyes on the drawing. The psychic was not particularly talented artistically, but even though the chalk drawing was crude, he had no trouble identifying what it was.

"The Callanish Stones." The location of the council compound that had been destroyed after demons had attacked it.

"That's not all." Barclay scrolled to the next picture.

This drawing was somewhat better, almost as if the psychic's vision had been clearer. "A council member's dagger." The nine intertwined rings on the handle were clearly in the right formation. It was no accident. No coincidence.

"She knows things about us, things no one outside of our confidence would know. If the demons get wind of her, if they can bring her to their side and use her visions against us ..."

"… they could annihilate us," Logan finished the sentence.

Barclay nodded gravely. "Yes. If she knows where our old council compound stood, we have to assume that she knows the location of the new one, and perhaps many other compounds around the world. Or if she doesn't know yet, her next vision might tell her. In either case, it makes us more vulnerable than we've ever been." He sighed. "And with her mental state in the condition it is, she has no chance fighting the influence of the demons once they set their sights on her. If they haven't already."

Logan exchanged a look with Manus. It would be a monumental task to protect this woman and shield her from the demons, an assignment that wouldn't just last a few weeks or months. She would have to be protected until she was strong enough to fight off the mental influence a demon could exert on her and make her turn to the dark side. And that could take years. In the meantime, word that the Stealth Guardians had found a true psychic could not be allowed to spread. Barclay was right to keep this secret under wraps. How long Logan and Manus would be able to keep this from their compound mates, however, was another question.

"We have to act quickly," Barclay interrupted Logan's thoughts. "I sent you everything we've been able to put together on her on short notice. I wish we could run a more thorough background check, but I'm afraid we don't have that kind of time. She's a free spirit, defies conventions." He pointed to the computer. "The file is only accessible under your logins. Pearce has no access to it. Study all the information carefully, but quickly. You can't afford to make any mistakes on this one. The existence of our species is on the line." Barclay met Logan's eyes. "That's why I chose you. I know you'll follow the council's directive to the letter."

"Yes, Primus."

Manus tilted his head to the side. "And I'm the comic relief?"

Barclay tossed him a derisive look. "You weren't my choice for this job, but I got overruled by the other members of the council. Apparently you have some fans who thought that the callousness you displayed in previous circumstances might be of use in this assignment."

"I didn't know I was known as callous."

"You're known for many things, Manus," Barclay admitted, "but I have neither the time nor the inclination to list them all for you. I'm sure you're aware of your own faults. Just be glad that we need every guardian who's willing to perform the duties of a warrior, and are therefore willing to overlook your many infractions. For now."

The reprimand shut Manus up. For now.

Logan had to hand it to Barclay: he knew how to handle his subordinates.

"Well, then," Barclay said, "let's go over the details."

Logan nodded. He knew the drill, but protecting a psychic would be different. Because of her visions, she couldn't be treated like a normal charge. She had to be let in on secrets that could never be revealed to others. "How much are we authorized to tell her about our species?"

"Tell her?" Barclay stared at him as if bitten by a hornet.

"Yes, so we can get her cooperation and protect her effectively," Logan elaborated.

"Protect her?" Barclay shook his head. "She's a security risk to us, one that calls for one action, and one action only. You're not charged to protect her. The council voted to eliminate the threat."

The last words echoed in Logan's head.

Eliminate the threat. He knew what it meant.

Kill her.

4

"Argh!"

Winter yelled out in pain and stared at the blood spurting from the wound. The blade had been razor sharp, the aim perfect—if she'd wanted to cut her own index finger off. Which hadn't been her intention. But the piece of the salami had slipped from her fingers when she'd tried to slice it thinly to make herself a sandwich.

"Goddamn it!"

Could she not do a single thing right today? First she'd overslept, then she'd almost burnt her hair with her hairdryer because she'd been distracted by a news report on the radio, and now this.

She ran to the other side of the kitchen and ripped open the top drawer. While she rummaged through it, she kept pressure on the injured finger so she wouldn't drip blood all over the counter. Without success. She tore a sheet off the kitchen roll and wrapped it around her finger, soaking up the blood, while she continued to look for the Band-Aids she knew she'd placed in the drawer only a week earlier—since she'd exhausted her supply of first-aid materials after a similar mishap.

Well, she just wasn't good with knives, or fire, or hammer and nail. Two left hands, her grandmother had commented many years earlier and suggested she find a job that didn't require her to handle any tools.

"That's just great," Winter griped, ready to throw a fit when she suddenly spotted the box of Band-Aids in the farthest corner of the drawer.

With difficulty she managed to pull one Band-Aid from the box and remove it from its protective sleeve. More blood oozed from the wound, before she managed to seal it with the bandage. She continued to keep pressure on it, and after a minute or two, it seemed that the blood had started to clot.

Winter sighed and cleaned up the mess she'd made, wiping the blood drops from the counter, then looked back at her attempt at making a sandwich. Suddenly she wasn't really that hungry anymore. She reached for the salami and looked at it.

"Uh, what the heck." She bit into it, biting off a large piece and chewed. She wasn't going to give slicing a second try.

She shoved the two slices of bread back into the bag and sealed it, when a sound startled her. Still chewing on the salami, she spun around and looked down the short hallway. The door that led to her shop was closed. She was sure that she'd hung the sign indicating that she was on a lunch break on the door. So why could she hear the old floorboards creaking in the shop? Had she forgotten to lock the door?

Winter wiped her hands on a towel, then marched to the connecting door and opened it. A tall man stood in the shop, his back turned to her as he looked at some of the drawings that hung on the walls. There was something familiar about him. She felt a spark of recognition ignite in her mind, yet no memory was forthcoming.

"I'm sorry, but we're closed for lunch," she said in a firm voice.

He turned confidently, as if he wasn't at all surprised that he wasn't alone anymore. Their eyes met. She froze, couldn't move an inch. The spark of recognition she'd felt when looking at his back returned, this time stronger. As if she'd seen him somewhere, though she didn't recognize his face.

And she would have. What living, breathing woman in her prime—and she was in her prime, despite the fact that she hadn't dated much lately—would ever forget a face like his? Chiseled features, strong cheekbones, pronounced black eyebrows, a straight nose, short black hair, all underscoring his classic good looks. A chin that spoke of determination, yet lips that promised something different, something that didn't jive with the stature of this man who looked like he belonged on an army recruiting poster. Army, yes, because his body was muscled, not in a bodybuilder kind of way, but like a man who'd seen combat. Everything about this man was hard, every muscle seemed to have a purpose, yet his lips were parted, betraying a softness, kindness, that lived inside him.

Nevertheless she saw that he was troubled. That he needed answers. That he needed them now. Couldn't wait.

"Miss Collins? Miss Winter Collins?" he asked.

The timbre of his voice reverberated in her chest as if he'd used her ribs to make the sound. "Yes," she murmured, feeling breathless all of a sudden.

She tried to shake off the feeling of lightheadedness. Why did she suddenly feel so dazed? She'd met good-looking men before and had never been so tongue-tied. Somehow she knew her reaction to him had nothing to do with his looks, but with the feeling of recognition.

He saved you in your dream.

It couldn't be. She knew lots about dreams, about the fact that you couldn't dream of a face you'd never seen before. That dreams were merely a way for your mind to work through the things you'd experienced during the day. But she also knew that her nightmares were different. That they showed her things that couldn't possibly exist. But if he was the man from her nightmare, the man who'd slain the green-eyed monsters, then why was he standing in her shop now?

She wasn't in the middle of one of her nightmares. She hadn't felt the pain that preluded them. She knew she was lucid. She had to be wrong about him. He was just another customer. One who'd clearly not seen the sign in the door that said she was on her lunch break.

"Take a seat," she blurted out, even though she'd planned to tell him to come back after her break.

"A seat?" he repeated, as if he hadn't heard her.

She pointed to the table and the two chairs. "Yes, for your tarot reading. That's why you're here, isn't it? Because you have questions. What's your name?"

"Logan," he said slowly, walking toward the table even slower, as if he was reconsidering his visit.

She'd seen that hesitation in first-time clients before. It had taken all their courage to come, and then, when they were inside the shop, they faltered and left. But Logan didn't strike her as the kind of person whose courage suddenly left him. No, it was something else. As if somehow he didn't really want to know the answer to his question.

Winter sat down and waited until Logan had taken the seat opposite her. "The reading is forty dollars. I hope that's okay?"

He nodded. "No problem."

She took the deck of cards and handed it to him. "Shuffle them."

She watched his hands as he did so. Long fingers, clean nails, yet these were not the hands of a man who worked in an office. Too many scars, too many injuries, too many calluses. He worked with his hands, with his entire body. She could imagine how he must look when he worked, his upper body bare, his muscles flexing, sweat making his skin glisten. She imagined her hands sliding over the tanned ridges...

Oh God, what was wrong with her? She felt like a bitch in heat.

She coughed.

"When should I stop?" Logan asked.

His question made her wonder how long she'd been staring at him, objectifying him, imagining him half-naked. "Uh, now is good."

He placed the deck on the purple velvet.

"Cut the deck," Winter instructed.

He followed her command and waited. Winter took the cards and laid out a Horseshoe Spread between them, glad to have something to do with her hands.

"Tell me your question, Logan." She looked up from the cards and found him staring at her.

~ ~ ~

He should have listened to Manus, who'd suggested approaching her invisibly, taking her out without her ever knowing what was happening to her. But Logan hadn't listened, because eliminating an innocent wasn't a task he took lightly. It was an irreversible step, and therefore he had to be sure that he was doing the right thing. It meant he had to confirm that she truly knew about the Stealth Guardians and presented a danger.

As sentinel, the leader of this mission, he'd overridden Manus's protest and ordered him to stay outside in the car and watch for any demon activity. Grudgingly, Manus had agreed.

Logan had waited until Winter had locked up for lunch to make sure they would be alone. He'd used his supernatural skill of passing through solid objects to enter the shop. Considering the report on her had claimed she was mentally unstable, he knew he could tell her she'd forgotten to lock the door with such conviction that she'd doubt her own recollections. It hadn't been necessary, because she hadn't questioned him on that point.

Instead, she'd stared at him. Just like she was staring at him now.

"Your question," she prompted.

"I have an important decision to make. I need to know if I'm making the right one," he said, because he had to give her something so she wouldn't get suspicious of him.

Winter nodded and turned over the first card. He didn't even glance at it. Instead he looked back at the various drawings that hung on the walls. One was the same depiction of the Callanish Stones Barclay had shown him on his cell phone, another the drawing of a council member's ceremonial dagger. There were a few more drawings, all black chalk on a white background.

"You're both giving orders and taking orders," Winter said and briefly looked up from the card.

He nodded.

She dropped her gaze back to the cards, and turned over another one, while Logan used the time to let his eyes wander to the wall behind her, where a door with the word *Private* led to the remainder of the small townhouse. He was about to look away, when he noticed the markings above the door frame: runes. The same kind of runes that adorned the Stealth Guardian compounds. The report hadn't made any mention of them. But if Winter knew what runes looked like, she already knew too much.

"This time you're not sure the order you've received should be followed."

Logan snapped his head back to Winter and noticed a frown on her face. As if she saw something she couldn't make sense of. As a true psychic, could she see what he was thinking, what he was planning? Because now that he'd seen the runes, seen for himself that just by her careless displaying of their secrets, she could harm their species, he knew his decision was made. He had to follow the order.

"You're struggling within you," Winter added.

No, she couldn't see inside him, or she would see that his struggle was over, his decision made. What she was doing was the usual mumbo-jumbo any tarot card reader dished up for their clients. A few meaningless sentences that could be interpreted any way. But the things she'd drawn, the things she was displaying on the walls of her shop, those were her visions, those were the truth.

"Fighting, struggling..." she stammered and pressed one hand to her temple.

More dramatics. He had to hand it to her, she was a great salesperson.

Her lips quivered, and her breathing accelerated. "No, not again, no..." Her face distorted in pain and she lifted both her hands to her face, pressing them against her head as if trying to stop it from exploding.

Alarmed, Logan said, "What's wrong?"

She shot up from the table, staggering, knocking her chair over in the process. "No! Please, no!"

Logan jumped up, just as Winter grabbed at the table for support, only managing to get hold of the purple velvet. Off balance, she fell backwards, sending the tarot cards flying. Logan lurched forward and caught her not a second too soon. They both crashed to the floor, but Winter landed on him and not the hard floor, where she could have injured herself.

"Winter, are you alright?"

She thrashed in his arms, but he knew that it wasn't to escape. She was in the middle of what somebody else might have interpreted as an epileptic fit, though it wasn't quite as violent. But he knew better: she was having one of her visions. The report had indicated that because she was unaware of what was happening to her, she was most likely fighting the visions physically, which manifested as a full-body spasm.

"You've gotta let go, Winter," he said softly and brushed a few strands of her dark hair out of her face.

He knew now was the perfect time to slip her the poison he'd brought. It was painless and almost instantaneous. Within a few seconds she would be dead, and she wouldn't even know. It was how he'd planned it. But to take her life now, when she was at her most vulnerable, repulsed him, though he knew it was his duty.

Would he hesitate if she weren't a beautiful woman? Would he hesitate if she weren't so sensual, so fascinating? He knew he wouldn't. But looking at her now as he cradled and comforted her, doubts rose in him. Doubts about his orders, his duty.

With Winter in his arms, he rose. She was still shaking, but less so now, as if the vision was fading. He carried her to the door, opened it and walked through, kicking it shut behind him. He passed the short hallway, which opened to a live-in kitchen. A table with four chairs stood in the middle of the large room, a ragged sofa against one wall. He lowered Winter onto the sofa just as she opened her eyes again.

Their deep blue color almost blinded him, and he froze in his movements, still holding her as if in a lover's embrace. Which of course it wasn't. This woman would never have another lover, because she would die today. For a moment, regret flooded him. But then he caught himself. He was here to do his duty to his kin, to protect his species from danger. He'd sworn it many decades ago, and he'd never broken that oath. He wouldn't break it now. No matter how hard it would be to kill this woman.

Winter looked at him awkwardly.

"You collapsed," he hastened to explain.

She swallowed visibly and nodded. Instinctively, Logan released her from his hold, and she quickly sat up.

"I'm sorry," she said, avoiding his gaze.

What had she seen? Did it have something to do with him? Or his brethren? Could he perhaps get some more information from her before he had to execute his plan?

"What happened?" he asked. "Is it epilepsy?" He knew it wasn't, but he wanted her to talk.

She shook her head. "No, no." She made a dismissive hand movement. "Just an episode of..." She hesitated, then cleared her throat.

He could see the lie before it left her lips.

"... dizziness. I probably need to hydrate and eat something."

She wasn't going to share her secrets with a stranger. Logan couldn't blame her. And she'd just given him the opening he needed.

"I'll get you a glass of water."

"You don't have to. I can do that myself." She made a motion to rise.

"I insist." He turned to walk toward the sink. "Where do you keep your glasses?"

"In the cupboard over the sink."

He opened the cupboard and took out a glass.

"But don't use the water from the tap. It tastes like chlorine. There is filtered water in a pitcher in the fridge."

He turned to the refrigerator, which was located on the other wall and realized that opening its door hid his actions from Winter entirely. He filled the glass with filtered water, then placed the pitcher back on the shelf, but before closing the door, he reached into his inside pocket and retrieved the small vial and emptied its contents into the glass. The poison was colorless and odorless. Winter wouldn't notice it.

After placing the empty vial back in his pocket, Logan closed the refrigerator and turned back to Winter. She'd gotten up and was walking to the kitchen table, where papers, crayons, and other knickknacks were strewn about.

"I'm sorry it's messy. I wasn't expecting any visitors," she apologized and grabbed some of the sheets of paper to put them in a pile.

More drawings like the ones in her shop. Yet different. On these she'd used colored chalk and crayons in addition to black.

"These your drawings?" he asked and moved closer to get a better look at them.

"Yes." She shrugged. "I'm not really talented. But it helps me."

"May I?" Logan reached past her to pick up one of the drawings.

"Do you draw too?"

He set down the glass of water. "A bit," he lied and reached for the next drawing in the stack. "Expressionism? Realism? What are you drawing?"

Another shrug. "Just things that come into my head."

She spread the stack, drawing Logan's attention to one sheet with a black circle surrounded by a swirling mass of fog or smoke. Inside the circle were dots of green, neon green.

He looked closer. Demon eyes. Winter had visions of the demons.

"This looks interesting. What is it?" he asked, though he knew it for what it was: a demon's vortex. A portal a demon cast in order to travel from the Underworld to the mortal world.

"Just some lights in the fog," Winter said casually, too casually. She was afraid of the image. Her hand shook as she shoved the picture underneath another one, bringing a different drawing into the foreground.

Logan's eyes fell on it. He held his breath. It wasn't another vortex, it was something much more important—that is, if he was interpreting it right. "What is this?"

"Oh, tunnels, underground tunnels. Like a maze," she replied, her voice scratchy now. She reached for the glass.

He bent over the table. It was a map. A map of the Underworld. He knew it instinctively. Virginia and Wesley, the only two non-demons who'd ever entered the Underworld and escaped it alive, had reported that the demons' lair was a maze of interconnected tunnels, but they'd only seen a small part of it and hadn't been able to bring a permanent record of it back. But this, Winter's drawing, seemed much more extensive, maybe even complete.

Winter didn't just have visions of the Stealth Guardians and their fortifications, she also saw demons and was able to draw their lair. She was valuable beyond all comprehension. If her visions could be focused, the Stealth Guardians would have a powerful ace up their sleeve.

A movement in the corner of his eye made him snap his head to the side.

Winter was bringing the glass to her lips, about to drink the poisoned water.

Shit!

He shot his arm across the table in front of Winter as if trying to reach for something and stumbled on purpose so he crashed against her. The fake fall knocked the glass out of Winter's hand. It fell to the floor and shattered there, the water spilling on the wood floor where the poison could do no harm.

Winter let out a gasp and braced herself against the edge of the table.

Relieved, he exhaled. Nobody would be drinking poison today.

"Oh, so sorry," he apologized to Winter. "I'm such a klutz sometimes. But I got so excited about these drawings. I think you're wrong about not being good." He was babbling, but he had to make her think that he was a hapless idiot so she wouldn't suspect what he'd been about to do: snuff out her life.

Change of plans. Winter needed to be protected. At all costs.

And in order to do that he needed to gain her confidence.

5

Logan insisted on cleaning up the mess that he'd made, and Winter let him, watching him as he carefully disposed of the glass shards and wiped the floor dry.

When he was done, he looked up at her, a hesitant smile on his face. "Sorry again."

"Don't worry about it. It's just a glass." She rose from her chair, feeling much better now.

The nightmare had been a powerful one, yet she'd managed to force it back, taking strength from Logan. Odd, how his arms around her had helped her calm herself during the episode, making her ordeal shorter and less scary than normal. Maybe if she had somebody who cared about her, somebody who'd be by her side during the nightmares, she would finally be able to conquer them and banish them from her life.

"Are you alright?" Logan asked, concern in his voice and a warmth in his eyes that hadn't been there earlier.

"Yes, yes, I'm fine, really. I can continue your tarot reading now. I'll lay a new spread for—"

His hand on her forearm stopped her. "It's not necessary."

She tried to ignore the way his hand made her feel, how it calmed her. How she wanted him to never let go. "But you came here with a question."

"It's not important anymore."

For the first time Logan smiled, and it was as if her entire kitchen suddenly lit up. Not only was he handsome, he had the most disarming smile she'd ever seen. Like a light in the darkness. Again the image of the man who'd beheaded the green-eyed monster of her nightmare flashed across her inner eye, but this time she tried to concentrate on the face of her rescuer. But before she could focus on her savior, he'd turned his back to her. She couldn't see his face. Only the back of his head and his short, dark hair.

"You still seem a little dazed," Logan said.

His hand on her arm was gone. She blinked and smiled at him, trying to ease his concern. "I'm perfectly well. Thank you. May I offer you something to drink? Or to eat?" Just so he would stay a few minutes longer and let her enjoy his company.

When he hesitated, she quickly said, "It's okay. I'm sure you've got somewhere to be. I shouldn't keep you. You've done enough."

"I don't have anywhere to be. Not right now anyway," he said. He shifted his weight as if he was uncomfortable—or nervous. "It's just... there's something I need to talk to you about." He motioned to the table.

She looked over her shoulder, but saw nothing of concern. Only her drawings, still strewn about. When she looked back at Logan, she noticed that he'd stepped closer, his expression unreadable.

"Those drawings," he started. "I know what they are."

Her breath hitched. Logan knew that the drawings were part of her art therapy and were meant to help her deal with her nightmares? But how? Doctor-patient confidentiality should have prevented her psychiatrist from breathing a word to anybody. So how did this stranger know? Or was he guessing? Was Logan going through something similar? Was he trying to tell her that he was just as crazy as she? That he was afflicted with the same disease? Was that why he'd been comforting her, knowing what it was like when the nightmares struck?

"They're nothing," she insisted.

"Listen," Logan said calmly, "I know it's difficult for you to talk about this to a... well, to a stranger, but if you'd let me explain."

Winter narrowed her eyes, suspicion creeping up her spine. "I don't know what you're talking about. I think it's better if you leave now. As I said before, I'm on my lunch break, and you're not interested in me continuing the reading." She pointed to the door. "Please."

Logan lifted his hands in a capitulating gesture. "I mean you no harm. And I wish I could make this easier on you, but there's no easy way to tell you what you need to hear."

Right now he sounded just like any conman who was trying to lure his mark into a trap. She'd allowed herself to drop her guard because of his good looks and kind demeanor. It had been a mistake.

Instinctively she took a couple of steps back, until the kitchen table halted her retreat. "Whatever you've got to say or sell or whatever, I'm not interested. Please leave."

He didn't move, neither making any attempt to leave the room, nor one to approach her. In fact, he remained frozen.

"I can't leave. You need to know the truth. The things you see in your visions are real."

"Visions?" She shook her head. "How do you know about the nightmares?"

"They're not nightmares. They're psychic visions. The green-eyed creatures you see, they're demons." He pointed to the table behind her.

"No." She snatched a quick breath. "You stole my medical file." She eased away from the table and toward the kitchen counter, where the knife with which she'd cut herself still lay. "What are you planning to do with it? Embarrass me? Ruin my business? Drive me crazy?"

She let out a bitter laugh and took another step toward the counter, avoiding looking at the knife so he wouldn't notice what she was trying to do.

"What for?" she continued, to buy herself more time. "If you've seen my file, you know I'm already going crazy. And you also know that I've got nothing you could want, no money, no possessions." She reached for the knife and gripped it, then pointed it in Logan's direction. "Now get out."

"Winter, please, hear me out." He pointed to the knife. "Put it away or you'll hurt yourself. I won't come any closer. I have no intention of hurting you, physically or otherwise."

He didn't seem to be intimidated by the sharp knife in her hand, and that fact made her nervous.

"Who are you?"

"My name is Logan Frazer."

"Your name is immaterial. Are you a criminal?"

"No, though I have to confess I entered your shop even though the door was locked."

She knew it! She'd been certain that she'd locked it.

"So you *are* a criminal! I told you already I have nothing. No money, nothing of value. I can barely make the rent every month."

"I'm not here to rob you. I'm here because—"

He interrupted himself and snapped his head in the direction of the door to the shop.

Her heart suddenly started pounding. Instinctively she held her breath, and then she heard it too: the wooden floorboards in the shop creaking under the weight of somebody's foot.

"You should leave before I scream and that customer hears me," she warned now.

He whirled his head back to her. "That's not a customer. The door is still locked. Whoever is in your shop broke in."

Confused, she opened her mouth to respond, but then Logan's phone pinged.

He pulled it from his pocket and looked at the display. "Shit! Demons!"

6

At first Logan had thought that Manus had entered the shop, passing through the locked door the same way he had done. But Manus's text message had squashed that assumption. Demons must have picked the lock and entered. How many, Logan didn't know. And there was no time to ask Manus.

In disbelief, Winter stared at him, mouth agape.

But the time for explanations had run out. The door was flung open, and several demons charged through the short hallway into the kitchen.

Winter screamed at the top of her lungs.

"Fuck!" Logan hissed. There were four of them.

Apparently these days Zoltan, leader of the demons, believed in throwing as much manpower as he could muster at a tiny problem such as a psychic. Clearly, he'd learned from his mistakes. And the demons had an advantage: there was no back exit through which he and Winter could flee.

"Stay back, Winter," Logan warned her, as she stood frozen at the kitchen counter. At least she still held the knife in her hand.

The four demons, their telltale green eyes glaring, charged at him. They were big creatures, humanoid in nature, but stronger and less vulnerable. Only weapons forged in the Dark Days could kill them. Logan now pulled such a weapon, an ancient dagger, from the concealed sheath inside his jacket.

"Come get me, you bastards!" he yelled. He had to keep them away from Winter until reinforcements arrived.

With blades aimed in his direction, the demons lurched forward. Logan made himself invisible, a skill unique to Stealth Guardians, and dove low to the left, avoiding his adversaries' daggers. Angry grunting sounds bounced against the kitchen wall.

"Get the psychic!" one demon ordered.

Over my fucking dead body!

Still invisible, Logan lunged in front of the demon who now separated from the other three and veered toward Winter. Logan sliced his dagger across the asshole's thigh, cutting deep.

Green blood spurted from the injured demon, accompanied by a cry of pain. He'd hit the femoral artery. Kicking him to the side with his foot, Logan managed to avoid being rained on. Relieved, he whirled around. The three able-bodied demons charged toward him like a wall.

"He must be here!" one of them grumbled in displeasure. "Fucking guardian!"

Still invisible, Logan jumped, aiming his foot at the demon to the left and kicking him back against the doorframe, while he let his right arm make a wide horizontal motion, aimed at the middle demon's throat. More blood spurted, but the demon wasn't dead. Logan had only grazed him.

"Gotcha!" one of the demons ground out.

Logan didn't have to look down at himself to know that he'd been sprayed with green demon blood, blood that gave away his position. Unlike any other substance, demon blood couldn't be made invisible.

"Shit!"

His advantage gone, Logan made himself fully visible to save energy and lunged at the demon again, but the two others came to his aid. And from behind Logan came the sounds of a struggle. The injured demon was trying to grab Winter, but Logan didn't get a chance to spin around.

He kicked one of his attackers in the balls and while the bastard toppled over, clutching himself and crying in pain, Logan aimed his dagger at the demon to his right, managing to deliver a cut across his chest.

Then a blade came toward him from the other side. Logan ducked away, but couldn't avoid it entirely. Pain seared his bicep. He drew back his other arm and flung the demon backwards. But the next one was already upon him. This time, Logan didn't have time to dive away.

Yet the demon's dagger didn't connect with Logan's chest. The creature suddenly froze, blood spurting from his neck, then he fell sideways. Behind him, Manus stood with a satisfied grin on his face and a bloodied dagger in his hand.

"You're welcome," Manus said and jumped at the demon Logan had just flung across the room.

Now free, Logan spun around.

Winter was fighting the injured demon at the kitchen counter. With one hand the bastard was trying to stem the flow of blood from his wound, the other was wrapped around Winter's neck. The knife in her hand was gone, though Logan noticed several cuts on the demon's arms.

Logan rushed toward them, gripping his dagger firmly. He snatched the demon by his shaggy hair, bent his head back, and sliced through his neck with such force that he severed the head from the torso.

He kicked the dead body to the ground, tossing the head after it like a useless piece of garbage. Which it was.

"You okay?" he asked Winter, who stared at him wide-eyed. He gave her a quick once over, but couldn't detect any wounds except for the redness on her neck where the demon had tried to choke her. Luckily he'd been so weakened by his blood loss that he hadn't had sufficient strength.

Winter's lips quivering, she nodded.

Angry grunting sounds made Logan whirl around. Manus was fighting the two remaining demons, holding them at bay as best he could.

Having reassured himself that Winter was okay for now, Logan went to help his compound brother. He ripped one of the demons off him, then aimed his dagger at the demon's chest. But the bastard was strong, stronger than the others he'd fought. Logan was surprised that Manus had been able to keep him at bay while simultaneously dealing with a second attacker. Logan could barely land a punch or a blow, let alone do any damage with his dagger.

"Shit!" Logan cursed. "Fucking demons!"

He couldn't see how Manus was faring with the other assailant, but he heard grunts and thuds, indicating they were still fighting. Finally Logan managed to kick the demon in his midsection, sending him back against the doorframe. Wood splintered, and an audible *ooph* escaped from his victim. The demon's knees buckled from the impact, and Logan saw the chance to end him. He lunged forward, but the demon, his green eyes flashing, turned tail and charged through the hallway and into the shop.

By the time Logan had caught up with him, the demon was casting a vortex in the middle of the shop. A mass of black fog and cold wind suddenly swirled in the center of the room, momentarily pushing Logan against the wall, the force of the magic blasting him away from the demon's portal. The blade slipped from Logan's fingers and slithered away in the opposite corner of the shop, out of reach.

But Logan caught himself quickly despite the loss of his weapon, and, using all his energy, he lunged for the demon entering the vortex, intent on preventing his escape.

His hand found purchase on the demon's forearm. Logan pulled, feeling the force of the vortex more intensely now. As if it wanted to devour him. But he wouldn't let it. The only good kind of demon was a dead demon. That was his motto.

The demon's second hand emerged from the dark fog and landed a punch. Logan's head whipped back, but he wouldn't be defeated so easily. With his free hand, he tried to reach for his boot, where he kept a second dagger, but his fingers couldn't reach that far, without releasing his grip on the demon.

"Shit!"

He had no choice now. Logan dove forward, into the vortex. But the demon was faster. A heavy boot connected with Logan's midsection, sending him flying out of the vortex and crashing against the wall of the shop. In the few seconds it took Logan to pick himself up, the demon disappeared, the vortex closing behind him, vanishing like a mirage.

"Fuck!"

But there was no time to cry over spilled milk. Logan turned and rushed back into the kitchen. Three dead demons lay on the ground, bathed in green blood. Relieved, Logan took a much-needed breath. But he didn't even get to enjoy that short moment of peace.

Winter screamed. Logan's gaze shot to her, his legs already moving. He charged toward where Manus was pressing her against the wall, his knife at her throat.

"Nooooooo!" Logan screamed.

Manus whipped his head to the side, staring at him, a look of resignation in his eyes. "It has to be done. The demons won't give up."

"No!"

But Manus turned his gaze back to Winter. Logan jumped, grabbed hold of Manus's wrist and slammed it against the wall so hard Manus lost his grip on his dagger.

"Fucking asshole!" Manus hissed and glared at him.

Logan didn't hesitate. He jerked Manus away from Winter, looped his arm around his fellow Stealth Guardian's neck and put him in a chokehold. Manus fought him, kicking his legs back and tearing at Logan's arm with his hands, but to no avail. Logan had the upper hand in this fight, and he was going to keep it. He couldn't lose. Not when Winter's life was at stake.

Later, he'd explain his actions to his friend and convince him that they had to protect Winter instead of killing her, but right now, with Manus running high on adrenaline from the fight with the demons, there would be no reasoning with him.

"Sorry, buddy," he murmured close at Manus's ear just as his friend stopped struggling and lost consciousness.

Slowly, making sure Manus didn't hit his head, Logan dropped him on the ground. Then he looked up at Winter, who stared at him, her face drained of blood, her lips quivering.

"He was trying to kill me." Then she looked toward the dead demons, motioned toward them with her hand. "Those things. Those monsters. They're like the monsters in my dreams. Green-eyed monsters." Her voice was shaking.

"They're demons. Demons of Fear. And they weren't dreams. You had visions of them, because you're a psychic, and that's why they came."

"To kill me," she stated.

Logan shook his head. "You're not worth anything to them dead. They wanted to kidnap you. Take you to the Underworld, so you would serve them."

A sob tore from her throat. "The fires, the caves..." She stared at him with a million questions in her eyes.

"I'll explain everything. But we have to leave. Now. You're not safe here anymore." He pointed to the hallway where the stairs led to the upper floor. "Pack a bag, just the barest necessities, medicines, a change of clothes, any cash you have, any valuables."

She nodded as if on autopilot. Logan watched her walk upstairs. When she was out of sight, he bent down to Manus and used his friend's cell phone to send a text message to the compound requesting backup and a cleanup crew at Winter's shop. He felt Manus's pulse. His friend would be fine, but in an extremely bad mood once he regained consciousness. It was best to be far away by then and explain everything over the phone.

After assuring himself that all the demons were indeed dead, Logan collected their weapons and tossed them in a plastic bag he found in a drawer. Since weapons forged in the Dark Days were rare, they were always a welcome bounty.

He heard Winter descending the stairs. Good, she'd followed his instructions and packed quickly. Logan glanced around the kitchen once more, and his eyes fell on the overturned kitchen table. Winter's drawings were scattered on the floor. He quickly collected several of them and shoved them into his jacket pocket.

"I'm ready," Winter announced from the hallway.

Logan turned to her. "Let's go."

7

Winter still felt numb as Logan led her to his car and helped her in. She couldn't speak. It felt as if she'd been in the middle of one of her nightmares, yet at the same time it had been different. It had been real. Which meant everything she'd ever seen during her episodes was real. The green-eyed monsters were demons and she had been right to fear them: they wanted to snatch her away and drag her to the Underworld. To hell. She'd actually seen herself there. As if it was her destiny. Or had Logan now altered her future? By killing the demons had he spared her from her fate?

"I'm not crazy," she murmured to herself.

"What?"

She met Logan's gaze. "I thought I was going crazy. I thought the nightmares meant that I was mentally ill."

"You're not," he confirmed and looked back at the street ahead of him as he weaved through light traffic.

And it was a relief. She didn't need the pills her psychiatrist had prescribed. Pills that made her feel like she wasn't really there. Like she was living in a fog. Now everything was clear again, but she still had questions. A million questions. And she had no idea where to start.

"What exactly is a psychic? I mean, does that mean I really am a fortune teller?"

Logan gave her a sideways glance. "In a way. Psychics can see into the past as well as the future. But that doesn't mean that what you see will necessarily happen. Just by communicating with somebody what you've seen, you may alter its outcome."

"What do you mean?"

"For example if you warn somebody of something that might happen, that person can prepare for it and thus change the outcome, change the future."

"Oh." Now she realized the impact any of her visions could have. And she'd had no idea, until these creatures had shown up and attacked her. "The demons... tell me about them. They seemed so strong. And their blood... I've never imagined a creature could have green blood," she said.

"They are evil to the core," Logan started. "Their blood and their green eyes are the only way they can be detected. And they've found ways to disguise their eyes, so we have a harder time spotting them."

"Colored contact lenses?" she guessed.

He nodded and tossed her an appreciative glance. "That, and sunglasses. The fact that they still use sunglasses makes us think that the colored lenses don't always work. We've suspected for a while now that the green color of their eyes is the result of some sort of chemical that might eventually burn through the lenses and render them useless."

"Hence the need for sunglasses as a backup?"

"You learn fast. That's good."

She had no choice. "I want to survive."

"And I'll make sure of that."

"You knew how to fight them."

"My people have fought them for centuries. And we'll continue fighting them until we've eradicated them," Logan said grimly.

"But they seem so strong. Even injured, that demon who pinned me would have choked me to death had you not killed him. I tried to fight him... I had the knife, but when I cut him, he just laughed as if it didn't hurt at all." She shook her head. "Don't they feel pain?"

"You fought bravely. But you didn't have the right tools."

"But I had a knife," she protested. "And all of you were fighting with knives." Which was strange in itself. Why not use guns against an enemy so strong?

"Daggers actually," he said with a sideways glance.

"No different than a knife."

"Our weapons were forged a very long time ago. From special metal. They are the only weapons that can kill a demon. Sure, your knife cut him, but it didn't really hurt him, nor would you have been able to inflict a mortal wound with it." He shrugged. "That's just how it is. You couldn't know. You really had no way of defending yourself."

Winter swallowed. It was true what people said, that during a dangerous situation a person wasn't really aware of how bad it was and what else could have happened. But afterwards, as the mind processed the events, all kinds of scenarios played out as the mind imagined the things that could have happened. She let the attack play out in her mind again, frame by frame—and stopped almost immediately.

Winter whipped her head to Logan. "You disappeared before the fight even started. I was in such a panic that I thought I was hallucinating, but now, looking back, I remember: you just disappeared."

He turned his head slowly, a hesitant look on his face. She saw him taking a breath.

"What are you not telling me?" she asked.

"A lot, I admit. Some of which I can't share with you. But this I have to, since you already saw it. I didn't disappear. I was still there, but I made myself invisible so the demons would have a harder time fighting me."

"Invisible?" she echoed, pressing her hand against her chest. "Like in the movie *The Invisible Man*?"

He nodded. "It's a skill we have."

"We?"

"My people and I."

Instinctively she edged away from him, her heart thundering now. "Who are you? What are you?"

He lifted one hand from the steering wheel and made a calming motion. "I'm an immortal warrior. We call ourselves Stealth Guardians. We're the defenders of the human race. Our only purpose in life is to protect humans from the influence of demons. We've been doing so for centuries."

She swallowed, let out a breath. "Immortal..."

"Yes. I'm two-hundred years old."

She shook her head in disbelief. But she knew it was true, felt it, just like she now knew that the demons of her nightmares—no, visions—were real. So why shouldn't immortal warriors be real too? At least that would level the playing field.

"I'm sorry. I know this is a lot to take in. I wish I could have given you more time to digest all this, but the attack took me by surprise. We weren't aware that the demons had already locked onto you. We only discovered your existence this morning." He stopped abruptly, as if the conversation was heading in a direction he'd rather avoid. "Anyway, it's a lot to take in."

"You knew I was a psychic when you came to my shop. You didn't really come for a reading," she said. It wasn't a question, just a statement she made to order her own thoughts. "How come I didn't know that I'm a psychic? That I have visions?"

"Most psychics, while naturals, need some guidance, some help so that they can master their gift. It's a powerful skill, one that can overwhelm a person. And the visions can indeed feel like nightmares. You saw demons, didn't you?"

She nodded. "They frightened me. I felt that they were coming for me. Their green eyes... when they looked at me with those poison-green eyes, my blood froze in my veins. I could feel their evil intent. I've never been so scared in my entire life."

"I understand. No wonder the visions felt like nightmares. But now you know better. You'll be better prepared next time it happens."

"Next time?"

"Your visions won't stop, just because you know they're real. Nightmares might stop once you've worked through the issues that cause them. Visions don't work that way. They're part of you. You're special. That's why the demons wanted you, so you can help them defeat us."

She frowned. "What?"

"You also saw other things in your visions, not just the demons. You saw our weapons, our strongholds. You can find us. And that makes you valuable to the demons."

"But I can't. I don't know anything about you and your people," she protested.

"You do. Even though you might not realize it." He put his blinker on and turned into a street that led into a park. "You drew things that could be used to identify us. In your shop hangs a drawing of a dagger. It's one of ours. And another drawing depicts the Callanish Stones, the place where one of our compounds was located. You drew those things without knowing their meaning, but the demons, they'd be able to put two and two together."

Winter put her hand over her mouth. "Oh no. But I didn't mean to. The psychiatrist... he said it would be good to draw what I see so that I could get over it."

To her surprise, Logan reached for her hand and squeezed it. His warmth was comforting.

"Don't beat yourself up. You couldn't know. And I got to you just in time."

"About that—"

"Later," he interrupted and stopped the car in a small deserted clearing with a bench and a hut that she identified as restrooms. "We need to get changed before we go any further."

"Changed? Why?"

He pointed to the green stains on his shirt and then to her. She looked down at herself and saw the same spots on her clothing.

"I need to bring you to a safe house. But to do so I need to make us both invisible, and—"

"Invisible? You can make me invisible?"

"Yes, with either my touch or my mind. But one substance defies my skill." He pointed to the green splotches. "I can't make demon blood invisible. If I made us invisible now, people would still see the blood on our clothes. And if demons were in the vicinity, they would find us. I can't risk that."

She nodded. "I understand."

He motioned to the restrooms. "I'll make sure nobody is inside. Then you'll go in and change, and I'll change out here, making sure nobody approaches. You'll be safe."

She looked into his eyes and knew he spoke the truth. Logan would keep her safe.

8

Zoltan rode the female demon hard. He had her bent over his desk in his study, her cargo pants down to her ankles, her ass bare, while he gripped her hips with both hands and slammed into her from behind. His pants were shoved to mid-thigh, just enough to give his cock and balls sufficient room to do the deed. This wasn't a romantic assignation, but a need he had to satisfy. There were always plenty of female demons willing to offer their services to him. After all, he was the Great One, and if they pleased him, he might even take one of them to his bed and favor her with more than just a quick fuck. Or he might not.

He pounded into the willing flesh, tuning out the sounds coming from the woman's lips, moans he knew were faked, and concentrated only on himself, his needs, his desires, his goals. Nobody else counted. Everybody else was expendable. Replaceable. Just like the woman at the end of his thrusting cock. He looked down at her, gazed at her long blond hair. Hers was straight, but he remembered a woman with curls, no, not curls, but braids, though he assumed once untied the hair was curly.

A loud knock on the door stopped his mind from pursuing the road he was on.

"What?" he yelled toward the door.

"Urgent news." It was Yannick, the demon responsible for all vortex circles in the Underworld, and thus the one who knew of all comings and goings.

Goddamn it!

Zoltan delivered two more thrusts, and with the second one, shot his semen into the blond woman. Then he withdrew and pulled his pants up. Not giving the woman any time to get dressed, he called out, "Come in, Yannick."

The door opened immediately. Yannick stepped in, while Zoltan zipped up and closed the button of his pants. The female grunted in displeasure at the interruption and hastily pulled her pants over her ass, but not before Yannick had gotten an eyeful.

"Off you go," Zoltan ordered and motioned to the door.

Scowling, she scampered away, and Zoltan made a mental note never to ask for her company again. Her attitude didn't please him.

Once the woman was out of earshot, he asked, "What news?"

"News from the group you sent to find the psychic."

"Ah, excellent!" His day was looking up.

Yannick cleared his throat. "Uh…"

Narrowing his eyes, Zoltan looked at him. He could see it in Yannick's demeanor. The news wasn't good. "Fuck!"

"One of them came back," Yannick offered and motioned to the door.

"Who?"

"Colton, oh Great One."

Zoltan glared into the dark corridor behind Yannick. "Colton! In here! Now!" Then he glanced at Yannick. "You stay."

Yannick froze and nodded, while Colton hurried into the room.

"Shut the fucking door!"

Shaking, Colton turned and shut the door, then pivoted to bow. "Oh Great One."

"Where are the others?"

"Dead. We were ambushed."

Zoltan narrowed his eyes in suspicion. "Ambushed?"

"By the Stealth Guardians. They were lying in wait for us when we got to the psychic's house. We never had a chance." Colton dropped his head.

"Elaborate."

"Uh… the, uh… Stealth Guardians knew we were coming. They were ready to fight."

"They're always ready to fight. You probably rolled in like a tank announcing yourselves. No wonder."

"No, oh Great One. We were careful. But they outnumbered us," Colton insisted.

But there was something in his eyes. His eyes flickered with an overproduction of the chemical that colored his eyes green. Like tears the substance oozed through his irises. A demon couldn't cry, however, other things could be conveyed through the eyes. Things like lies.

Zoltan had studied his demons closely over the last few years and learned to recognize the signs. He was by no means infallible in detecting a lie, but he didn't need to be. Better to stamp out one demon who turned out to be truthful than let one liar live.

"Outnumbered, you say? How many guardians did you encounter?" Zoltan asked calmly, almost casually, though inside his fury was already boiling, ready to burst from him.

"Many, a whole group." Colton's voice sounded less sure now, and there was a slight trembling in his hands, which he tried to disguise by clasping them together.

Zoltan stepped closer. "How many?"

"Maybe six or seven."

Another lie. This time so much easier to detect.

"How many?"

"Four?"

Zoltan snatched Colton by his throat. "The truth now."

Colton struggled to breathe. Zoltan eased his grip, giving him just enough air to answer.

"Two. There were two. But they were cunning, stronger than others."

Zoltan let go of Colton's throat. "Now was that so hard? Telling the truth, I mean?"

Wordlessly, Colton shook his head.

"I'm glad I was able to teach you something. Sadly, however, this lesson comes too late for you."

Zoltan pulled his dagger from the sheath at his hip and plunged it into the demon. "Never lie to your master, because he'll always find out."

Colton gurgled helplessly, and Zoltan twisted the knife in his gut until green blood bubbled up from Colton's mouth and spilled over his lips. Then he pulled his dagger out and kicked the demon backward, so he fell onto the hard stone ground.

Zoltan tore his gaze from the dying demon and addressed Yannick, "Put together my best warriors and send them out to find the psychic. Have them kill every Stealth Guardian they encounter, and everybody in their way. I want that psychic. Alive."

"Yes, oh Great One!" Yannick answered. Then he bowed and charged toward the door.

"And have the garbage taken out," Zoltan ordered, motioning to the floor. "It stinks of cowardice in here."

9

Logan tossed his stained shirt into a bag in the trunk of the car, pulled out a fresh one and slipped it on. He did the same with his pants, which also sported green bloodstains. It was standard to keep a change of clothes in the car for incidents like this.

He was zipping up when his cell phone rang. He retrieved it and looked at the display. He'd expected the call.

Logan looked toward the restrooms, where Winter was getting changed and stepped farther away from them, so she wouldn't overhear his conversation. He pressed *answer* and brought the phone to his ear.

"Man—"

"You fucking asshole!" Manus yelled into his ear, forcing him to hold the phone a foot away for a moment. "What the fuck were you thinking knocking me out like that? Are you out of your bloody mind? You practically ambushed me. Me! Your friend. You've got a beating coming, you fucking jerk! Explain yourself! Where the fuck are you? You left me amongst a load of dead demons!"

"Are you done with your rant?"

"No, I'm not done. I'm not done by a long shot! We had a job to do. And you stopped me from doing it. What the fuck got into you?"

"If you stopped ranting, I'd explain."

Manus mumbled something unintelligible.

"Now listen. We can't kill her. She's too valuable to us."

"The council took a vote. And neither you nor I can question it."

"They didn't have enough facts to come to the right conclusion."

"Oh, and you do? Fuck you, Logan!"

"Would you shut up and listen for a moment? The things she sees, it's not just about us. She sees the demons, too. Hell, she's drawn a maze that I believe is the tunnel system of the Underworld."

"So? You don't think the council knows that?"

"Don't you get it? With the information she can provide, we can find the demons' stronghold. We can destroy them."

Manus huffed. "*You* don't seem to understand that the council already took all that into account when they made their decision. They're not stupid, Logan. I'm sure they weighed the pros and cons. And the cons weighed heavier. Their decision is law. And you know it."

"We have to change their mind. If we show them the drawings I found in her place, we can convince them that she's more valuable to us alive than dead."

"We? No, buddy, no way. I'm not committing treason. And you'd better not either."

"I'm not committing treason. This is—"

"Tell me where you are. Where did you take her? We have to finish this job. Before the demons launch another attack. If she falls into their hands—"

"She won't." Logan looked toward the restrooms. He was running out of time to convince Manus. Winter could emerge at any moment. "So are you with me or not?"

"Not," Manus shot back. "I urge you to change your mind, because the council will never change its vote. And if you flee with her, we'll find you. The council will prosecute you. Don't do this. Come back now. The council need never know what happened today. I won't breathe a word of it."

Logan shook his head. "I can't do that. I'm sorry. She needs to live. We need her."

He disconnected the call and stared at the phone.

Going to a safe house was out of the question now. Manus would be able to find them. Just as he would be able to trace Logan's cell phone and the car just as soon as he spoke to the Baltimore compound. Pearce would run a trace in minutes, and soon after, several of his brethren would come to take him in and kill Winter. He couldn't let that happen. Now he not only had to hide from the demons, but also from his own people.

"Shit!"

"Something wrong?" Winter's alarmed voice came from the entrance to the restrooms.

Logan's gaze shot to her, as she walked toward him quickly, her eyes darting around as if looking for danger. She'd changed her gypsy outfit for jeans and an oversized sweatshirt and removed the dozens of bangles from her wrists.

Knowing she wouldn't believe if he told her that nothing was wrong, he decided to dish up a lie instead. "The safe house I was planning to take you to isn't available. We'll have to go somewhere else. And we'll have to cover our tracks." He motioned to the car. "Get in. We need to leave."

He took her bag and tossed it on the backseat, then slid into the driver's seat, waited until Winter was seated, and drove off.

"Where to?" she asked.

"I'm working on that." He tapped on the navigation system in the car and expanded the map so he could get a better overview of the area. "We have to ditch the car." And he'd already figured out where.

"But without the car—"

He tossed her a comforting look. "We'll be fine. There's other transportation. I'll keep you safe. I promise."

She met his look and held it for a few seconds. She nodded. "I trust you."

He swallowed hard and looked back to the street in front of him. She trusted the man who'd saved her life back there in her apartment. But would she trust the man who was supposed to kill her? What would she do if she found out? Would she still trust him then?

Logan pushed away the thoughts. It wasn't important right now. The only thing that mattered was getting Winter to a safe place, hiding her from the demons and the Stealth Guardians, and then figuring out how to convince the council to let her live under the protection of their people.

The Philadelphia bus station looked depressing, like an old mental hospital with fluorescent lighting. For a large city like Philadelphia, it was rather small. Located only a block

from the Convention Center and a few short blocks from
City Hall, it was smack-bang in the heart of the city.

Logan parked the car at a metered parking spot on the
same block and turned to Winter. "Take your bag. We're
leaving the car here."

While Winter retrieved her bag from the backseat, Logan
set an alarm that would disable the car until a Stealth
Guardian entered a code. It would prevent thieves from
absconding with the vehicle. Then he looked around to make
sure he hadn't left anything that could identify him or Winter
and got out of the car.

From the trunk, he pulled the bag with his soiled
clothing. He quickly navigated to an app on his cell phone,
typed in a short command, then memorized the three results
the app offered him. Then he locked the cell phone, dropped
it in the bag with the dirty clothes—leaving it switched on—
and zipped it back up. From the bag with the daggers he'd
taken off the dead demons, he took two blades, slipped one
into the sheath in his boot, the other into the inside pocket of
his jacket. Then he locked the doors with his key remote and
put several coins into the meter to mitigate the risk of the car
being towed within the next two hours. He needed to give his
colleagues enough time to follow the trail he was laying out
for them.

"Where to?" Winter was waiting for him on the
sidewalk.

Logan pointed to the bus station. "We need to buy
tickets."

Winter walked by his side as they headed for the glass-
fronted entrance of the building. "We're taking the bus?"

"Something like that."

He felt her eyes on him, her brows raised inquisitively.

"You'll see in a minute."

Logan opened the door and let Winter walk inside ahead
of him, while he looked around. There were a couple of short
lines at the ticket counters, about two dozen people sitting on
benches waiting for their bus, and a few lowlifes lingering
near the restrooms. As he walked farther into the hall, Logan
looked out through the side doors that led to the depot. More

people were waiting outside, some boarding a bus. He read the destination listed on the side: Chicago.

He steered Winter toward one of the ticket windows.

"I need your credit card," he said in a low voice.

She looked at him. "But won't the demons be able to trace us if we use a credit card? I mean, if they know how to use a computer."

"That's the point. I want them to follow our trail."

Looking confused, she shrugged, then dug into her jacket pocket and pulled out her wallet. She handed him her credit card a moment later.

The female clerk finished with the customer she was serving and called out, "Next."

Logan took Winter's elbow and walked toward the window with her. "Good afternoon. Do you still have tickets for the bus to Chicago?"

Bored, the clerk looked at the clock. "Bus leaves in eight minutes."

That didn't exactly answer his question, so he went a different route. "Two tickets, please."

The clerk typed something on her computer, then looked up and said, "That'll be $87 per person. $174 in total. Will that be cash or card?"

"Card." Logan tossed Winter's credit card into the tray beneath the glass window that separated them, and watched as the clerk turned a handle to retrieve the card on her side.

"Debit or credit?"

"Credit."

While the clerk entered the transaction, Logan exchanged a quick look with Winter, then glanced over his shoulder to the door through which he could see the bus to Chicago. The bus driver was helping passengers load their bags into a compartment underneath the seating area.

"Please sign here," the clerk said.

Logan looked back at Winter, pulled the credit card receipt, the pen, and the credit card from the tray and stepped aside. "Winter?"

She took the pen and signed the receipt, then shoved both back into the tray for the clerk.

A moment later, Logan held two tickets for the bus to Chicago in one hand, Winter's credit card in the other. He stepped away from the window and brought his head close to Winter's.

"I want you to pretend to put your credit card back into your pocket, but drop it instead."

She stared at him, stunned. "What?"

"Do it. This will be the last time you use it. It's no use to us anymore. I've noticed a few guys in here that are just the type to pick it up and use it. That's what we want. Somebody else using your card to cover our trail."

"But they'll ruin my credit."

"That should be the least of your concerns. You're running from demons."

Winter sighed. "I guess you're right."

"I am. Now do it."

He watched as Winter attempted to slip her card back into her jacket pocket, but dropped it to the floor instead.

"Good. Now let's go. We've got a bus to catch," he said and took her hand.

He led her to the bus and walked to the area where the bus driver was loading bags into the luggage compartment. Logan handed him his bag and watched him place it inside the compartment. When Winter made a motion to hand her bag to the driver, Logan stopped her.

"We'll keep this one with us."

He smiled at the bus driver then led Winter toward the line of people getting onto the bus. But instead of getting in line behind the other passengers, he led Winter past them and around the bus.

"But, the bus," Winter protested, looking over her shoulder.

"We'll take a different mode of transportation," he assured her. "The bus was just a diversion."

"But your bag—"

"All part of the plan. My cell phone is in there. If they've locked onto my GPS, they'll think we're indeed on our way to Chicago." Winter didn't need to know that by *they* he meant his own colleagues and not the demons. It would buy them some time until he'd devised a plan for how to convince the council to let Winter live, and figured out where to go in the meantime.

"Together with the fact that we bought tickets with your credit card, they'll believe we're headed to Chicago and will try to follow us."

Winter's expression changed to one of admiration. "This is not the first time you've done this, is it?"

"It won't be the last either." He steered Winter toward two parked buses.

"What are we doing?"

"Listen carefully." He looked around, but nobody could see them here. And there were no cameras either. He'd checked. "I'm going to make us both invisible now. You need to keep holding my hand so I won't have to expend too much energy. While we're invisible, don't talk unless there's an emergency. People can still hear us. And they can bump into us. Understood?"

"You don't want any of the traffic cameras in the city to pick us up," she stated, understanding.

"Or the cameras on the SEPTA."

"SEPTA?"

"The public transportation system here. The trains. We need to get out of here without being seen, without any of the cameras picking us up."

"Okay." She nodded, then she bit her lip.

"What?"

"When I'm invisible, what will it feel like?"

"How do you feel now?"

She shrugged. "Normal. Why?"

"Because you're already invisible. As am I."

Her breath hitched. She looked down at herself. "But I can still see myself. And you too."

"There are different levels of cloaking. I made it so you can still see me, and I can still see you. But nobody else can." Not even his fellow Stealth Guardians would be able to spot them now. And that was the whole point. He hated having to go against his own people's rules, but sometimes a warrior had to refuse an order and follow his gut. Now was one of those times.

"Okay then," Winter said, a brave expression on her face.

He had to admit he was surprised how much courage she showed. Another woman would most likely have turned hysterical by now. But Winter was strong. The council was wrong in thinking that she was unstable, that she wouldn't be able to hold her own against the demons. Somehow, he had to convince them of it, so they would let her live.

"This way," Logan instructed. "There are several lines that converge in the city center. From now on, we'll need to be silent until we reach our destination." He squeezed her hand. "Are you okay?"

"I will be."

10

Holding onto Logan's hand, Winter walked next to him, not questioning where he was taking her. He'd saved her from certain death at the hands of the demons, and he was protecting her now. Wasn't that enough reason to trust him? It was for her. Life had suddenly become very precious, knowing that she wasn't crazy, that she could live a productive life without having to worry that she would end up in a mental institution. Of course, that didn't mean she was without problems. Only that her problems were of a different nature.

Yes, she was now on the run from demons. But at least she had a supernatural protector, an immortal who could make himself and her invisible. That should help, though being invisible wasn't quite as cool as she'd imagined.

For starters, nobody could see them, which meant people walking on the sidewalk didn't get out of her and Logan's way. She and Logan constantly had to dodge people who would otherwise collide with them. It made for a very awkward walk through the busy downtown area. But she soldiered on without complaint, Logan's strong hand providing guidance and security. She took strength from him, from the confidence with which he navigated the streets, the same confidence with which he'd laid the false trail for the demons to follow.

They walked for several blocks, until Logan stopped in front of the entrance to a subway station. He pointed to it. She nodded and together they descended the stairs, dodging more people. Logan used himself to shield her so she could walk behind him and avoid crashing into people. She was grateful for it, because the obstacle course was tearing at her nerves, wearing her out. And who knew how long they would be on the run? She needed to preserve her energy until they could find a safe place to rest.

When they finally arrived at the turnstiles, Logan stopped and turned to her. He made a motion with his hand, indicating for her to wait. Then he released her hand and walked through the turnstile without turning it.

She blinked in confusion. How was that possible? Was it because he was invisible? She walked to the same turnstile and bumped against it. But she couldn't get through. Without a ticket, it didn't yield to her. Logan suddenly reached for her hand from the other side.

She met his eyes, and he made a motion indicating that he would lift her over it. He set the bag he was carrying for her next to the floor beside him to have both hands free. A moment later, with his help, she cleared the turnstile and was now in the area reserved for paid subway riders. Logan took her hand again, her bag in his other hand, then dragged her toward the area where a train was just rolling into the station.

There was no time to ask him how he'd simply walked *through* the turnstile, *through* solid matter as if he were made of air and not flesh and bone. But she wouldn't forget the question. She would ask him later when she could speak again without drawing attention to them. Clearly, he hadn't told her everything about himself. Who knew what other skills he had? As an immortal, a preternatural creature, maybe he could do all kinds of wild things, aside from making himself invisible and walking through solid objects.

Then it suddenly struck her. What if he wasn't all that different from the demons? After all, in order to fight evil creatures like the monsters who'd attacked them, wouldn't he need skills that were out of this world?

The subway train stopped, and people streamed onto the platform and toward them. Logan quickly pulled her toward the wall, pressing her back flat against it, while he covered her with his broad body. She couldn't even see the passengers rushing past them, because he was so much taller than she, but she could feel whenever somebody bumped into him, because the action pushed Logan against her. She should feel claustrophobic, being sandwiched between the wall and him, but she didn't. She felt cocooned instead. As if nothing could happen to her when she was with him.

Don't be stupid!

He might be immortal, but that didn't mean *she* was. She was still human—though a psychic—and therefore vulnerable.

She looked up at Logan and found him staring at her. Was he aware of the intimacy of their situation? Could he feel her heart beating against her ribcage? Could he see that his nearness didn't leave her unaffected? Because, yes, she could admit it to herself, though not to anybody else, that she found Logan attractive. That his body so close to hers ignited desires in her that had nothing to do with gratitude for him having saved her life.

Logan's head came closer, slowly, but undeniably. She swallowed hard, her pulse racing now. He dipped his head lower. Was he going to kiss her? She parted her lips, feeling a breath rush over them.

"We need to get onto that train," he whispered at her ear. "Let's go."

Heat rushed to her cheeks.

Logan turned abruptly, clasped her hand and rushed toward the doors. A beeping sound reached her ears. The doors were starting to close. Logan jumped into the train, pulling her with him. Behind her, the doors closed and the train started moving.

The train was relatively full. There was no spare seat, so they remained standing near the doors. At each station, they dodged the entering and exiting passengers, as the train emptied more and more the farther they got from downtown. Finally, they found seats away from the other passengers and took them.

Winter didn't dare look at Logan. What had made her think that he'd wanted to kiss her? How silly of her. He didn't even know her. Had only met her a few hours earlier. And there she was imagining things. As if this was an adventure like *Romancing the Stone* where the heroine ended up with the man who was helping her. This wasn't a movie. Or a book. This was life! Real life with real demons. There was no time for romance. There was barely enough time to escape.

Several stops before the end of the Broad Street Line, they got off the train. But Logan didn't seem to be satisfied with how far they'd traveled invisibly. He ushered her toward a regional rail line. Without questioning him, she walked alongside him, onto the first train out of the station. She didn't even look where it was going. It didn't matter.

The regional train was less busy than the subway, and they were able to find seats quickly. Logan was still holding her hand, her bag now sitting on the floor between his legs. She sighed silently and caught Logan's look. He made a motion with one hand while tilting his head and closing his eyes.

She nodded. Yes, she was exhausted, could feel the tiredness in her bones.

He angled his body, lifted his arm and pulled her toward him, so she could rest her head against his chest. Without protest, she accepted his offer and closed her eyes. The vibrations of the train and the warmth of Logan's body allowed her to rest. She didn't sleep, didn't know whether she could ever sleep again, but she dozed, resting her eyes and her body as much as she could.

She felt Logan's steady heartbeat, but she knew he wasn't sleeping. He was watching out for her.

Like a sentry in the night. Like the immortal warrior he was.

Like her hero.

11

Logan hadn't put his arms around a woman in a long time. Not that this—sitting on a train, Winter's head leaning against his chest—really constituted an embrace. All he was doing was providing support so she could rest for a few moments. Yet at the same time, he enjoyed feeling Winter snuggled up to him. It reminded him of a woman after sex, when she wanted to cuddle, and he wanted nothing more than to get out of bed and run. Only there hadn't been any sex, and he felt no urge to run from Winter.

For a few minutes, Logan allowed his mind to wander and follow a road that was paved with *what-ifs*. Many decades ago he'd chosen to become a warrior to serve his people and protect them. He'd gone into it knowing full well what it meant: sacrifice. All warriors were forced to live in compounds with five to ten other warriors as their constant companions. It was almost like living in a monastery, though there was booze and partying like in any place where more than two men were assembled. Nobody demanded that warriors be celibate. But the demands of their work and the living conditions had turned many a warrior into a monk.

The opportunities for finding sexual gratification were few. Due to their birthrate being skewed toward males, there were much fewer Stealth Guardian women than men. And even fewer female warriors. His compound had one. But Enya was a prickly one. She wanted nothing to do with any of them, and he had to admit, he wasn't interested in her in a romantic way either. He'd practically grown up with her. He knew the others felt the same way.

The lack of women of their own race meant warriors had to sow their oats with human women. In general, it wasn't an issue. After all, Stealth Guardians looked no different from humans, and no woman would know that she was sleeping with a preternatural creature. A creature who couldn't even impregnate her, because a Stealth Guardian's sperm wasn't fertile until he'd gone through a bonding ritual with a woman. One-night stands were a popular option for any warrior who felt sexual frustration, but if he wanted more, if he wanted a relationship, things got difficult.

For starters, no human was allowed in the compounds unless they were bonded to a warrior. Of course, that rule had been broken a few times by his own compound mates. However, a warrior trying to stick to the rules had a hard time making a woman trust him, when he could never take her *home*, home being his compound. And many women got suspicious of men who had to keep secrets like that. They could feel that the man was hiding something. Which led to the second big obstacle: a warrior wasn't allowed to reveal that he was a preternatural creature until he'd made the decision to bond with the human.

Logan sighed. Why was he even thinking about all this? The situation with Winter was entirely different. She wasn't a woman he'd picked up in a bar or a chatted up in a supermarket. She wasn't a potential one-night stand or fling, though had he met her under other circumstances, he would have asked her out and explored if there was a spark between them. If, at least for one night, they could connect. But that was impossible now. Winter was under his protection and he couldn't exploit the situation. It would be unethical. Winter was his charge. He was her guardian, her protector. Even if the council had ordered otherwise.

When the train slowed, Logan looked out the window. They were approaching the final stop: Trenton. He shook Winter's shoulder gently, and she immediately sat up straight and looked at him. He motioned to the window, where the Trenton station was coming into view. She nodded, having understood that they would alight here.

Logan waited until most people had gotten off the train, then stepped onto the platform holding Winter's hand. It was still best to cloak her with his touch, an action that required less energy, since making her invisible with his mind would become less secure if he lost his concentration. And right now he had to concentrate on figuring out the safest place to go.

By the time Logan had examined the map in the entry hall and found a hotel that would be suitable for their purposes, the sun had set. He looked around. There were cameras in the train station, which meant it wasn't safe yet to become visible. He led Winter outside. It would have been more comfortable to take a taxi to the hotel, but the CCTV system around the train station could pick them up, and once Manus realized that the trail to Chicago was a diversion, he would ask Pearce to run a facial recognition program against traffic cameras and the like. Logan knew the drill.

When they were out of earshot of others, Logan whispered to Winter, "We'll have to walk. It's about a mile. You gonna be okay?"

"Yes. We're still invisible?"

"Yes. But once we get to the hotel, and I see that it's safe, I'll make us visible again."

"We're going to a hotel?"

"Yes, for tonight. Then we'll move on." Where to, he hadn't figured out yet, but he would. Right now it was important to get off the street.

Logan was glad when they finally reached the budget hotel he'd spotted on the map in the train station. Checking in and paying cash rather than credit at a place like this wouldn't be unusual. As much as he would have preferred to take Winter to a better place, he couldn't risk using one of his own cards to pay for the room. His fellow Stealth Guardians would be able to trace him in a nanosecond.

The hotel clerk at the front desk didn't flinch when Logan asked for a room on the second floor and paid cash. Nor did he question the lack of luggage besides the small bag Winter had packed.

"Is there a place to get some dinner close by?" Logan asked while he took the keycard from the clerk.

The clerk pointed over his shoulder. "Take the alley behind the hotel. Next block has a good grill." He glanced at Winter, looking her up and down with interest. "They do takeout, too."

"Thanks." Logan turned away from the front desk and took Winter's hand again. They walked around the corner to the elevators. "I'll get you settled in the room. Then I'll get us something to eat."

"That sounds good. I'm starting to feel a little hungry," she said, a grateful expression on her face.

The room was clean and functional: two queen beds, a built-in desk with chair, a TV mounted on the wall, a small table with two chairs, and an ensuite bathroom. The curtains were already drawn when Logan entered the room ahead of Winter to make sure it was safe.

He ushered her inside and dropped her bag onto the floor next to the desk, then looked back at Winter and caught her looking at the beds.

"I'm sorry, Winter, but I can't let you stay in a room by yourself. I need to be with you to keep you safe," he said.

Her gaze connected with his. "I wasn't complaining."

"No, you weren't. And I appreciate it. You're taking all of this without much fuss. Many people wouldn't." And that made his respect for her rise even more. She was no shrinking violet.

"I'm grateful for what you're doing to help me. You put yourself in danger for me."

"That's my job." But as he said it, guilt nagged at him. It had been his job to kill her, not save her. Didn't she deserve to know the truth, to know why he'd really come to her shop? But if she knew, she wouldn't look at him like she did now, her eyes brimming with admiration and gratitude.

He was a cad for letting her believe he was a hero, a man of honor.

"Winter, there's something you should know," he started. It was best to wipe the slate clean, tell her the truth, or it would eat him up from the inside.

She plopped down on one of the beds and let out an exaggerated breath. "There's a lot I should know. Starting with how you just marched through those turnstiles at the subway station. How did you do that? You could have warned me."

"Oh that."

"Yeah, that."

He shrugged. Maybe in the course of their conversation, he'd get a better opportunity to tell her why he'd been at her shop in the first place. It was best to establish trust between them first, so that she would understand when he came clean.

"It's one of the skills every Stealth Guardian has. We can dematerialize our bodies and pass through solid objects." All but lead, but there was no need to expose his people's vulnerability to her. "It assures that we can enter any building, any location we need to gain access to. It's come in handy once or twice."

Winter chuckled unexpectedly, and it brought out a softness in her face that made his heart skip a beat. "That sounds like an understatement."

It was.

"So why did you make me climb over the turnstile? You could have just—"

"I couldn't." He shook his head. "A human's body is too fragile. If dematerialized, the cells would never rematerialize in the correct order."

"Oh, you mean like in that episode of *Star Trek* when the transporter was malfunctioning?"

Not having seen that episode, he said, "I guess. It wouldn't be a pretty sight. Unfortunately that means we have to make sure there's always an escape route that our charges can actually navigate."

"Your charge? Is that what you call people like me?"

He wanted to call her other things, but this was neither the time nor the place. In fact there would never be a time or place where it would be appropriate for him to see her as anything other than his charge. "Yes. But now I should get us some food. You said you were hungry."

She nodded. "A burger and some fries wouldn't go amiss right now."

"That can be arranged. I'll be as quick about it as I can. But promise me you won't leave this room, not even to go to the ice machine down the hall."

"I have no intention of going anywhere on my own."

"Good. And don't answer the door for anybody."

She suddenly stood up as if she realized something. "And the demons? I mean, can they walk through a locked door like you?"

Logan smiled at her. "No. The only person who can walk through this door is me."

Or one of his brethren. And he was certain that they hadn't caught onto his trail yet.

12

Manus stormed into the command center, fury coursing through every cell of his body.

"Fucking bastard!"

Logan had betrayed him. Hell, he'd betrayed not only their compound, but their entire race. And if he didn't find him fast, Logan would pay for it with his life.

Manus marched to the computer console, where Pearce was working. "Anything?"

Behind him more people entered the command center. He knew that Aiden and Hamish, who'd helped with the clean-up at the psychic's shop and apartment, had followed him. But now he saw Enya, the only female warrior in their compound, enter too.

"I got something," Pearce said. "Not sure if it'll help."

"Can somebody fill me in on what's going on here?" Enya asked and approached.

"Later," Manus said and motioned to the computer. "What have you got? Where is Logan?"

"Well, I can tell you where his car is." Pearce pointed to a map on the screen. "He parked it right outside the Greyhound station in Philadelphia. It's still there. Somebody had better pick it up before it gets towed."

"Yeah, later," Manus said impatiently. "What about Logan?"

"I figured since he left his car outside the bus station, I'd start there. And bingo, a camera picked him up entering the ticket hall with a woman."

"And then?"

Pearce swiveled in his seat. "How about you give me a little bit more information about what's going on here. It's kind of hard to figure out what he's planning when you've only given me half the facts. What went down on your mission? Or is it too super-secret to tell even us?"

Manus looked back to where Aiden and Hamish were standing. They'd come to get him in Wilmington and helped dispose of the demon bodies, but he hadn't told them much either, only that Logan had left with the woman.

"Ah, fuck confidentiality. I don't know why Barclay bothered." When he caught Aiden's raised eyebrows, Manus shrugged. "Your father can be a pain in the butt sometimes."

"You're preaching to the converted," Aiden said. "Now tell us what's really going on. Logan wouldn't just run from demons."

"He wasn't running from the demons. He was running from me."

Enya let herself fall into a chair. "Well, this sounds like it's going to be an interesting story."

"What did you do to piss him off this time?" Hamish asked.

"I'm not the one at fault here." Manus shook his head. "Logan didn't follow the order the council gave us."

"Could you be any more cryptic?" Pearce asked, sarcasm dripping from his voice.

Manus tilted his head to the side, grimacing. "Fine. Here's the deal. Logan and I were tasked with eliminating a psychic."

Several gasps filled the room.

"Yeah, and before you all start talking at once, I'll tell you what you need to know. The psychic, a woman named Winter Collins, is apparently unaware of her psychic abilities. She's mentally unstable, and she displays drawings of her visions in her shop." He motioned to Aiden and Hamish. "I mean, you saw it. We had to wipe down the runes she'd scribbled on the door frame with chalk. And the pictures she'd hung on the walls, we had to take them down. Anybody coming into her shop could see them. That's probably how she drew the demons' attention to herself."

He sighed. "Anyway, Logan was supposed to go in and slip her the poison, kill her quickly. I was waiting in the car outside, and I saw the demons break in. I rushed after them as quickly as I could. And when I got there, Logan was fighting them, and the psychic was still alive. He hadn't killed her." He looked at his colleagues. "We fought the demons together. Killed them all except for one, who escaped through a vortex. But I knew they'd come back. We'd been lucky to defeat them at all without them snatching the psychic. So I figured, I'd do the deed myself, since Logan hadn't managed to."

Manus huffed angrily. "And what the fuck does he do when I'm about to slice her throat? The asshole attacks *me*! *Me*! And puts me in a chokehold until I lose consciousness."

"Mmm," Aiden hummed. "I don't understand why he would do that. I mean, it was an order from the council. They voted, right?"

Manus nodded. "Five to four to eliminate the psychic."

"Bit odd that they'd vote to kill her, when she could be of use to us," Enya threw in.

"Apparently the council didn't think so," Manus griped.

"And Logan?" Hamish asked.

"When I called the asshole, he gave me this whole spiel about how useful she could be, that she has visions about the demons and could help us destroy them. Don't you think the council didn't discuss that before they took their vote? But no, Logan thinks he knows better. He said he has to save her. That he'll prove to the council that she's worth more to us alive than dead. Idiot! They'll never change their vote!"

Enya shrugged. "Given the right evidence, they might."

"Oh please!" Manus glared at her. "Are you going soft, or what?"

Enya narrowed her eyes at him. "Don't you—"

"Stop, both of you!" Hamish ordered. "Your bickering isn't gonna help us find Logan."

"Hamish is right," Aiden said. "We have to find him. Quickly, before the council gets wind of this and figures out that he ran off with the psychic instead of killing her. That's treason. And I'm not letting my friend go down for treason."

"I'm not either," Pearce confirmed.

"Same," Enya said tightly.

Hamish only nodded.

Manus snorted. "Yeah, well, I'm not letting him do that either. But he's still an asshole!" Asshole or not, Logan was his friend, and he couldn't let his friend be tried for treason, an offense punishable by death.

He turned to Pearce. "Did you run Logan's credit cards already to see if he used them at the bus station?"

Pearce nodded. "Yep. No hit. He wouldn't be so stupid as to use his credit cards if he's trying to evade us."

"Then check the woman's. Winter Collins. Maybe they used hers."

"Give me a second to find her records." Pearce started typing on his computer. Windows popped open, then closed again. It seemed to take an eternity, when in reality it probably took Pearce only several minutes to located the woman's credit card and review her latest charges. He pointed to the screen. "Here. Purchase of two tickets on the Greyhound bus from Philadelphia to Chicago."

Manus stared at the entry. "Why would he want to go to Chicago? It doesn't make sense. Why travel by bus?"

Pearce met his look. "I get it. Why risk being exposed for so long, when he could just go to the next portal and travel anywhere without us being able to track him?"

"Exactly," Manus said. "He meant for us to track him. But why?"

"Can we check if he even got on that bus to Chicago?" Hamish asked. "How about his cell phone? Can you ping it?"

Pearce turned back to the screen. "I did it earlier, but couldn't get a good reading. He might have been in an area with bad reception. Let me try it again."

A few moments later a map appeared on one of Pearce's screens. A red dot flashed.

"He's moving," Pearce said. "Currently outside of Pittsburgh. That's the route the bus would take from Philadelphia to Chicago. Looks like he's on the bus."

Manus shook his head. Something wasn't right. He turned to his compound mates. "Tell me something, if you were on the run from us, would you leave your cell phone switched on, knowing that we can trace it with our software and find your location?"

All of them shook their heads.

"That's what I thought." Manus grumbled. "Fucking bastard. He's laid out breadcrumbs for us to follow, leading us on the wrong trail. He's nowhere near Chicago."

"Then where?" Aiden asked.

"He's making his way to a portal so he can disappear." Manus turned back to Pearce. "Get me a list of all known lost portals within reach of the public transport system of Philadelphia. Because unless Logan stole a car, he couldn't have gotten far. He would have had to use the rail system. And check reports about any stolen cars in the area, just in case."

Pearce tapped away on his keyboard, then cursed. "Shit, there are too many portals. Their rail system is too extensive. There's no way that between us we can have a man at every portal in the area to lay in wait for him. And we can't ask another compound for help. Nobody can know about Logan going rogue. We need to narrow down the number of portals."

"How?" Aiden asked.

"We have to put ourselves in his shoes," Pearce said. "What would Logan do?"

13

The food had been just what Winter needed. She felt better after filling her belly with the burger Logan had brought her. While they'd eaten, she'd asked Logan more about the demons and their ultimate goal.

"World domination?" she echoed.

"Nothing less." Logan grabbed the paper plates and food scraps and put them in the plastic bag in which he'd brought the food. He tied a knot in the top, then walked to the bathroom.

She heard him place the trash in the bin, then wash his hands.

She rose and walked toward the open door to the bathroom. "And you and your fellow Stealth Guardians have been fighting them for centuries without success? When you fought against those four, you held your own. I can't believe that you can't defeat them. You're so strong."

Logan dried his hands. Their eyes met in the mirror. "They're just as strong."

"But you can make yourself invisible and walk through solid objects. In a fight, that gives you an advantage."

"That's true, but there just aren't enough of us. There are too many demons. And their numbers are growing by the minute."

She made a face. "You mean they can reproduce?" That thought made her feel sick to her stomach.

"Not in the traditional sense, although we're not even sure about that. No, their numbers grow because whenever they turn a human to their evil ways, whenever they make a human commit an atrocity in their name, the human turns into a demon, their soul lost forever. That's how they grow their ranks. There's so much evil in this world, so much anger, so much division, even just in our own country. Add to that the wars all over the world, and you've got a perfect breeding ground from which to draw your next demon."

She stared at him wide-eyed. "A never-ending supply."

Logan walked out of the bathroom, and she stepped aside. She followed him as he leaned his butt against the table and gave her a sad smile. "It's a never-ending battle."

"How do you not lose hope in the face of such overwhelming evil?"

He shrugged. "I take one day at a time. Kill one demon at a time. That's all I can do."

She shook her head and moved closer to him. "And now you have to take care of me." She sighed. "I'm sorry."

She took his hand and squeezed it. He stared at her in silent surprise. What she'd meant as a gesture of comfort suddenly felt different. Logan's eyes turned molten, and she lost herself in them. Such beauty, such power. Winter lifted her hand and ran her knuckles over his cheek, feeling a shiver go through her at the touch. It felt as if electricity was charging through her. Not realizing what she was doing, she drew closer to him. Logan's lips were slightly parted and looked more tempting than anything she'd ever seen. She took a breath and leaned in.

But he suddenly shifted, moving away from her.

Startled, she gasped and tried to turn away from him, but he snatched her arm.

"It's best if you don't kiss me."

Heat shot into her cheeks. Had she really just lost her mind and tried to offer him her lips? She tried to step back, embarrassment rushing through her, but he didn't let go of her arm. She snapped her gaze back to his face. To her surprise, she saw regret in his eyes.

"I'm sorry," she said.

"No, don't be," he said in an even voice. "I would welcome your touch. I would have kissed you back. But there can't be anything sexual between you and me."

He would have kissed her back? So he'd felt the attraction between them, too? Then why did he have scruples? Or wasn't it that at all? What if the reason wasn't because he didn't want to have sex with her but because he *couldn't*? *Physically* couldn't. That thought made her suck in a breath of air and pause. Yes, that had to be it. "Oh." She swallowed hard and lowered her eyes. "I didn't realize. I thought because you look so human that... you know... you'd have all the same... uh, parts." She cleared her throat. "I didn't mean to—"

"Parts?" Logan interrupted, his voice raised.

"Uh..." Was he going to make her say it? Oh God, how embarrassing. She made a motion in the general direction of his groin, then averted her eyes quickly. "You know..."

"You think I don't have the right equipment?"

Winter coughed nervously. "Please, I'm sorry I made an assumption. I'm sorry I tried to, uh... Can we please drop the subject?"

"No, we can't."

She looked back up at him. There was a struggle going on inside him, a struggle that reflected on his face.

"You don't understand," Logan said. "It's my fault. I probably sent you the wrong signals. I'm not immune to you. I'm attracted to you. But you're my charge. My responsibility. It doesn't matter what I want, because I won't give into my needs. I can't do that." He released her arm. "I won't take advantage of a woman in my care. It's not right. You're vulnerable. Impressionable. You probably think you owe me something. You don't. But I need your help to resist the temptation. Please don't try to kiss me again. It will only lead to one thing." He motioned to the bed. "Knowing that we'll sleep in the same room tonight is going to be temptation enough. I might be an immortal warrior, but I'm also a man." He let out a weak laugh. "With all the right parts."

Winter gaped at him. He was attracted to her. And despite being different species, they were *compatible*. And his objection was that he thought he was taking advantage of her? That couldn't possibly be it.

"So let me get this straight. You find me reasonably attractive," she started.

"Not just reasonably."

She registered his comment with satisfaction. "And you have *all the right parts*." She glanced at his groin. "And I'm assuming they work?"

Logan growled. "They work just fine," he pressed out through clenched teeth.

"But you think you're taking advantage of me, if you sleep with me." She rolled her eyes. "Men! No wonder I don't date much. They're just too complicated."

"You're calling me complicated?"

"No, *you*"—she drove her index finger into his chest—"I call boneheaded."

He narrowed his eyes at her. "Care to explain why I deserve such harsh criticism?"

"You still don't get it, do you? I could die tomorrow. Hell, we could both die tomorrow. The demons could catch up with us and murder us in our sleep for all I know. And you're concerned about taking advantage of me, when I'm the one making a pass at you?" She shook her head and turned away. "Honestly! If you're trying to spare my feelings, because you're not actually interested—"

A firm hand on her shoulder spun her back around to face him. Suddenly both his hands were on her, gripping her shoulders. "I'm interested."

He pulled her to him, his hands sliding down her back until they came to lay on her behind. He pressed her against his groin, where she felt hardness rub against her soft stomach. Her breath hitched.

"Is that proof enough of my interest?"

Winter snapped her gaze to him. He didn't look angry anymore, nor had his voice sounded annoyed. Instead he had a smirk on his face. Stunned, she froze.

"Well, now, look at that. Suddenly the little seductress isn't quite so brave anymore, is she? Are you gonna back away now that you know I'll take you up on your offer if you make it again? I hope that's a warning to you. Don't play games with me."

She felt him loosen his grip and shove her back, but before he could release her, she put her hands on his biceps and held tight. "I wasn't asking for a warning. And I don't play games."

"Goddamn it," Logan ground out, but dipped his head toward her nevertheless. "This is a mistake."

"But one I'm going to enjoy," she murmured. "And I don't need to be a psychic to know that."

"Winter?"

"Hmm?"

"Stop talking."

"Then start kissing me already."

A second later, she felt Logan's lips on hers, pressing gently, flooding her with warmth and the knowledge that for a short while she would be able to forget everything that had happened in the last hours.

14

Logan felt Winter respond to his kiss and knew there was no going back now. She was a free spirit like Barclay had mentioned, and she didn't care about conventions. The fact that she didn't know him at all didn't stop her from offering her body to him in the most trusting way. And he was a scoundrel for accepting the offer. Because he knew what he was doing was wrong. Wrong on so many levels.

Wasn't it enough that he'd gone rogue, betrayed his friends and defied his superiors' orders? Wasn't it enough that he was still lying to her about why he'd been in her shop? Did he have to top it all off now by sleeping with her?

Fuck! He should stop, should confess everything. But he couldn't. Winter's body in his arms felt too good. Her mouth yielded to his, her lips parted to invite him in. And what man, what living, breathing creature could resist such temptation? She was young and beautiful, her body soft, her curves round and tantalizing.

Kissing Winter was like a sensual dance. A dance between two strangers who had no secrets from each other. Two strangers who trusted each other. Was it Winter's free spirit, her unconventionality that contributed to what was happening between them now? Or had the horror she'd gone through only hours earlier driven her to this act, an act that reaffirmed life?

With every stroke of his tongue against hers, every press of his lips to hers, Logan felt his body temperature rise. It had been a while since he'd felt desire like this, since he'd been aroused by a mere kiss. But it wasn't just the kiss. He felt her hands on him, touching him, exploring him with almost desperate anticipation, with a wildness he now welcomed.

She was already opening the buttons of his shirt as if she feared he would change his mind and suddenly stop if she didn't undress him fast enough.

Logan drew his head back and took a hold of her hands.

She stared at him, disappointment instantly flaring up in her eyes.

"Easy, Winter, we've got time." He let go of her hands and put two fingers under her chin, tilting it up. "If we're really gonna do this, I'm not gonna rush it. You're right, we might die tomorrow, so let's at least enjoy this together."

A slow smile built on her lips, while she released a relieved breath of air. "You scared me there for a moment."

"You should never be scared of me. I mean that, Winter." He slanted his lips over hers and captured them for another kiss. And another.

At the same time he slowly began to undress her. Layer after layer he peeled away. First her sweatshirt, then the camisole. Beneath it she wore a bra. He let her keep it, for now. He wasn't ready to lay her bare there.

But he did want to feel her curves, so he let his hands slide over her naked shoulders, down her torso to where the simple white cotton bra covered her shapely breasts. Under the many colorful layers she'd worn in the shop and then the unshapely sweatshirt she'd changed into later, he hadn't been able to guess what treasures lay beneath. Two perfect globes, firm and yet soft, beckoned to be explored.

He ran his thumbs along the bra's seams, delving below the fabric to touch the silken skin. Her chest rose in invitation, and a ragged breath tore from her chest.

"Beautiful," he murmured and dipped his head to kiss the indentation between her breasts. She smelled of lavender there, of innocence and sensuality. When he lifted his eyes to look at her face, he saw her watching him, her eyes hooded, her lips parted, still moist from his kisses.

The sight made his cock spasm in anticipation. He was already hard. Had been since the moment she'd started talking about *parts*. Had she really believed he didn't have the right equipment to make love to her? How silly, and how charming at the same time.

"Aren't you gonna continue?" she suddenly asked.

He chuckled. "Trust me, only one thing can stop me now."

"What's that?"

He brought his face to hers. "You changing your mind. There's still time for that."

Winter shook her dark curls. "No, there isn't." She slid her hand down his torso to the front of his pants, cupping the hard bulge there, making him gasp in response. "See? There's no going back now. I need to feel you, skin on skin."

"I think my people got it wrong: you're not a psychic, you're a witch."

She chuckled. "That's what men call women when they can't tame them." Her eyelashes fluttered, and her pink tongue emerged to lick her lips. "But I bet you can tame me with what you've got here." She squeezed his cock through his pants.

Her boldness surprised him—and turned him on.

"Fuck!" he cursed under his breath and pressed Winter against the wall behind her.

He lowered his head and kissed one breast through the thin cotton, until the nipple was rock-hard and the fabric was so wet it became transparent. Then he unleashed the same torture on the other breast. Meanwhile, his hands weren't idle. He made quick work of the button of her jeans, then lowered the zipper, before yanking her pants down to her thighs. She wore cotton panties without any frills. He slid his fingers underneath the fabric, combing through the coarse hair at the juncture of her thighs until he found what he was looking for: a warm wetness oozing from her core.

He moaned against her nipple and bathed his fingers in her arousal.

"Logan, oh God!" she uttered on a moan.

Knowing his touch was welcome, he started rubbing along her slit, then brought the moisture up higher to where her clit was hidden underneath a protective hood. He swiped upwards, covering the sensitive organ with her juices.

Another moan, this time even more breathless.

He let go of her nipple and lifted his head, kissing a path up her neck until he could suck her earlobe into his mouth. "You like my fingers there?"

"Y-yes," she stammered.

"Good, cause I'm gonna make you come with my fingers first, so you'll be nice and relaxed when I make love to you with my cock."

Her breath hitched, and he felt her nipples rub against his chest.

With her jeans down to her knees, Winter's range of motion was restricted. She couldn't open her legs any wider, but Logan didn't mind. He had enough space to slide three fingers back and forth to reach her clit without any problem. Winter couldn't escape his caresses. She was at his mercy.

Planting open-mouthed kisses on her neck, he continued to stroke her center of pleasure, feeling how her clit became more and more swollen, while Winter thrust her pelvis toward his hand, demanding more friction. He complied with her demand, rubbing her hard and fast, adjusting his tempo to her breathing pattern, to her frantically beating heart.

"Logan, oh yes, yes, please!"

Even without her words he could tell how close she was. Her skin was perspiring now, a soft rose blush covering it, her chest was heaving, her breaths ragged, her pulse racing. He loved seeing her like this, loved being the reason for it. He felt her clit throb now, and knew she was ready. He slipped his middle finger deep into her pussy, then pinched her clit with his thumb and index finger.

Her body spasmed, her inner muscles clenching his finger tightly. Then he felt her shudder as her orgasm crashed over her. He stilled his fingers, allowing her to ride out the pleasure now coursing through her body, kissing her neck, her shoulders, dipping down to her breasts, and kissing her there too, until the tension in her body finally ebbed and she sagged against the wall.

Slowly, gently, he eased his fingers from her. Then he lifted her into his arms and placed her down on the bed.

"I'll take care of you now," he promised and continued to undress her.

~ ~ ~

Winter felt like she was in a daze. A dream. But it wasn't a dream. She was lying on the bed, and Logan was undressing her. She felt cool air blow against her skin and knew he'd taken off her pants. But she was too satiated from her orgasm to lift her head and look down at herself.

Then she felt his hands on her chest. She watched him as he freed her of her bra. He tossed it aside, then dipped his head to one breast and licked over the nipple. Her entire body still hypersensitive, she let out a moan.

He briefly looked at her, smiled, then reached for her panties and slid them off her. She felt no shame about being exposed to him like this. She wanted him to see her like this. Just like she wanted to see him. Every immortal inch of him.

"Take your clothes off," she said, barely recognizing her own voice. When exactly had she turned into a breathy-voiced vixen?

Logan stood up straight. "Only if you watch."

She braced herself on her elbows and looked at him, more alert now. "Oh, I'm watching."

There was something intimate about watching a man getting undressed. But watching Logan as he took off his shirt and unbuttoned his pants, was even more of a turn-on. Was it because he was an immortal? Or because he was a stranger, and she had no expectations? Maybe it was both.

His chest was covered with only the lightest dusting of dark hair, just as dark as the hair on his head. His pectorals were defined, not in a bodybuilder kind of way, but in a, well, warrior kind of way. He looked as strong as he was. His abs were just as well-developed, the ridges reminding her of ripples the ocean waves left in the sand. Down the middle of his abdominal muscles, the hair grew slightly thicker where it disappeared into his pants.

Her eyes were glued to his hands, his strong, yet elegant fingers, when he lowered the zipper revealing black boxer briefs beneath the khaki pants he wore. When he stopped, she lifted her head to find out the reason why and found him looking at her.

"Just wanted to make sure you want me to go on," he said with a smirk.

"Now you're just being a tease," she said.

"Or maybe I'm simply enjoying the way you look at me."

"I'll enjoy it even more once I get to see more." She tossed a pointed look at his groin.

Finally, he continued his slow undressing. He bent down and undid his boots. He pulled a dagger from one of them and put it aside, before stepping out of them. Then he stripped himself of his socks, straightened again, and pushed his pants down. When he stepped out of them, she was rewarded with the sight of two muscular legs. But her interest lay farther up, where the black fabric of his boxer briefs stretched over a thick bulge.

Winter licked her lips. A groan came from Logan, then he hooked his thumbs into the waistband and pushed his last item of clothing down, freeing himself. His cock sprang free. Hard and heavy it curved toward his abdomen, and below, his balls hung in a tight sac.

"You do have all the right parts." She raised her eyes to meet his. "Perfect parts."

"I'm glad you approve." Slowly he bridged the distance to the bed and slid one knee onto the mattress. "Now let's put this part to good use."

"Let's." She reached her hand out, sliding it along the underside of his cock, reveling in the smoothness of his sensitive skin. "Perfect."

Logan pressed her back into the mattress and rolled over her. "It'll be even more perfect inside you."

"We need a condom." How could she have forgotten about that?

Logan froze. "I don't have a condom." He sighed. "Our race doesn't use them. We don't need to. As preternatuals we carry no disease."

"Ah, makes sense," she said, relieved to a point. "But I'm not on the pill."

He shook his head. "You won't have to worry about that. I can't get you pregnant."

She looked into his eyes and saw the truth in them. "Well, then I guess…" She pulled him down on her and spread her legs wider, making space for him.

Logan slid into the space as if they'd done this a thousand times. She locked eyes with him and saw passion reflected back at her. His eyes were light brown with flecks of a darker color throughout. They seemed to sparkle. And then she felt it, felt his cock nudge at the entrance to her body and slide between her moist folds. His eyes still holding her gaze, he thrust deep into her, stretching her, filling her.

A breath escaped her and with it a soft moan.

"See?" he murmured. "We fit perfectly."

She loved the feeling of his hard root inside her, loved the fullness. She squeezed her interior muscles wanting to feel more of him.

Logan moaned, his eyes closing for a moment, then he looked at her again. "Keep that up and this'll be over in no time," he warned.

"Then maybe you should do something about that." She moved her hips, pressing toward him.

"Maybe I should."

Before he'd even spoken the last word, he withdrew from her sheath and plunged back in. This time not as gently as before. But she didn't mind. On the contrary, she welcomed it.

"Now we're talking."

"Talk's over," he said and kissed her.

Farther below, his hips started moving, his cock thrusting back and forth, in and out of her drenched pussy. Oh, yes, she was wet. He'd made her climax so violently that even now her body was still hypersensitive. And with every thrust, every stroke of his magnificent cock, he was driving her toward that same abyss.

Winter slid her hands onto his back, touching, caressing, exploring what she could reach. His butt muscles flexed with every thrust into her, and she couldn't help but urge him on by digging her fingers into his backside and driving him deeper with each stroke.

All the while, Logan was kissing her, her lips, her neck, her shoulders, her breasts. As if he couldn't get enough. His chest was covered with a light sheen of perspiration, his breaths came in short pants, and his cock thrust relentlessly.

The sound of his breathing was mixed with deep moans, and the cords in his neck were strained, as if holding onto his control was costing him the last ounce of his strength.

How she loved a man who gave his all when making love. How she loved a man who only lived in the here and now, only worked for this one moment of pleasure and pure bliss. How she loved a man who made her feel desired. A man who drove her to such heights.

With every movement, every stroke, every kiss, every thrust, her body heated more. Her pulse was racing now, and she knew she was heading for another monumental orgasm.

"Oh Logan!" she cried out.

As if he knew what she was trying to tell him, he shifted his angle, and with every thrust of his cock, his pelvic bone rubbed against her clit, igniting her. Waves of pleasure rushed over her. Then a different kind of wave followed. Logan's cock spasmed inside her, and liquid heat flooded her as his seed released inside her.

Logan's moans mingled with hers, before his movements slowed and he finally came to rest on top of her, his weight braced on his knees and elbows, his cock still inside her.

When she met his gaze, he smiled.

"You felt so good," he said and brushed his lips over hers. "Thank you for allowing me to make love to you."

She couldn't remember any man ever having thanked her after sex. "I feel I should thank you." After all, he'd made her come twice, and she'd really needed that after the many revelations she'd had to deal with today.

He slowly withdrew his cock halfway, then slid back inside, wringing another moan from her lips.

"You keep doing that and we won't sleep tonight," she warned.

"Don't worry, I'll make sure you sleep like a baby tonight. I'll watch over you."

She stared at him. "You won't sleep?"

"Only with one eye closed."

Winter raised her hand and combed it through his hair. "Don't you think we're safe here for tonight?"

"We probably are." He pressed a kiss to her lips, then slowly rolled off her. "You should sleep." He made a motion to get out of bed.

She reached for his arm and stopped him. "Won't you stay in bed with me?"

Logan gave her a hesitant smile. "You don't want me to use the other bed and give you some space?"

She shook her head. "Unless you're the one who wants the space."

"I don't. But my… uh *parts* might react to holding you in my arms all night." He pointed to his groin, where his cock was still semi-hard.

She moved closer until her lips were only inches from his mouth. "We'll cross that bridge when we get to it." She slanted her lips over his and kissed him. Moments later, she felt the mattress at her back again and Logan's naked body sliding against hers.

15

Logan had slept on and off. And though sharing a bed with Winter had raised his desire for her even more, he hadn't acted upon it and let her sleep. She needed her rest. Instead, in the darkness of the hotel room, he'd worked on a plan for how to proceed. He knew he had to be careful. Not only were they running from the demons, they were also hiding from the Stealth Guardians—at least for now, until Logan could figure out a way to convince the council that Winter should live. Until then, he had to take every precaution to evade his fellow guardians. Which meant he couldn't ask them for help. He had to find help elsewhere.

He'd already showered and gotten dressed by the time Winter stirred. He walked to the bed and sat on the edge. When he pressed a kiss on her shoulder, she hummed softly.

"Time to get up," he said. "We've got a lot ahead of us today."

She turned and wiped the sleep from her eyes. Her hair was rumpled, and there was a soft glow about her. She looked rested. And irresistible. But guilt was churning in him again this morning. He'd slept with Winter, but hadn't told her that he'd gone to her shop to kill her. He felt like a cad for deceiving her like this, but right now he couldn't tell her the truth. What if she ran from him once he confessed that he wasn't only an immortal guardian, but that on occasion he also had to be an assassin?

"Good morning," she murmured and wrapped her arms around him.

The gesture was so trusting, it made him feel even worse. But he couldn't let her believe that something was wrong, so he hugged her back and pressed a kiss into her hair. "Being with you last night was amazing." It was true, though that wasn't the reason he was saying it. He knew only too well that on the morning after, regrets could surface, and he didn't want her to regret her actions from the night before. Even if he regretted having been too weak to resist her allure. What he'd done was wrong. Still, having Winter in his arms, making love to her had been the best thing he'd ever done.

Slowly he eased out of her embrace and stood up.

"Why don't I get us some breakfast from downstairs while you take a shower and get ready?"

It would be best that way. At least then he wouldn't be tempted to follow her into the shower to make love with her again. And repeat his mistake.

"Sure." She shrugged, looking somewhat disappointed, just as disappointed as he felt inside. Why couldn't he have met her under other circumstances?

He forced himself to smile at her. "Eggs? Bacon? Pancakes?"

"Bacon and eggs, and coffee. Black. Thanks."

"Be right back."

Logan left the room and made his way downstairs to the breakfast buffet. A dozen other people were already chowing down on their food and gulping down their coffee. On one wall, a mounted TV screen showed the news. The TV was muted, but Logan read the closed captioning. No news about any dead men with green blood found two states over. Had the police found men oozing green blood, every TV station in the country would be reporting on it. It meant that his compound mates had cleaned up Winter's shop and disposed of the demons.

By now they would also have found his car and traced his cell phone. Whether they were following the fake trail he'd left was another question. His compound mates weren't stupid. The diversion wouldn't keep them off his trail for long. They had to assume that he would eventually use one of the lost portals to transport them somewhere without being traced. But how quickly would they figure out which portal Logan intended to use?

Logan had memorized the location of three portals in the area. He could, of course, travel farther afield, but it would mean logging into the Stealth Guardians' system from an unsecured public computer to research the location of other portals. Once he did that, his compound mates would be able to determine his location by the IP address of the computer he was using. He couldn't risk it. There was a more complicated way of figuring out the location of a portal, but unfortunately Logan wasn't sufficiently well versed in the intricate mathematical calculations necessary to perform such a task. He had no choice but to choose one of the three portals close by.

Minutes later, Logan entered his hotel room with a tray of food. Winter was already showered and fully dressed, her hair still damp at the tips. Her eyes were wide, and she looked scared.

He set the tray down on the desk, then rushed to her. "What's wrong?"

"I saw him again."

"Whom? Where?"

She gripped his arms tightly. "The demon who tried to kill me. The one you choked to death."

Logan didn't correct her that the man who'd tried to kill her wasn't a demon, nor did he tell her that he knew that Manus wasn't dead.

"Did you leave the room? Where is he? Where did you see him?"

Winter shook her head. "I was in the shower. I had a vision. It was different this time. Maybe because I knew what it was. I didn't fight it, not at first. But then I saw him. I thought he was dead. I thought you killed him. But he's still alive." Tears brimmed at her eyes.

Logan pulled her to his chest and stroked his hand over her head. "Tell me exactly what you saw."

She looked up at him. "It was a warehouse, I think. Red brick. He was staring at something. At a wall. It looked like something was carved into it, but I couldn't make it out. It was too dark. But I saw the dagger at his belt. He was waiting. I think he was waiting for me. For us. As if he knew where we would go."

Because Manus did know. He'd figured it out. He'd put two and two together and deducted that Logan would go to a portal to disappear with Winter. And at one such portal, Manus was now lying in wait. And Logan had to figure out which one, and whether any of his other compound mates were guarding the other portals. Luckily, he knew there were too many portals within a fifty mile radius of Philadelphia for his fellow guardians to guard them all. They would have to make an educated guess where Logan would appear, and that's all it would be, a guess. Because they couldn't rely on transit cameras to find him and Winter, nor on credit card charges. Logan had made sure of that.

"You've done well," he said to Winter.

"Well? But he's chasing us."

Logan shook his head. "He's waiting for us at a place he believes I'll go. Which means we'll have to make sure not to show up there. I need a computer." He pointed to the tray. "Eat something and be ready."

He walked toward the wall that connected this room with the one next to them.

"What are you planning?"

Logan looked over his shoulder. "I'll use another guest's computer to check three possible addresses on Google street view. If one of them looks like the one you saw in your vision, we'll avoid that address and go to one of the others."

"What will we find at those addresses?"

"Portals."

When her mouth opened for another question, he stopped her. "I'll explain later." Then he made himself invisible and stepped through the wall into the other room.

~ ~ ~

Logan had thought it safer to walk to the portal he'd chosen rather than take public transportation or steal a car. Safer to walk invisibly. Winter didn't mind. At least the cool air helped her clear her head.

On the way, Logan explained what a portal was.

"You mentioned *Star Trek* yesterday. Think of it as the transporter room. The door to a portal is marked with a carved dagger. Only the hand of a Stealth Guardian can open it. You step inside, like you would step onto the pods in the transporter room in *Star Trek*. But our portals don't need an engineer to work."

"What do you mean?" Winter asked. "Then how do you beam from one place to another?"

Logan tipped his finger to his temple. "With my mind. I concentrate on my destination, and it takes me to the portal closest to that destination."

"And the demons? How do they do it? In my visions I saw something different, yet strangely similar. Fog and smoke, all swirling around. And they disappear in it." And it had scared her.

He nodded. "It's a portal of sorts. We call them vortexes. But they are mobile, not tied to any specific place."

She stopped walking for a moment, her heart pounding. "Are you telling me that they can appear anywhere?"

"Almost anywhere. They do have restrictions."

"Such as?"

"A demon can only conjure a vortex on the ground."

"What does that mean?"

"It means the surface on which they project their vortex has to be directly connected to the earth. So, for example, it's possible for them to project a vortex on the ground floor of a building, but not on a floor higher up."

Winter thought about it for a moment. "In that hotel we had a room on the second floor."

Logan nodded. "Otherwise a demon following us would have had a chance of entering our room without having to kick the door in."

"Oh my God! So, really, nowhere is safe."

"Not exactly. A demon has to have a visual of his destination to transport him there. Either he has to have been there before, or he needs a picture of it, needs to know what it looks like."

"How do you know so much about them?"

"We observe, we analyze, we learn. Occasionally we get the opportunity to capture a demon and torture him for information."

"And torture, it works?"

"Sometimes. But the demons have a very high tolerance for pain. It's hard to get information out of them. They'd rather die. So we oblige them."

There was something matter of fact in Logan's voice, as if the killing of demons was a daily occurrence. Maybe it was. Just another day in the office. She almost laughed at that. Almost. But the situation was too dire.

Logan seemed to misinterpret her silence, because he said, "They have to be killed. You do understand that, don't you?"

She quickly glanced at him. "Of course. They deserve to die. I'm not judging you for killing them. I'm grateful that men like you exist. Or I would be dead now." Or worse, living in the Underworld, doing the demons' bidding.

She shuddered at the thought.

"We're almost there," Logan suddenly said and pointed to a building.

Winter read the inscription over the double doors. "The library? The portal is in a library?"

"Come on. Once we pass those trash containers over there, I'll make us visible. Then we'll go in like ordinary citizens wanting to check out some books. Ready?"

She nodded.

They had no problems entering the library. It was late morning and not busy. Once in the stacks, Logan turned to her and lowered his voice. "We're looking for a wall, either made of stone or wood with an ancient dagger carved into it. Keep your eyes open."

Winter knew what a portal would look like. She'd seen several in her visions. "Let's split up. I'll walk around the second floor wall, you take the first floor."

Chuckling, Logan shook his head. "Not a chance. Have you never seen a horror movie? When did *let's split up* ever turn out well?"

She grimaced. "You've got a point."

He took her hand and ushered her toward the outer wall of the old building. "This way."

For several minutes, they searched for the telltale dagger that would reveal the entrance to the portal, but found nothing.

Back where they'd started, Winter met Logan's eyes. "Maybe upstairs?"

He shook his head. "Extremely unlikely." He pointed upwards. They were standing in a small atrium that allowed them to see the walls of the upper floor. "The walls are too new. Probably an add-on to the original building. They wouldn't have used old stone or salvaged wood up there that could contain the portal's entrance."

"But where then? Are you sure this was the address?"

"Yes. I'm sure."

Footsteps behind them made Winter spin around. Logan did the same. A woman in business attire and with a nametag that read *Chief Librarian* smiled at them.

"I'm sure you're wondering where it is," the woman said in a pleasant voice.

Winter felt Logan tense next to her, his hand already reaching inside his jacket.

"Uh, yeah, uh," Winter stammered.

"You wouldn't be the first," the librarian continued and pointed to an area behind the history stacks. "The permanent exhibit is still in the history section. We thought of moving it, but it would have been too costly. Feel free to browse and come back to my desk if you have any questions." Then she moved her hand toward them, and only now did Winter see the brochure she held out. "Here you go, you forgot to pick up a leaflet on your way in."

Logan, still on alert next to her, didn't move, but Winter forced a smile and reached for the leaflet. She glanced down at it quickly, not wanting to let the librarian out of her sight, just in case she was a demon. But one look at the photo displayed on the leaflet, and she jabbed Logan in the ribs.

"Thanks so much," she said to the librarian, then looked at Logan, and in a much lower voice she said, "Look at this!"

Only when the librarian had walked back to her desk, did Logan finally look down at the leaflet.

"You've gotta be kidding me!" he murmured.

Winter nodded, her eyes scanning the text on the brochure. "They think it's a stone the Vikings brought to North America during their explorations."

Already walking toward the history section, Logan said, "It's much older than that."

Holding onto Logan's hand, she rounded the corner just behind him. And there it was. A monolith with an engraving. It was hard to make out what the engraved symbol was if one didn't know already. But she knew what it was, and therefore she recognized the dagger instantly.

"The portal," she murmured full of reverence.

She exchanged a look with Logan.

"We've gotta be quick before she comes back," Logan said and stepped over the cordon.

Winter followed him and watched as he put his palm flat over the dagger. A few seconds later, the monolith was gone and in its stead, an opening leading into darkness appeared.

Logan turned to her and must have seen her fearful look, because he said, "Trust me."

She took a steadying breath and nodded. Then Logan walked into the darkness and pulled her inside. When she looked over her shoulder, she could still see the stacks of books, but a moment later, everything went dark.

"Hold on to me. Don't let go," Logan said.

Winter put both arms around his torso and held on for dear life.

Logan put one arm around her waist and brought his mouth to her ear. "It might get a little bumpy."

"Okay."

Then she lost the ground beneath her feet and gasped in shock.

16

San Francisco was its usual foggy self, particularly in the Corona Heights neighborhood where Logan had brought Winter after arriving in a portal inside a station of the Bay Area's public transport system. He'd cased the house until he was sure that only one person was inside, the person he needed to see.

Clasping Winter's hand and giving her a reassuring nod, Logan rang the doorbell. He didn't have to wait long. The door was opened within seconds.

A stunned Wesley greeted him, "Logan?"

"Hey, Wes."

"What a surprise. Come on in."

Wesley motioned them inside, and Logan was glad for it. He didn't like standing outside where he and Winter could be seen. "Thanks."

"You just missed Virginia. She didn't mention that you were coming. I'll call her."

Logan put his hand on Wesley's forearm. "Don't. We came to see you. In fact, I'd appreciate it if this visit remained between us. No need to involve Virginia."

Now Wesley's eyebrows rose. It was evident that he didn't like keeping secrets from his Stealth Guardian wife. His shoulders lifted a fraction. "Okay?"

Logan turned to Winter. "Winter, this is Wesley Montgomery. He's a witch. A very good one."

Winter spun her head to Wesley, staring at him open-mouthed. "A witch?"

Wesley rolled his eyes at Logan. "You do have a way with words," he said, his voice dripping with sarcasm, before he extended his hand to Winter. "He's right about one thing, I am indeed very good."

"Yeah, and very humble," Logan added, while they shook hands. "Wes, Winter is a psychic. A true one."

Now Wesley's eyes widened, and he held on to Winter's hand, looking her up and down. "I'll be damned!" He grinned. "I'm honored. I've never met a psychic."

"I've never met a witch," Winter said.

Finally, Wesley released Winter's hand and waved toward the back of the house. "I was just finishing breakfast. Come on back to the kitchen." He was already turning and walking down the hallway. "Are you guys hungry?"

Logan took Winter's hand. "We've had breakfast already. We came from the East Coast."

"That explains it."

Logan entered the large kitchen behind Wesley, Winter by his side. He motioned to one of the barstools, and Winter took a seat, while he set down the bag next to her and leaned against the bar. Wesley busied himself at the stove.

"So, what's up? You said you came to see me, not Virginia?"

"We need your help," Logan said.

"Sure, what do you need?" Wesley pointed to the coffee pot then to Winter, who nodded. He took a mug from a cupboard and poured the coffee.

"Thanks," she said and took it.

"Winter needs help controlling her visions. And since psychics are extremely rare, we can't exactly ask another one for help. I figured you're the next best person," Logan explained.

Wesley grimaced. "Ah, so I'm your second choice. You do have a way of making me feel special."

"This is serious, Wes."

"Gee, you're tense, can't even take a joke these days?"

"Demons attacked me," Winter suddenly said, drawing Wesley's gaze to her. Fear had returned to her eyes. "It was horrible. Their eyes..." Winter shuddered visibly. "There was green blood everywhere."

To his credit, Wesley gave Winter a kind smile, all joking forgotten. "Oh, I've been there, believe me. I met those bastards. They're no joke. But you've got a good protector by your side. One of the best. Right, Logan?"

Logan nodded. "We have to lay low for a while, until Winter can get her visions under control. Will you help us?"

"Sure. But when you say get the visions under control, what exactly do you mean?"

Logan put his hand on Winter's and squeezed it. "Winter found out only yesterday that she's a psychic. She thought the visions she was having were nightmares, her psychiatrist thought she had PTSD."

"Some psychiatrist!" Wes commented.

"Well, he didn't know any better. Anyway, Winter's been fighting the visions, because they were too horrible to face. But now we need to help her control her psychic powers."

Wesley poured another cup and set it in front of Logan. Logan nodded thanks and took a sip.

"Hmm," Wes said, "this reminds me of how I started." He looked at Winter. "I was in a similar situation as you. I didn't know I was a witch. I really had no powers to speak of. But I studied, I practiced, and then practiced some more. It's a hard road. But once you have your powers under control, it's very rewarding. Not to mention useful."

"I wish I could just extinguish these powers, then the demons wouldn't be after me," Winter said with a sad smile.

"I'm afraid that's not possible," Wes replied. "A psychic's powers are hereditary, passed down from generation to generation."

"You mean I could have inherited this from my parents?"

"Most likely, though it can skip a generation, sometimes even two, and not every sibling inherits the powers. Do your parents exhibit any signs of being psychics?"

"They died when I was nine. In a car crash."

"I'm sorry," Wesley said. "Any siblings?"

She shook her head. "I'm an only child."

"Any other relatives? Grandparents?"

"All dead."

Wes exchanged a look with Logan. "At least you won't have to worry about protecting another psychic apart from Winter." He turned to the coffee machine and switched it off. "I think I need to hit the books to read up on psychics and see how they channel their visions. That's what you want, right? To be able to direct your visions so they can be of use."

"If Winter's visions can be channeled so she'll be able to reveal secrets about the demons, we might be able to defeat them." And Logan might be able to convince the council to let Winter live. But he couldn't say that, not in front of Winter.

"I figured as much. I might have to confer with another witch in case I don't have all the information in my library."

"Just do it on the downlow. The fewer people who know about Winter and where she is, the safer it is for all of us," Logan cautioned him. "We have to assume that the demons have their spies out listening for any chatter about a psychic."

"Don't worry, nobody will find out."

"In the meantime, Winter and I need a place to stay. Just for a few days."

Wes made a motion with his arm. "You can stay here. I'm sure Virginia won't mind."

Logan had expected Wes to offer his own house, but as soon as Virginia was back and found him and Winter in her house, the gig would be up. "Ahem, do you mind if we have a little chat, Wes? Just you and I."

When Winter gave him a wary look, he squeezed her hand. "Nothing to worry about."

"It's something bad, isn't it?"

Logan forced a smile. "Nothing bad." He hesitated, then let the lie roll over his lips like water over a waterfall. "Just some history Virginia and I have."

"You and her?" she murmured and cast a quick look at Wes. "Oh."

"Wes? Your office?"

Logan marched out of the kitchen, Wesley on his heels. Moments later they were in Wesley's home office, the door shut.

"History between you and Virginia? What a load of bollocks!" Wesley said. "Why did you lie to her? What are you not telling me?"

Logan swallowed away the knot in his throat. "We're not just on the run from the demons. I'm a fugitive from my own people."

Wes visibly jolted. "What?"

"I defied a direct council order. And now I'm on the run with Winter. Virginia can't find out where I am, or they'll bring me in."

Wesley slumped down into his armchair. "Oh for fuck's sake! What have you done? Are you crazy? And you came to my house? What if Virginia had been home?"

"I waited until she left."

"Oh, well, that's just great. That makes it alright." Wesley shook his head. "She's my wife, you know. And I'm not one to keep secrets from my wife."

"You have to keep this one. Or Winter dies."

Wesley jumped up. "What?"

"The council ordered her execution."

"Does she know?"

"No, she has no idea. Nor does she know that I was the one supposed to kill her. But I couldn't do it…"

"Well, she *is* pretty. I give you that."

Logan glared at him. "That wasn't the reason." He sighed. "At least not at first. When I was at her place, about to kill her, I realized that she would be of more value to the Stealth Guardians if she remained alive and if she could guide her visions. If she could channel them toward the demons and become an asset for us."

Slowly Wesley shook his head, but in his eyes understanding blossomed. "You mean to make the council members change their votes."

Logan nodded. "I need to convince only one council member. Only one, and the execution order will be reversed."

"You're absolutely crazy. You're risking being tried for treason."

"The reward is worth it."

"What reward are you talking about? The advantage she might represent in your fight against the demons, or your personal reward?"

Wesley's eyes bored into him.

"How dare—"

"Oh, come on, Logan, I'm married, not blind! And I don't have to be a witch or a psychic to see what's going on between you and her."

"What I want for her has nothing to do with that." And yet it had everything to do with it.

"But if you can convince the council, you'll get both. Two birds with one stone. Right?"

"You can be very annoying sometimes. You know that, Wes?"

Wesley shrugged. "Hearing the truth can have that effect on people. But I'm a sucker for a good love story."

"So you'll help us?"

"Yeah, and I'm probably gonna get in trouble with Virginia over it."

Logan smiled. "Way I remember it, you can be very charming when you want to be. I'm sure you have a way of taming that warrior wife of yours." He slapped Wesley on the shoulder. "Thanks, buddy."

Wes huffed. "Easy for you to say." Then, almost casually, he added, "When are you gonna tell Winter that she's marked for death?"

"And tell her that I was the one who was supposed to kill her? I hope never."

"I suggest you tell her sooner rather than later. Lies have a way of finding their way to the surface."

Logan shook his head. "If I tell her now, she might run from me, and I won't be able to protect her."

Wesley shrugged. "It's your funeral."

17

After a couple of hours at Wesley's house, their host had found a safe place for Winter and Logan to stay and driven them there in his fancy Mercedes. This was Winter's first time in San Francisco, and during the drive she'd caught glimpses of some of the sights the city was famous for. But she didn't really look around. Instead she thought about what Wesley had told her, that a psychic inherited her powers from her parents or grandparents. Could this mean that her grandmother had been a psychic? That she hadn't been mentally ill? It all made sense now.

Her grandmother had always insisted that she saw things, that she knew what was going to happen. And nobody had believed her. Everybody had thought she was losing her mind, when in reality, she hadn't had anybody to help her with her gift, just like Winter hadn't had anybody to explain to her what was happening to her. Until now.

The building in front of which Wesley finally stopped was somewhere downtown and looked a little dirty and rather run down.

"Don't mind the homeless," Wesley said, when he caught her assessing look. "They're mostly harmless."

"If you say so." She waited for Logan to round the car and take her hand.

Together they followed Wesley to the front door.

"Where are we?" Logan asked.

Wesley unlocked the front door and ushered them into the dark interior. "This building belongs to Amaury. He and Nina live on the top floor, but their boys have their own flat just beneath them. The twins are on a training mission for the next four days, so the flat is empty. You can stay here. Nobody will disturb you."

Logan said, "And Amaury and Nina. Did you—"

"I didn't breathe a word to them," Wesley interrupted just as the elevator doors opened. He ushered them inside, then pressed the button. "They're gone too. Some dirty weekend or something." He shrugged and grinned. "You know how these lovebirds are."

"I do," Logan said.

"Who are they? You know them well?" Winter asked, looking at Logan. She felt uncomfortable sneaking into a stranger's home without them knowing or having given permission.

The elevator doors opened and Wesley stepped out, already heading for a door.

Following him, Logan said in response to her earlier question, "I've worked with Amaury before. He's a good man. He's one of the directors of Scanguards."

Wesley opened the door to the apartment wide and walked in.

"What's Scanguards?" Winter asked as she followed Wesley inside.

Behind her, Logan closed the door. "A security company."

She caught Wesley exchanging a look with Logan and asked, "There's more. What are you not telling me?"

Wes jerked his thumb toward her. "She's a psychic, you know. Might as well tell her. She's gonna find out eventually. All she has to do is open the fridge and see the blood. Besides, she's seen demons, and I think vampires are way less scary than demons."

"Vampires?" The word left her throat on a breathless whisper.

Logan glared at Wesley. "Thanks, bro. Way to break the news gently."

"You're just way too slow, buddy, beating about the bush all the time." He pointed to Winter. "She's survived a demon attack. She can take it."

Wesley's encouragement felt good. Winter smiled at him, then shook her head at Logan. "I'm not that fragile, Logan. You don't have to keep stuff from me because you think you need to protect me from everything. I can handle it." Though knowing vampires existed was kind of a shock.

She put on a brave face. "So, vampires, huh? Amaury and Nina? Friendly vampires? You trust them?"

Logan approached her and took her hands. "With my life, and so can you. And only Amaury is a vampire. Nina, his mate, is human. They are good people."

"But you don't want them to know that we're here," she stated.

"The less people know about you, the better."

"I get that." She looked around the apartment. "I didn't expect such a nice place in this neighborhood."

Wes chuckled. "Amaury doesn't spare any expense when it comes to his precious sons."

"Vampires can reproduce?" Winter asked in astonishment. Common lore had always suggested otherwise, not that she'd ever given it much thought. She'd never believed in the supernatural. Not until yesterday.

"They can, under the right circumstances," Wesley said, "but I won't bore you with the details. I'm sure you guys want to get settled. There should be food in the freezer."

"Food?" Confused, Winter gaped at Wesley. "But didn't you just say they're vampires?"

"Amaury is, but his sons are hybrids," Wesley explained. "They are part vampire, part human. They eat regular food, but they also drink blood. Keeps them strong."

"Oh." Her head was spinning already. So much to digest. But maybe it was best to get as much information as she could all at once. Then at least she would be prepared for anything.

"Don't worry, you'll get the hang of it," Wesley assured her.

She liked him. He was easy going and charming. Not to mention practical. "Thank you for helping us, Wesley. I hope I can repay your kindness one day."

"No need. We're all one big family here, and that's what family does."

Logan let go of her hand and offered his hand to Wesley. They shook hands. "I appreciate it."

Wesley handed the key to Logan. "Oh, before I forget, I think you should go see Gabriel."

"Gabriel, why?"

"Because of his gift. He might be able to unlock memories of some of Winter's visions. I mean it's just a thought. No idea if it even works. But it's worth a shot. I'm sure he'd be happy to do it."

Logan's face lit up. "That's a brilliant idea. I'll discuss it with Winter."

"You do that. Oh and before I forget it..." He reached into his jacket pocket and pulled out a cell phone. "This is a burner. Only I have the number so I can get in touch with you. My number is programmed in."

"Thanks, Wes."

Then he smiled at Winter. "Nice meeting you, Winter. I'll be in touch soon and let you know what I can find out about psychics."

She raised her hand to wave goodbye and watched him leave. Silence descended on the apartment when the door shut behind Wesley.

"Are you alright? I know it's a lot to take in."

She met Logan's gaze. "Please stop asking me if I'm alright. You don't have to walk on eggshells around me. I can handle it." She lifted one shoulder in a shrug. "I mean, compared to demons, vampires sound like kittycats. And witches are basically just humans doing spells, right?"

"You're right. You can handle it. But when it gets too much, when you feel it becoming too overwhelming, you'll have to let me know. Promise?"

"And then what are you gonna do?"

"Everything in my power to make things right."

She gave him a hesitant smile. As if anybody could make things right again. This was a world of demons, vampires, and witches. A world she knew nothing about. A world that was frightening, a world where evil reigned. And a single Stealth Guardian couldn't change that. Maybe an army of them. An army who knew where the demons were vulnerable. She knew now where she was needed. "You'll need my help for that. You'll need my visions to fight them." She looked into his eyes. "Let's do what Wesley suggested. Let's go to this Gabriel and see if he can help me dive deeper into my visions."

"Even if that means you'll have to relive the horrors of those visions?"

She swallowed away the fear. "What I see can't hurt me now. Not anymore. It can only help us." It was time to face her fears. And with Logan by her side, she was strong enough to do it.

~ ~ ~

The walk to Gabriel's house in Nob Hill, a fancy downtown neighborhood, wasn't far, but the streets leading to it were steep. Logan didn't break a sweat, but he noticed Winter breathing heavily on the sharp incline, so he slowed his walk. He wasn't going to ask her if she was alright, since clearly, she didn't like him fussing about her. He liked that about her, too. She wasn't prissy. She played the cards she was dealt and made the best of it.

"We turn right here," he said and pointed to the next intersection. He'd been to Gabriel's house on a couple of occasions in the last two years, and though he didn't remember the exact street address, he recognized the street and the house visually.

Like so many houses in San Francisco, Gabriel's was an old Victorian, a magnificent home he shared with his vampire mate and their three children. It was early afternoon, and though Logan hadn't called ahead, he expected Gabriel to be at home.

"That's his house?" Winter asked with awe in her voice. "It looks amazing."

"Wait till you see the inside."

Side by side they walked up the steps leading to the dark wooden door. There, they stopped and Logan put his hand on Winter's arm, making her look at him.

"There's something you should know about Gabriel."

"Yes?"

"He has a disfigurement, a long scar reaching from his ear to his chin. It's not a pretty sight, and it may give the impression that he's a violent man. The contrary is the case. I don't want you to be afraid of him."

"Thank you for letting me know. I'll do my best to ignore it."

"Good." Logan pressed the doorbell and heard the chiming sound inside the house.

Moments later, the intercom crackled and the light of a camera shone into his face.

"Is that you, Logan?" a male voice came through the speaker.

"It is. Who's this? Ryder?"

"No, it's Ethan."

The buzzer sounded, and Logan pressed against the door, opening it. He held it open for Winter, ushered her inside, and followed.

Within seconds, Ryder and Ethan, as well as their sister Vanessa, appeared in the entrance hall, each coming from a different direction. They were young adults now, with Vanessa being the youngest at age twenty, and Ryder the oldest at twenty-three.

"Oh my God, did something happen?" Vanessa asked. "Does Dad know you're here?"

Vanessa, who reached him first, hugged him quickly then stepped back.

"He doesn't, though I really need to see him." Logan reached his hand out to Ethan and shook it. "Hey, Ethan. Good to see you."

Then Ryder offered his hand in greeting. "Did you bring us some d—" He stopped himself when his gaze fell on Winter. "Oh, hi, I'm Ryder."

"Hi, I'm Winter."

"You can speak freely in front of her. She knows everything about us." Then he nodded at Ryder. "And, no, I didn't bring you any demons to blow up."

"Blow up?" Winter asked, her gaze darting between Logan and Ryder.

Ryder grinned. "I'm doing explosives training right now. With Quinn. And blowing up some demons would be immensely fun."

"So gross!" Vanessa said. "Splattering green blood all over the place. Yuck!" She shook her head then smiled at Winter. "I'm Vanessa. And don't listen to those two oversized blowhards. So far none of them has blown up any demons yet."

Logan noticed Winter smile and was glad that the hybrids' sibling rivalry was putting her at ease. After all, the three were just like any other young adults, carving out their place in life, and testing their boundaries with each other.

"I wouldn't mind seeing them all blown up," Winter said.

Ryder and Ethan exchanged a conspiratorial look and chuckled.

"I guess somebody should wake Dad," Vanessa said and turned toward the staircase.

"Not necessary," a deep male voice came from the top of the stairs. "With the ruckus you're making down here, you could wake the dead."

Gabriel came into sight a moment later as he marched down the stairs. He wore a pair of low-slung jeans and a white shirt, which was unbuttoned. His long brown hair, which reached to his shoulders and was normally tied into a ponytail, was open. He looked to be in his mid-thirties, but of course he was much older.

"Logan, don't tell me you're bringing us even more work than we already have?" Gabriel greeted him with slap on the shoulder and a firm handshake.

"Nothing you can't handle," Logan replied. "May I introduce Winter Collins? Winter, this is Gabriel Giles, second-in-command at Scanguards."

Gabriel extended his hand and Winter shook his, but barely lifted her eyes.

"Nice to meet you," she said and dropped her lids.

There was an awkward pause, before Gabriel said, "Pleasure. By the way, it's okay for you to look at me. I prefer people staring at my scar rather than avoid looking at me altogether."

Winter gasped and lifted her head to face Gabriel. "I'm sorry. I didn't mean to offend you." Her gaze lingered on his face, and Gabriel didn't move, allowed her the time she needed to get used to his appearance. "It's not as disfiguring as Logan made me believe. In fact, you're an attractive man, even with the scar."

"I've always thought so," a female voice proclaimed from the stairs.

Winter's eyes snapped to the woman, barefoot and dressed in a bathrobe, descending the stairs. Logan followed her gaze. Maya was a beauty with long dark hair and a sensual figure. And despite having three grown children she still looked like she was in her early thirties. Being a vampire did have its advantages.

"I'm Maya, Gabriel's mate," Maya said with a charming smile and took Winter's hand into hers. "You're human." She turned to look at Logan. "It's nice to see you, Logan. Though I get the feeling this is not a social visit."

"It's not."

Gabriel motioned to the end of the hallway. "My study?"

Logan nodded. "Lead the way."

18

A half hour later, Gabriel, sitting in a comfortable leather armchair in his study, let out a breath.

"So you're a psychic. Never thought I'd ever meet one," he admitted.

Logan watched Winter meet the vampire's gaze, this time without avoiding looking at their host's gruesome scar. "I guess we're all having a lot of *firsts* today. I never thought I'd meet a witch or a vampire, or any kind of immortal creature."

"Hmm." Gabriel looked at Logan who sat on the couch next to Winter. "So you think I can help Winter with my gift?"

"That's what I'm hoping. I think it might help to restore some of the memories she's suppressed of the visions, trying to forget them because she thought they were nightmares. If you can unlock them, we might be able to unearth useful information about the demons." Logan took Winter's hand and squeezed it. He'd done that a lot in the last twenty-four hours, and he liked the connection he felt to her when he touched her like this. "And perhaps it'll help with future visions, too."

"I can certainly try," Gabriel offered and looked directly at Winter. "With your permission, of course. You must understand that if I delve into your memories, I might see things you'd prefer I didn't. It's an invasion of your privacy. So if you have secrets you don't want revealed, you need to tell me now."

Winter hesitated.

Did she have secrets she didn't want him or Gabriel to know? After all, everybody had secrets. And sometimes those secrets could burn holes in a person's conscience, just like the secret Logan was keeping from Winter was burning a hole in his.

"It's your choice," Logan assured her.

Winter took a breath and let it out. "I have no secrets."

"Then I have your permission?" Gabriel asked.

She nodded. "How does it work?"

"You won't feel anything. I'll put my hands on your head—it works best with a physical connection—and I'll concentrate on your mind and try to connect with it. I'll see only the things you've seen and if I see blockages, I should be able to unblock them for you, so any suppressed memories will rise to the surface again. I have to warn you, though." He made a small pause. "If there are painful memories within the visions that I'm trying to unlock, you'll feel the pain again. Be prepared for it."

"I'm ready. Do what you need to do."

"Well then," Gabriel said and motioned to Logan. "Would you mind if I took your seat?"

Logan rose and changed seats with Gabriel, so Gabriel was now seated on the couch next to Winter, facing her. Logan knew from others who'd been through this process that there wasn't actually anything to watch. All he would see was Gabriel laying his hands on Winter's head, eyes closed, and minutes later the vampire would be able to retell what he'd seen in her memories. Logan leaned back in the armchair and waited.

Gabriel put his hands on Winter's head and closed his eyes. His breathing seemed to calm, his chest rising and falling evenly. Not a sound could be heard in the study. Logan glanced toward the only window of the room, which offered a partial view of the garden. Anybody else would have been surprised to see that the curtains weren't drawn, though it was daytime, but Logan knew that all the vampires associated with Scanguards had vampire-proofed their homes by applying a special UV-impenetrable film to the windows, shielding the inhabitants from sunlight.

Logan was admiring the invention, when he suddenly heard Winter give a loud gasp. He snapped his gaze back to her and Gabriel.

Logan shot up from his seat, but whatever was happening was already unfolding and couldn't be stopped. Gabriel screamed, a cry of agonizing pain like a wounded animal, his hands still connected to Winter's head. Winter's hair was standing up in all directions as if electrified, the tips shimmering with blue light, throwing off sparks that shot right into Gabriel's face.

"No! Stop!" Logan cried. He charged toward them, hoping to separate the two, but a wave of electrical current hit him and flung him back, making him crash against the armchair.

Helplessly, he watched as burns spread on Gabriel's hands and face and Gabriel continued to cry out in pain.

"Winter! Stop! Let him go!" Logan yelled, as he scrambled back to his feet and lunged for the couch.

He would have thrown himself between the two, had somebody not pushed him out of the way in that moment. By the time he managed to snap his head back to the scene, the person who'd charged in had ripped Winter and Gabriel apart and catapulted Winter against the wall next to the window. There, Maya was squeezing Winter's neck with one hand, baring her fangs.

"No, Maya! Stop!" Logan yelled and rushed toward her, knocking over the armchair in the process. "She didn't mean it! Stop, Maya! Don't hurt her!"

But Maya wasn't listening. She growled at Winter, whose eyes were open now, staring at the vampire woman with naked horror—as if she'd just woken up and didn't know what had happened to her.

Logan reached Maya and grabbed her arm. She turned her head, snarling at him, her fangs fully extended, her eyes glaring red, looking at him as if she didn't even see him. Only rage controlled her now. Rage, and the need to protect her mate.

Logan had always known that a vampire would protect his mate to the death. Now he saw with his own eyes that a vampire female was no different.

"Maya! Baby, no!" It was Gabriel's voice, raspy, but firm, that now sounded from behind them.

Logan whipped his head to him. He'd landed on the floor next to the couch and had burns all over his hands and face, but he seemed otherwise unharmed.

"Gabriel, please stop her. Please! Don't let her hurt Winter."

Gabriel managed to jump up and rush to them. "Maya, baby, look at me, I'm fine. I'm unharmed." He put his hand on his wife's arm. She turned her head and looked at him. "See, I'm alright, baby, nothing happened." Slowly he eased Maya's hand from Winter's neck and pulled his wife into his arms.

~ ~ ~

Winter, finally able to breathe again, coughed, knowing she was lucky to be alive. Maya had been prepared to kill her. She'd seen it in her eyes.

Logan snatched her and pulled her to his chest. She was grateful for the comfort, because she was shaking.

"It's alright now, love, it's alright," he murmured to her and stroked his hand over her head.

A sob tore from her throat. What had she done?

"Easy, easy," Logan cooed and pressed kisses to her forehead. "I've got you. I won't let anything happen to you."

Winter's breathing grew steadier, and she chanced a look at Gabriel. His arms were around Maya, and she was holding on to him just as tightly as Winter was holding on to Logan.

"What happened?" Logan asked. The question wasn't directed at her, but at Gabriel.

Maya spun her head around. "What happened? She attacked my husband! What the fuck is she?"

Winter shuddered in Logan's arms, and he held her even closer to comfort her.

"She's a psychic," Gabriel said and pulled his wife's head back to him to force her to look at him. "And it wasn't her fault. She felt attacked by me diving into her memories."

Both Logan and Maya shook their heads.

"But—"

Gabriel lifted his hand. "I know, she gave her permission, but it appears that a psychic's mind works differently than a human's. The psychic in her didn't appreciate the invasion and was fighting back."

Winter stared at them. They were talking about her like she wasn't even there. But she was. And she had to say something. "I'm so sorry." She choked the words out amidst tears. "I didn't know how to stop it."

Gabriel looked at her directly, a kind expression on his damaged face. "I don't blame you. I should have realized that it wouldn't be so easy. That a psychic is a psychic for a reason. Nobody can get into your head. It's like a fortress." Then he ran his hand through Maya's hair. "Don't be angry with her, baby." He pressed a kiss to his wife's lips. "Would you get me a bottle of blood? I need to heal."

Maya tossed a look back at Winter, as if to check whether it was safe to leave her husband in the same room with her.

"I won't let her near him, I promise," Logan assured her.

Winter wanted to give the same assurance, but she didn't dare address Maya directly.

"You'd better keep that promise, or I'll rip your head off." Maya marched out of the room.

Gabriel followed her with his eyes. "She is a fierce woman." He smiled and looked back at Winter. "Please don't take it personally that she attacked you. She would kill for me. And I for her."

"I'm so sorry, Gabriel, I didn't mean to..."

Gabriel lifted his hand to stop her. "As I said, it wasn't your fault." Then he sighed. "But it also means that whatever you've got locked away in that head of yours, isn't for me to unlock. I won't be able to help you."

"Thank you for trying, Gabriel," Logan said. "I'm sorry we caused you so much trouble."

"Please, don't apologize. What are friends for? I wish I could help. But maybe this is a job for Dr. Drake."

"Dr. Drake?" Winter echoed.

"A vampire psychiatrist here in San Francisco. His methods are unorthodox, but he's had some successes. And unlike a human psychiatrist he's familiar with preternatural creatures. He might know how to help you."

"But I'm not a preternatural creature," Winter protested.

"You're not human, Winter," Gabriel said. "A psychic is a preternatural. Their closest relatives in our world are witches."

Winter's mouth fell open. "I'm a preternatural creature?" That couldn't be. She was human. She felt human. How could she suddenly be a preternatural creature?

Logan stroked his knuckles over her cheek. "I thought you realized that when I told you that you were a psychic."

She shook her head.

"It's not so bad." Then he sighed. "But maybe for right now, you've had enough excitement. We should let you get some rest." Logan looked at Gabriel. "Could you give me the address for Dr. Drake so we can visit him later?"

"I'll call him for you and set it up. You'll have to wait for nightfall anyway. He doesn't see patients before dark."

19

Logan flipped the deadbolt. They were alone again, in the twins' apartment. After the incident in Gabriel's house, Winter had barely spoken, clearly shaken by what had happened. He'd been rather silent himself on the walk back, mulling over what Gabriel had said: that Winter's mind was like a fortress that could withstand any invasion. He considered this a good thing, even if it had resulted in injuries to Gabriel and an attack on Winter by Maya. Winter was strong. Maybe stronger than he'd thought at first. Strong enough to hear the truth, the truth about why he'd come to her shop.

It was time. The guilt of keeping this secret from her was weighing heavily on him, particularly since they'd made love the night before. He'd been looking for an occasion to tell her the truth ever since, without having to worry about the weight of it crushing her and making her run from him. But now, after seeing how strong Winter was, he knew she would be able to handle the truth. Whether she could forgive him, he wasn't sure, but as long as she didn't run from him, he'd accept the consequences of his deception. Even if it meant she would never allow him to touch her again.

"Winter," Logan said softly and looked across the open-space living area that connected to the kitchen. "There's something I need to tell you."

She met his gaze, her body rigid as if she already knew what was coming. "What is it?"

He reached her and took both her hands in his.

"Is it about what I did to Gabriel?" She shook her head, more tears brimming in her eyes. "I couldn't control it, Logan, I felt like I was in somebody else's body. It just happened. I didn't mean to hurt your friend."

Logan put a finger over her lips. "Shh. Don't worry about Gabriel. He's a big boy, and vampires heal faster than any creature I've ever met. Trust me, for him, it was just a scratch."

She let out a mirthless laugh. "You say that so easily. But I feel terrible. I've never hurt anybody."

"I believe that." He brushed a strand of her silken hair from her face. "You were only defending yourself. It's self-preservation." He sighed. "But that's not what I wanted to talk to you about. It's about what I did. Or rather what I was supposed to do."

She gave him a quizzical stare. "What do you mean?"

"I need to tell you why I came to your shop. Why—"

"But you already told me, to save me from the demons."

His heart clenched. This would hurt, maybe him more than her, because she would lose faith in him and see him for what he really was.

"I was there to…"

Winter's eyes widened, her lips parting. "Demon!" She pointed to a spot behind him and screamed, "Demon! Oh no!"

Logan spun around, pulling the dagger from inside his jacket, ready to slay any demon. When he laid eyes upon the intruder, however, he froze in mid-movement and a ragged breath tore from his chest.

"Shit!"

"Yeah, no shit, Logan!" Manus glared at him. "You really thought I wouldn't find you?"

"Kill him, Logan, kill him before he kills us," Winter cried out behind him.

Manus tilted his head a little to one side and glanced past him. "A bit bloodthirsty, your girlfriend. And where are your manners, buddy? Aren't you gonna introduce us properly?"

"Shut up, Manus." Logan suddenly felt Winter's hand on his arm.

"You know his name?"

Logan put his dagger back into his jacket.

"What are you doing?" Winter asked, panic coloring her voice.

Logan turned to her. "He's not a demon. He's the same as me. He's a Stealth Guardian."

Winter stared at him in disbelief, then gazed past him to Manus, shaking her head. "That's impossible." She pointed to Manus. "I recognize him. He's the one who tried to kill me in my apartment. He was with them. With the demons."

"It's the truth," Logan said with a sigh.

"You let her believe I was a demon?" Manus threw in. "Not cool, bro, not cool at all."

Logan glared over his shoulder. "You mind shutting up for a second?"

Manus shrugged.

"What is going on here?" Winter said, her voice even tenser than before, her eyes now scrutinizing Logan as well as his fellow guardian. "I'm not crazy. I know he was trying to kill me."

Logan sighed. "He was."

Winter shook her head in confusion. "But why, if it's true what you say? If he is a Stealth Guardian."

"Because I wasn't able to do it."

Winter shrank back from him, her eyes widening. Logan saw shock start to mingle with fear on her face. A breath rushed from her lungs. "What?"

Logan dropped his lids, unable to look her in the eye any longer. "That's what I was about to tell you before Manus stormed in. I was ordered to kill you. That's why I was in your shop. That's why I came. But—"

"But what?" she spat. "You decided to screw me first? Is that it? And now that you got what you wanted, you're gonna kill me? Or does your friend here get a turn first?"

"No!" Logan protested. "That's not—"

"Way to go, Logan," Manus interrupted. "You screwed her? Are you fucking nuts?"

"I said, shut up!" Logan yelled at his friend. "You're not making this any easier."

Manus cursed. "Fuck that! You know why I'm here. If you don't do what you were ordered to, the council will get wind of it. You know what happens then. And I'll be damned if I let my friend be tried for treason, because he couldn't follow an order. Now, be smart, man. Finish the job and nobody needs to know what you did."

"No! I won't kill her. And if you lay one finger on her, I'm going to—"

"What? Kill me?"

"If it comes to that, yes. Winter is under my protection. If you want to kill her, you'll have to kill me first."

~ ~ ~

Stunned, Winter listened to the exchange between the two men. Logan was ready to fight his friend to protect *her*? That couldn't be right. She had to have misheard, because only a few moments earlier he'd confessed that he'd been in her shop to kill her.

"Is she such a good lay?" Manus mocked.

"It has nothing to do with that. Winter is more valuable to us alive than dead. She's the key to fighting the demons. Once the council realizes that, they'll reverse their order of execution."

Order of execution. Those words sent a chill down her spine and turned her blood to ice. A race she didn't know existed until less than two days ago had decided to kill her. And she didn't even know why.

"Why? Why do you want me dead?" she murmured. She met Manus's eyes. "What have I done that's so terrible that it warrants death?"

"It's not what you've done, but what you will do," Manus said and motioned to Logan. "Tell her, explain it to her. It's your mission. It's your mess to clean up."

Logan cast her a long look. "Our ruling body, the Council of Nine, believes that you're too weak to withstand the demons and will eventually give in to their demands."

"Their demands?"

"To tell them everything you see about us in your visions. To become their seer so they can destroy us. And once they've destroyed us, they'll have free rein over mankind. But I know you won't do that. Because I've seen how strong you are. How good you are."

"Bullshit," Manus hissed. "Did you not read her file? She's not strong enough. If she were, the council would have voted for us to protect her."

Slowly, she tried to piece together what it all meant. "But I didn't even know that I was a psychic. They didn't even give me a chance to make my case."

Her words were directed at Manus, but Logan answered instead. "That's why I'm going to make it for you."

"No, you won't!" Manus griped. "You won't even get that far. The moment they find out you let her live, you'll be thrown into a lead cell to wait for your execution."

Winter swallowed hard. Manus had said something about treason earlier. "Execution? They'll kill him if he helps me?"

Logan glared at Manus. "Not another word."

"And why not?" Manus replied. "You don't want her to know what you're risking for her?" Manus directed his gaze to her. "The punishment for treason is death. And by letting you live, he's already committed treason. I'm giving him a chance to rectify this without the council having to find out. So, tell me, Winter, do you want to be responsible for Logan's death?"

A sob worked its way up her throat and she slammed her hand over her mouth to stop it from escaping. Somebody would have to die, either she or Logan. Neither choice was acceptable. How could they be so cruel?

"You're scaring her," Logan said.

"None of this would have happened if you had slipped her the poison without her knowing. It would have been easy." Manus jammed his finger into Logan's chest. "You made it hard and painful. For all of us." Then Manus's eyes traveled to her, softening a little. "I'm sorry, lady, I wish I didn't have to do this, but we have orders and somebody has to follow them."

Fear choked off her ability to breathe, even though Manus wasn't approaching her. Logan had clamped his hand over his fellow guardian's arm. The two were staring at each other as if locked in a battle of wills.

"There's another way," Logan said.

"There's no other way," Manus said. "You should have never come to San Francisco. Anybody who knows you would know you'd seek help from Scanguards."

"I had no choice. Winter needs help guiding and channeling her visions. Wesley is going to figure out a way to help her do that."

"Wesley? Are you fucking crazy? If he knows that you and Winter are here, Virginia will find out."

"You mean she would snitch on us, because of her relationship with Logan?" Winter asked, remembering that Logan had said they had history.

"Relationship?" Manus said and exchanged a look with Logan. "What the fuck?"

"I had to cover," Logan said quickly.

"You mean you lied about that, too?" Winter asked. "Why?" Was anything he'd ever said to her the truth? Could she believe even a single word?

"Because Virginia sits on the Council of Nine, the council that determined your fate. If she finds out you're here, the gig is up," Logan said.

This time she couldn't hold back the sob in her throat. It managed to escape and burst over her lips. "Oh, no."

"Wesley won't say anything to Virginia, he knows what's at stake," Logan assured her then looked back at Manus. "Wesley will help us. He'll find something that will help us convince the council to change their vote."

"You're delusional," Manus said. "Besides, your imminent problem isn't convincing the council, it's convincing me."

"I was getting to that," Logan said quickly. "You remember Gabriel?"

Manus nodded. "Ponytail, big scar, fangs, sure."

"You might be aware of his gift of being able to access people's memories."

Manus shrugged. "Might have heard people talk about it. So what? The file didn't say that she's got memory issues." He jerked his thumb toward Winter as if she wasn't even there. And maybe in Manus's mind she wasn't, because to him she was marked for death.

"Wesley suggested asking Gabriel to try and access some of the visions that Winter has suppressed because they were too terrible to deal with. So that we could use any information we might glean from them to fight the demons more effectively."

Manus raised an eyebrow, for the first time showing some interest. But Winter knew it would be dashed just as quickly. After all, Gabriel hadn't even been able to get into her head. She didn't know why Logan was bothering to tell Manus this when it would lead to nothing.

"So, what did he see? Anything of use?"

"He didn't see anything," Logan replied and paused.

"Well, great." Manus's voice dripped with sarcasm. "If this is your way of buying time, all you're doing is pissing me off."

"Then let me say it again: Gabriel saw nothing, because Gabriel couldn't access Winter's mind. She shut him out. She fought him with so much power that she burned his skin. Do you see it now, Manus?"

Manus's gaze shot to her. His eyes bored into her as if he was looking for something.

"I didn't mean to hurt him," Winter said quickly.

Slowly Manus directed his eyes back to Logan. "So you think she's strong enough to withstand a mental attack by the demons?"

"A mental attack? What does he mean?" Winter asked, a different kind of fear welling up in her.

"The demons first try to bring a human to their side by seducing them with their greatest desires: a loved one cured, a better career, money, anything really. They use their powers of suggestion and for that, they need to get into the person's mind. If they can't get in, they can't seduce."

She digested the words quickly. "They won't be able to get into my head. If they try, the same thing will happen that happened to Gabriel."

Logan nodded. "Exactly."

Expectantly, she looked at Manus. Would he agree with their conclusion?

"I admit," Manus said slowly, as if carefully weighing each word, "that this eliminates one method the demons could use to gain influence over you. But that doesn't mean you're safe. It doesn't mean they won't get you to do their bidding."

"But I won't—"

"Will you be able to stay strong if they drag you down to their lair in the Underworld and torture you until you'll do anything to make the pain stop? Will you?"

Winter's breath hitched. Her chest heaved, and her heart galloped. She had a low pain threshold. She would crack quickly.

"Didn't think so." Manus turned his head to Logan. "So unless you can convince the council that Winter can provide us with actionable intelligence on the demons, then you've got nothing."

"Wesley is still working on figuring out how to guide Winter's visions," Logan said quickly.

"Then he'd better work quickly."

Logan met Manus's eyes. "Are you saying you're giving me time to work this out?"

Manus mumbled something to himself. "I should be stabbed for saying this, but you've got twenty-four hours to take care of this mess. Either you kill her in that time and come back to the compound, or you go before the council and make your case. Don't even think about going on the run again. We trained together. I will always find you no matter where you hide."

Logan extended his hand. "Thank you, brother. I appreciate what you're doing for me."

"It had better be worth the risk." He tossed a look at Winter, then pivoted, marched right through the door and disappeared.

20

Winter suddenly felt her knees buckle and braced herself on the backrest of the armchair she'd sought shelter behind when Manus had appeared in the apartment.

"Are you alright?" Logan asked and hurried toward her, but she lifted her hand to stop him.

"Don't."

She didn't want to feel his arms around her now, not even to support her. He'd lied to her from the very start. He'd been there to kill her. It wasn't something a girl could easily forgive and forget.

"Why didn't you tell me?"

His eyes shone with regret. "I was afraid you'd run from me. And I couldn't risk that. It would have put you in danger. But after what I saw today, what happened with Gabriel, I felt you were ready to hear the truth." He shrugged. "But then Manus beat me to it…"

She shook her head. "I'm not some brainless damsel from a 1950s movie who's too stupid to know who keeps her safe. I wouldn't have run. You could have told me earlier."

The answer seemed to surprise him. "I should have known that."

"You should have," she murmured under her breath.

"I'm sorry."

Well, at least he said all the right things. It was a start. But it didn't change anything about the facts: Logan had been there to kill her.

"Your plan was to poison me. Why poison?"

He didn't lift his lids when he answered, "Because it's painless. We don't let innocents suffer needlessly."

She didn't know whether she should consider it a mercy or not. Was it merciful to not even know that death was coming?

"Why didn't you do it?"

This time Logan did meet her eyes. "I witnessed one of your visions and realized what you were going through. You seemed so vulnerable. At first I thought maybe it would be a relief to end it for you, to end what you were going through." She saw his Adam's apple move. "So I handed you the glass of water."

"The water," Winter murmured, realizing now how close she'd been to drinking it. "But you spilled it. It wasn't an accident, was it?"

He shook his head. "When we talked about your drawings, when I saw the things you'd seen in your visions, I couldn't go through with it. I knew that if you were dead, it would be a loss to all of us, humans and Stealth Guardians alike. I knew you could help us." He blinked his eyes shut for a short moment. "But there was also a selfish reason why I couldn't let you drink the poison."

Winter didn't say anything, didn't ask a question, just let him take the time he needed.

"When I first saw you, I imagined what it would have been like had we met in a bar or run into each other in a supermarket. I wondered whether..." He shook his head. "It doesn't matter now. We met the way we did. And I'm glad I defied the council's order. You deserve to live."

"You committed treason."

He shrugged. "Manus can be very dramatic."

"Dramatic, sure, but I don't think he lied. By not killing me you're risking your own life."

"Maybe they'll be lenient."

"You don't believe that."

The look on his face confirmed her assumption.

"Well, I guess we have no choice now, do we?" she asked. "Either we prove to your council that my visions can help your race in the battle against the demons, or we both die."

It didn't help anybody to lament the fact that Logan had lied to her, had hidden his true purpose. She would deal with all that later. What mattered now was that Logan hadn't executed his orders. He hadn't executed *her*. She was still alive, and she wanted to stay alive.

"Gabriel mentioned a psychiatrist," Winter said. "I think we should see him sooner rather than later."

~ ~ ~

One phone call to Gabriel and an hour later the meeting with Dr. Drake was set up. His office was located in the basement of a stately Edwardian mansion not far from Gabriel's house, which meant it was also within walking distance of the twins' flat.

During the walk there, Logan and Winter didn't talk. He didn't attempt to start a conversation, sensing that Winter had said what she wanted to say for now. He didn't blame her for her silence. In fact, he was surprised that she hadn't hurled any heavy objects at him. Maybe she carried her anger toward him inside her like women did often.

After her initial outburst when Manus had still been in the apartment, she hadn't mentioned their sexual encounter again. He could guess what that meant: she wanted to forget as quickly as possible what they'd done in that motel in Trenton. As much as it pained him to know that she regretted their lovemaking, he knew that by telling her that he'd initially come to kill her, she would reject any further intimacies. Well, he'd have to live with that now. At least Winter wasn't doing anything rash that would expose her to the demons. He was grateful for that.

She was a smart woman. And he should have been smart enough to realize that earlier. Maybe then he could have saved their relationship. Relationship? He had to shake his head. They had no relationship, none that extended beyond protector and charge. And even that was a tenuous one.

If—no, *when*—he had convinced the council to let her live, Winter would insist on a different guardian as her protector. But he didn't want to look that far into the future. He had to concentrate on the task at hand.

Logan looked at the number on the gate. "This is the place."

Winter stopped next to him, and he pushed the iron gate open to let her enter ahead of him. He didn't attempt to take her hand, needing no confirmation that his touch wasn't welcome. "The door at the end of the tradesmen entrance. Gabriel said it's unlocked."

He closed the gate behind him and followed Winter down the narrow walkway along the imposing building. The door at the end was unassuming. There was no sign indicating that a psychiatrist practiced at these premises. Apparently vampires didn't have to or want to advertise their business. Word got around.

Inside, Logan was greeted by a Barbie-doll receptionist with a too-tight top and an aura that identified her as a vampire. No surprise about the latter.

"How may I help you?" she purred in a way that had nothing to do with kittens. Her gaze only briefly drifted to Winter as if she wasn't important at all, yet clung to Logan like static to packing material.

"Miss Collins and I are here to see Dr. Drake. Gabriel Giles made the appointment for us," Logan replied.

"Oh yes, the last-minute change to our schedule." She batted her eyelashes at him. "The doctor is expecting you." She motioned to a door. "Go right in."

Logan nodded, then walked to the door. After a perfunctory knock, he opened the door and let Winter enter ahead of him, then followed her into the room and closed the door.

He didn't really know what he'd expected to find in a vampire psychiatrist's office. But it wasn't this. He shot a look at Winter, wondering about her reaction, and saw that she too was taken aback by the rather unorthodox décor.

A black coffin-couch with faded red velvet cushions was the centerpiece of the room. Two armchairs in a plain style and a coffee table that looked suspiciously like a tombstone completed the seating arrangement. Gothic murals graced the walls, making the room look like a crypt. File cabinets with handles shaped like mini-stakes lined one wall.

"Welcome," Dr. Drake said.

Logan was grateful that the tall, skinny man wasn't wearing a black cape, but a white doctor's coat over his business suit.

"Thank you for seeing us on such short notice," Logan said and shook his hand, then stepped aside and motioned to Winter. "This is Winter Collins."

"The psychic," Drake said with appreciation, offering his hand to Winter. "It's a pleasure, Miss Collins."

Hesitantly, she shook his hand, then pulled back.

"Please, take a seat."

Drake motioned to the coffin-couch, but Logan walked to the normal-looking armchairs instead, pulled one out a little and made eye contact with Winter. She took the seat, and Logan slunk into the chair next to her. Drake, his eyebrows raised a bit, had no choice but to sit on the god-awful couch.

Drake cleared his throat. "Mr. Giles filled me in to save time. I took the liberty of reviewing some lore about psychics to understand how best I can assist."

"I appreciate that, Dr. Drake," Winter said, speaking for the first time.

"But of course. May I just say I'm honored to finally meet a psychic face-to-face. There aren't many of you to start with, and then of course there was a purge a few centuries ago that diminished your numbers even more..."

"A purge? You mean psychics were exterminated?" Winter's gaze flitted to Logan. He knew what she must be thinking. That his race was responsible for it.

"It was a war between the witches and the psychics," Logan explained quickly. "The witches felt threatened by the psychics' powers."

Winter stared at him. "Then why is Wesley helping us?"

"The remaining psychics negotiated a peace agreement with the witches. Besides, Wesley is of a different generation. The old wars, the old disagreements, mean nothing to him," Logan assured her. Then he looked at Drake. "Therefore, there's really no need to speak of it."

"Well," Drake said with a tight smile, "it's always good to know one's history." He turned to look at Winter. "Anyway, my understanding is that you need help in guiding your visions. In controlling them."

"Yes. They hit me out of nowhere. And I feel powerless when they come."

"Powerless? It doesn't have to be that way." He nodded as if nodding to himself, then continued, "Your visions are a powerful thing. Look at them like you look at emotions. Either you exert control over them, or they will control you. It's always a matter of what you allow them to do. Take love and hate for example. Two very powerful emotions. Which one do you believe is more powerful?"

The doctor looked at Winter expectantly. When she didn't say anything, he prompted, "Miss Collins?"

"Oh, you're asking me."

He nodded. "Yes. Which emotion is more powerful, love or hate?"

She hesitated. "Hate?"

Smiling, Drake shook his head. "Love. You know why?"

She shook her head, while Logan wondered where the shrink was going with this.

"It's the strongest emotion, because it comes straight from the heart, from the very essence of your being. You see, you can move mountains with love. There is infinite energy in it. It's up to you, how to use this energy." He cleared his throat. "What I'm trying to explain to you is that you have to start to love your visions if you want to have any power over them. If you want to start to control them."

Winter sighed. "It's a little hard to love something that causes me so much pain."

"Well, it will come, with time. In the meantime, there are several other things we can do: guided meditation, an in-depth psychoanalysis, and relaxation exercises." He pulled a small notebook from his coat pocket. "The guided meditation we can start right away, then you'll need to repeat it daily. I could fit your first psychoanalysis session in tomorrow night. But you'll need to come alone. And the relaxation exercises, for that I actually have a Tuesday night group."

Logan had heard enough. "Dr. Drake, I don't think you understand the time constraint we're under. We have twenty-four hours to get a handle on Winter's visions."

Drake gave him an undignified look. "And *you* don't seem to grasp that the mind of a psychic is a fragile thing."

"I disagree." What he'd seen of Winter's mind wasn't fragile at all.

"There's no way she'll learn to control her visions in twenty-four hours, when it's taken other psychics years to handle them. This takes practice and careful nurturing."

Winter shot up from her chair. "Then what are we doing here?"

Logan heard the desperate tone in Winter's voice and rose. "We're leaving." He nodded at the shrink. "Sorry to waste your time and ours."

He ignored Drake's protests, and took Winter's arm to lead her outside.

In the darkness of the alley, he stopped. "I'm sorry. If we had more time, maybe some of the things he mentioned would work…"

"What are we gonna do now?" She looked at him then, fear and desperation colliding in her beautiful eyes.

He hated seeing her like this, without hope for a future. He wouldn't let her cry, not under his watch.

"I'll call Wesley, see what he's got so far. I'm not giving up this quickly."

He pulled the burner phone Wesley had given him from his jacket pocket and selected the only pre-programmed number. It rang once, twice, three times.

Suddenly, there was a click on the line.

"Logan?"

"Yes."

"I was about to call you. I'm here with another witch. I think you and Winter need to join us."

His heart began to beat excitedly. "Tell me where."

Logan memorized the address Wesley recited, then said, "We'll be there as soon as we can."

21

A taxi took them through the city, turning so many times that Winter lost track of which direction they were going. During the drive she stared outside, not really taking anything in. Disappointment was starting to mount inside her. One failure after another, first Gabriel, now Dr. Drake. Not that she blamed either of them. They had tried. But what if nobody could help her? What if she was a lost cause?

When the cab suddenly came to a halt, Winter looked around. The taxi had stopped outside an unassuming-looking house that backed up to a large green space with tall trees and thick brush.

Logan paid the driver and helped her out of the car.

"Where are we?" she asked.

"On the edge of the Presidio. It's a former military installation." He tipped his chin in the direction of the wooded area, then pointed to the house. "Come on, let's see what Wesley has for us."

When they reached the front door, it was already opening.

A curvy woman with flaming red hair stood there to greet them. Winter stared at her. She looked exactly how she'd always imagined a witch would look.

"I'm Roxanne," the woman said and stepped to the side. "Come on in."

Winter accepted the invitation and walked into the cozy foyer from which a dark wooden staircase led upstairs and several doors led into other parts of the house.

"Thanks, Roxanne," Logan said behind her.

When Winter heard the door snap closed, she turned back to Roxanne. "Thanks so much for offering to help me. You're our last hope."

The redhead chuckled unexpectedly. "Oh, you think I'm the witch?" Her eyes sparkled. "Did you hear that, babe?" she called out toward a door that stood ajar. "Our guest thinks I look like a witch."

"I didn't mean to—"

But Winter didn't get a chance to apologize, because the door opened fully and a tall, broad-shouldered man walked through it, coming up the stairs from the basement.

"Well, you could be. You sure managed to bewitch me," he said with a smile. Then he offered his hand to Winter. "I hope you're not disappointed, but I'm the witch in this family. Name's Charles. My wife is a vampire."

Winter shook his hand, heat suffusing her cheeks. "Pleased to meet you. Uh, both of you." Would she ever be able to figure out which preternatural species she was dealing with?

"Logan," Charles now said, shaking Logan's hand, "nice to finally meet you, too. I've heard a lot about you and your friends. And you're valued at Scanguards. John speaks highly of you."

"Thank you. He's a good man."

"You work at Scanguards, too?" Winter asked.

Charles shook his head. "Roxanne does."

"I'm a bodyguard for them," Roxanne confirmed.

Stunned, Winter stared at her, but she was saved from finding an appropriate comment, when Roxanne said, "I'm gonna have to leave you guys. My shift's starting shortly." She kissed her husband on the lips. "Don't blow up the house while I'm gone."

Charles chuckled and gave her a loving slap on her backside. "What do I get in exchange?"

She rolled her eyes and, shaking her head, walked past Logan and out the door.

Charles laughed, then waved them toward the stairs leading down. "Wesley is helping me get things ready."

Winter followed Charles down the old staircase, Logan on her heels, and adjusted her eyes to the dimly lit staircase. "Getting what ready?"

"The spell, of course," Charles said, as if it was the most natural thing.

She froze for a second and felt Logan stop behind her. "You're doing a spell?"

Charles looked over his shoulder. "Come, I'll explain everything. I won't do anything you don't agree to. Deal?"

Slowly she nodded, then followed him down the stairs. It smelled a little musty, but the smell quickly dissipated when she approached the door to another room. From there, different smells emanated: spices, herbs, perfumes.

When she reached the open door, she stood there for a moment and looked inside the large room. It was a witch's lair—if "lair" was the right word. Maybe they called it a brewhouse. After all, there was a large caldron in one corner and lots of large mortars sitting on wooden shelves. Glass jars were filled with various herbs and spices, and bottles with different colored liquids lined several shelves. A low fire was burning in a hearth. In another corner, there was a desk with several old books lying open on its surface. A bookcase on the wall held even more books, many with titles printed on their spines in languages she couldn't decipher.

Wesley stood hunched over a bowl, mixing different herbs. He raised his head. "Hey, you made it."

Winter walked into the room. "Hi, Wesley."

"Hey, Wes," Logan said. "Nice setup you've got here, Charles."

"Thanks," their host replied. "Keeps me busy and out of trouble while Roxanne saves the world."

Wesley shook his head. "Charles likes to pretend that he's the tame house husband. Don't be fooled. I've learned a lot from this guy. He's a very powerful witch." He looked at Winter. "And he's found something that we believe will help you with your visions."

"Charles said you're going to do a spell," she said. "What kind of spell?"

Wesley looked to Charles, who nodded and explained, "Right. Here's the gist of it. Normally you would have been guided by the person who passed the gift on to you. Like a mother or father, or grandparents. Or an aunt or uncle."

"I have no relatives. My parents died in a car accident when I was young. My grandmother raised me, but she's dead now too. There was nobody else."

"Well," Charles said, "in cases where the psychic didn't get a chance to learn about his or her gift from a relative, it can often be misunderstood—like in your case, so Wes tells me. It's not uncommon to experience the visions as nightmares. How long ago did you experience your first vision?"

"Maybe eighteen months ago."

"Hmm. Enough time for your mind and body to form an automatic response. You conditioned yourself to reject the visions, because you feared them. By knowing that you're not dealing with a nightmare, but a vision, you've already made one step in the opposite direction. Eventually, you'll train yourself to accept the visions as normal. But retraining yourself takes time, and I understand that you don't have a lot of it."

"We have even less now," Logan interrupted. "Less than twenty-four hours."

"What?" Wes asked. "What the fuck happened?"

"Manus found us. He's given us twenty-four hours before he turns us in. I have less than a day to convince the council that Winter will be a great asset to us, and to do that we need to prove that she can control her visions. I need to give them something."

Charles let out a breath. "Well, we'd better get this show on the road then." He paused for a moment. "Winter, here's what this spell will do. Think of it as a time lapse spell. What it'll do is to make your brain believe that a lot of time has passed since you found out that your nightmares are really visions. Your mind will adjust to this new truth and new neuropathways will forge in your brain, allowing the visions to be processed without your conditioned responses blocking them. Next time you have a vision, you should be able to guide it in the direction you want to explore."

"Guide it how?"

"Let's say, you have a vision about, I don't know... what have you seen before?"

"I've seen a cave with demons."

Charles nodded. "Okay, let's say you see this cave again. With your new control, you should be able to walk inside the vision, a little bit like an avatar. You know what that is?"

She nodded.

"So you'll be able to walk in the direction of where you want to see more. For example, if you want to see what's behind a demon, or you see a door and want to know what's behind it, you'll be able to go and open it. But be careful. Don't go too deep into the visions, or you can get hurt. The longer you stay inside, the more of yourself goes into the place and the things you see, and the harder it will be to come back. Do you understand?"

She wasn't sure if she should nod or not. She understood his words well enough, but did she really understand the implications? Was she ready for this? There were so many more things she needed to know.

"Will I be able to force a vision?"

"At will? No. The vision will come whenever it comes. But once it's there, you'll be able to guide it."

Winter looked at Logan. "What if I don't have a vision that'll help you to convince the council by tomorrow?"

"We'll figure it out somehow," Logan assured her.

"I've heard that sometimes it helps to touch an object or a person, and a vision about that object or person emerges. It's by no means foolproof, but on occasion, it helps," Charles mused.

Winter swallowed hard. She had no choice. It was either this, or death for both her and Logan.

"Do the spell."

She watched as Charles and Wesley sprang into action. Wesley went back to the mortar where he was mixing herbs. Meanwhile Charles walked to the desk, took one of the books and brought it to the center table, where he placed it next to an ornamental dagger.

"Wes?" Charles looked over his shoulder. "Ready?"

Wes carried the stone bowl with the herbs to the table. "It's all there. Now for the last ingredient." He looked directly at Winter. "Your blood."

Her heart skipped a beat, and a breath rushed from her lungs.

"Don't worry," Charles added, "we only need a few drops. Step closer."

She moved closer to him, while he lifted the dagger.

"Give me your left hand," Charles demanded.

She stretched out her hand, and he took it, turned it palm up.

"This might sting a little."

Before he'd even finished his sentence, he cut into the tip of her thumb and held it over the mortar to let the blood drop over the herbs.

"Now, Wes," Charles said, still holding on to Winter's hand.

Wesley poured a clear liquid over her hand and into the bowl, letting it mix with the herbs, while simultaneously he and Charles began to chant an incantation from the open book on the table.

The words sounded like a mixture of Latin and Greek, or some other old, long-dead language Winter didn't recognize. The words seemed to build to a crescendo, and she felt a sudden pressure in her head as if a migraine was coming on. Red smoke started to rise from the bowl and travel up her hand, then along her arm, beginning to engulf her. Panic rose in her, and she wanted to pull away, afraid the red smoke would suffocate her, but Charles held on to her hand with an iron fist.

The red smoke entered her nostrils, and she was forced to inhale the substance. With it, the pressure in her head eased just as suddenly as it had started, and she felt as light as if floating on air.

Charles let go of her hand, and both witches stopped chanting. The floating feeling was gone again.

"How do you feel?" Charles asked.

She hesitated, mentally checking her body. Nothing ached. "I feel fine."

Charles and Wesley exchanged a look.

"That's good," Wesley said.

"What now?" she asked.

"Go and rest, your mind is adjusting now," Charles explained.

"How do you know if it worked?" She glanced at Logan, who stood a few feet away from her, a concerned look on his face. "I mean, I don't feel any different."

"It worked," Charles said. "There is a calmness about you now that wasn't there before. Your body knows it. Your mind just has to catch up."

Slowly, she nodded. She had no choice but to trust his words. She'd done that a lot the last couple of days: trust strangers.

22

From the twins' apartment, Logan stared out into the night, letting his eyes roam over the adjacent buildings. Despite the late hour, there was still light in some of the hotel rooms across the street. A few night owls emerged from bars that were closing for the night, and taxis searched for late-night fares. Druggies and homeless people looked for a comfortable corner, and vampires looked for a quick meal among them.

Behind him, Logan heard Winter pacing. After returning to the apartment, they'd put a frozen pizza into the oven and eaten it, then waited, and waited some more. But so far, Winter hadn't had a vision. There was no way of verifying whether Charles's and Wesley's spell had worked. Logan had done his best not to let Winter feel his anxiety. She was worried enough. He had to be the calming influence now, even though inside he felt anything but calm. If he couldn't prove to the council that Winter's visions could be controlled and therefore be of use to them in their fight against the demons, they would kill her.

"There's no use in waiting around," Winter suddenly said, frustration coloring her voice.

He spun around to look at her. "There's nothing else we can do. We just have to be patient."

"I'm not good at being patient." She shook her head. "For all I know, this time tomorrow I'll be dead and you'll be on trial for treason."

"Winter, please—"

"I can't waste my last few hours in this world just... waiting. I need to do something."

"There's nothing you *can* do. Charles said it might take a while for this to work."

She took a few steps toward him. "Why are you so calm? I mean, your life is on the line too."

He sighed. "My life is always on the line. It's been on the line ever since I was born. This is nothing new for me." Though this time, it was different, because he feared for another person, for Winter. "But I wish I could do something for you. To take your fear away. You were thrown into this without any preparation. This is new and scary for you."

He met her gaze and gave her a long look.

"But it's my destiny, isn't it? As a psychic. As a preternatural creature." Her voice trembled a little, though he could see the effort with which she tried to show strength.

"You're part of this world now." He took a few steps closer, close enough so he could reach for her if he wanted to. But he didn't follow his desire to touch her, even if it was only to comfort her and lend her strength. "One day, you'll look back at this, and realize how strong you are and that you can survive almost anything." He smiled at her. "I've never met a woman as strong as you."

She shook her head. "Don't they have female Stealth Guardians? I bet they're much stronger than I could ever be."

"That's not what I meant. Sure, female Stealth Guardians are physically as strong as their male counterparts, but you, Winter, you're strong in a different way. You're resilient. You can weather any storm. You're a survivor. And that's more important than physical strength." He lifted his hand, wanting to run it through her hair, but stopped himself.

Winter froze and stared at his hand, then back at him. She swallowed hard, and quickly, he lowered his hand again.

"I'm sorry," he said hastily and tore his gaze from her face. "I didn't mean to take liberties. I know you don't want this. Not after everything that I've done."

"What you've done?" She shook her head. "Oh, Logan, I'm not sure about all that anymore."

"What do you mean?"

"What have you really done? You were given orders. You tried to follow them like a good soldier." She put her hand on his bicep, surprising him with her touch. "But you didn't do it. You didn't kill me, even though you were ordered to. You defied your council to save me. At great risk to yourself." She sighed. "Yes, I'm mad that you didn't tell me, that you let me believe you came to save me from the demons. But even though that wasn't your intention at first, in the end it was what you did. That's all that counts."

Hope expanded his chest. "Are you saying that you forgive me?"

She shook her head. "There's nothing to forgive." She ran her hand up to his shoulder. "I'm sorry for the way I reacted when Manus showed up here. For accusing you of using me." She let out a breath. "What happened in Trenton, in that motel, wasn't something you initiated. It was all my doing."

"I didn't stop you."

She looked straight into his eyes. Instinctively he drew closer, unable to resist the lure. Everything he wanted was reflecting in those eyes.

"No, you didn't stop me…"

"Winter…"

Her lips came closer. "Tell me you won't stop me now either."

His heart pounding with excitement, Logan raised his hand to her cheek and caressed it. "Oh, Winter, I don't deserve you. You're too good for this world."

She turned her head to press a kiss into his palm. "Take me to bed, Logan."

If ever there was a siren call, it was Winter's voice murmuring those five words to him. He couldn't have resisted, even if he wanted to. And he didn't want to. Because all he wanted, all he needed right now, was Winter in his arms.

He brought his mouth to hover within an inch of hers. "Tomorrow, vision or not, I'll fight for you before the council." But tonight he would love her.

Logan sank his lips onto hers, capturing them in a tender kiss. How he'd missed her. Now, finally, he could be with her without guilt, without a secret between them.

"Come," he murmured and took her hand, leading her to one of the two bedrooms and closing the door behind them.

When he pulled her back into his arms, she stopped him. "I want to be in charge tonight."

His heartbeat accelerated in surprise. Slowly, he released her. "What did you have in mind?"

Winter put her hands on his chest and started opening the top button of his shirt. "I was thinking of undressing you first, then kissing every inch of your skin..." She let her hand slide down to his groin, where his cock was already pumping full of blood. "And then I thought..." She squeezed his growing erection and licked her lips. "I think you get the idea."

He let out a groan. He knew exactly what she had in mind. He put his hand over hers and pressed his cock harder against her palm. "Yeah, I think I do." He slid his other hand to the back of her neck and pulled her face to him. "And selfish bastard that I am, I can't wait for you to suck me."

"Then maybe I shouldn't waste my time taking off your shirt when we both know what I really want." She brought both hands to his pants now and opened the button, then slid the zipper down. She pushed his pants over his hips until they came to rest at mid-thigh. Again she put one hand over his cock, but this time the contact was even more intense, with only the thin fabric of his boxer briefs separating them. "Especially when you're ready for me."

She hooked her thumbs into his waistband and stripped him, dropping to her knees in the same instant.

"Fuck!" He hadn't expected her to get down to business this quickly. This wasn't the slow seduction he'd had in mind when he'd taken her to the bedroom. He ripped his shirt open and rid himself of it, so it didn't hinder his view of what Winter was going to do to him.

Kneeling in front of him, she looked up to him, her face at the same height as his heavy erection. If he moved forward only a couple of inches, his cock would touch her lips.

"I love a man with a beautiful cock." She ran one finger along the underside of his hard-on. "So thick and long." She wrapped her hand around its root, making him gasp in response. "So delicious."

She inched closer, bringing her mouth to the swollen tip of his erection and licked over it as if licking an ice cream cone.

"Fuck!" he repeated, any rational thought or the ability to form proper sentences having deserted his mind.

"Hmm. Yes, just like I imagined." Her breath teased his sensitive skin, and all of a sudden, warmth engulfed him and he sank deep into Winter's mouth, her lips sliding down on him, lubricating him as she took him inside.

A shudder charged down his spine, making his knees weak. He reached back and braced himself against the door. Breathing as if he were running a marathon, he looked down at Winter and found her looking up at him. Fuck, he'd never seen a more innocent, yet sexy look. He moaned, then felt her hands on his hips, before she pulled her head back slowly, letting him slip out of her mouth but for the tip. There, she hovered, staring up at him, before she slid down on him again, taking him inside her delicious mouth as far as she could.

"Fuck, baby!" His heart pounded. He wanted this, wanted to possess her like this.

Winter worked him beautifully, took him deep, then slowly released him inch by inch, making him shiver with pleasure. With every thrust into her heavenly mouth she increased her tempo, while she brought her hand to assist, wrapping it around the base of his cock. In concert with her sucking motions, she squeezed him. He couldn't stop watching his cock disappear inside her mouth, her eyes ever so often looking up at him. Such passion, such pleasure, such innocence.

Winter's moans vibrated against his hard flesh, sending more shivers through his body. If she continued like this, he wouldn't last much longer. Still, he couldn't stop her. His desire for her was growing with every second, the need to possess her becoming more urgent now.

In an ever-increasing tempo, Logan thrust his cock into Winter's mouth, meeting her movements. He loved the way she welcomed him, her tongue sliding along the underside of his erection on every descent, her lips clinging tightly to him on every withdrawal.

When she suddenly cupped his balls and squeezed them gently, he pushed her away with a groan, his cock slipping from her mouth. "Enough!"

He pulled her up to him, her lips red and swollen, and too tempting to resist. He slanted his lips over hers and kissed her, hard and deep, while making quick work of her pants. He dragged them off her, feeling her stumble, but held onto her so she wouldn't fall. Then he tore at her panties and rid her of those too. It was all he had time for.

Logan ripped his lips from hers and gazed into her passion-filled eyes. "By God, you deserve better than this, but I need to take you now."

He whirled her around so she faced the door, positioned himself behind her and spread her legs, then thrust into her, ramming his cock forward and upward in one swift movement, wringing a deep moan from Winter. Her pussy was warm and wet, her muscles tightening around him like a vice he didn't want to escape from.

"Logan," she cried out on a moan. "Yes!"

She braced herself against the door, both hands flat against it, and received his next thrust with a counterthrust of her own, driving him deeper and harder into her. But he needed more. Needed to feel her.

He pulled on the T-shirt she was still wearing and dragged it over her head. Then he opened the clasp of her bra and disposed of the pesky garment. Finally, he could touch her. He slid his hands over her breasts, delighting in feeling her hard nipples rub against his palms, and delivered another thrust with his cock.

Dipping his head to her neck, he kissed her there and felt her shudder. "I can't get enough of you. You're so gorgeous, so hot. And the way your pussy grips me…" He groaned and squeezed her breasts in his hands, while below he plunged in and out of her. He couldn't remember ever having felt so passionate about a woman. Was it real, or was it the fact that this could be the last night they would ever have together?

He shook off the thought. He didn't want to think of what the future held for them. Not now. Now all that mattered was the beautiful woman who was allowing him to fuck her like a beast when she deserved so much better.

Fuck, what was he doing? What a bastard he was! Selfish and without finesse.

Panting, he pulled himself from her sheath and released her.

"Something wrong?" she asked, turning her head.

"Yeah, everything." He pulled his pants all the way down, stripping himself, then lifted Winter into his arms and carried her to the bed.

She stared up at him wide-eyed.

"Don't look so surprised," he murmured and lowered her on the sheets. As luck would have it, they were crisp. It appeared that the twins had a housekeeper.

"I was enjoying the way you were taking me," she said with a wicked smile. "Why did you stop?"

"Because I'm not the kind of man who just takes. No matter how much I want something. And you, Winter, you I want." He kissed her softly, before sliding down her body. "All of you."

He pushed her thighs apart and settled in the space he'd created for himself. "Now relax and let me take care of you."

"Logan," Winter murmured and sighed. "But I didn't even ask for this."

"If you have to ask, you're not with the right man." Because the right man knew what his woman needed.

Logan lowered his head to her pussy and pressed a kiss into the damp hair, then dipped lower, licking his tongue over her pink folds. He'd been rough with her, but he would make it up to her now. With tender strokes, gentle caresses, and loving kisses.

She tasted like a mountain spring, her dew like a magical elixir. A symphony of sighs and moans accompanied the shudders that traveled through her body the longer he licked and sucked her. Feeling her let go in his arms, under his tongue, his lips, his mouth, was confirmation that he still had her trust, that despite everything he'd done wrong, she forgave him. He thanked her for it by showering her with passion and tenderness, the kind of tenderness he wasn't used to displaying, the kind that came straight from the heart. A tenderness born from deep affection. An affection he could feel expand in his heart.

He caressed her with more fervor and felt her pulse quicken, her breath become ragged as her body raced toward a climax.

"Logan, please, I'm so close."

"I know, baby." He doubled his efforts and caressed Winter's center of pleasure with his thumb. The little organ was swollen. He licked over it and felt Winter tremble. He repeated his action and at the same time plunged a finger into her warm channel.

A moan tore from Winter's lips, and her back arched off the mattress. He stilled his fingers and felt her interior muscles spasm around him. Feeling her climax almost made him come. Quickly he withdrew his finger from her pussy and rolled over her, feeling her legs pull him into her center, while she looked at him.

Winter in the throes of passion. He'd never seen a more beautiful sight. With their eyes locked, he plunged into her, seating himself to the hilt. Her pussy was still spasming, contracting around him, and it was all he needed. One more stroke, one more thrust, and he joined her in her bliss, letting his orgasm take him to a place where nothing mattered, nothing but the two of them.

"Winter…" he murmured.

But she suddenly stiffened. Her eyes stared blankly, becoming unfocused.

"Winter? What's wrong? Did I hurt you?"

Panicked, he pulled back to pull out of her, but she gripped his biceps and stopped him.

"No!"

Her voice was different. As if she wasn't herself. Naked fear gripped him. Something was wrong.

"I see it now. I'm there, Logan, I'm inside it."

Her eyes were still unfocused, and now he understood why. She was looking at something else. She was *seeing* something. Something only she could see.

"Tell me what it is, Winter, tell me what you see," he coaxed softly now, not wanting to break her concentration.

"It's dark. Flames… demons everywhere." She murmured something unintelligible, then her voice normalized again. She wiped her eyes. "I knew it was you. I knew it all along. You came." Her eyes suddenly focused and she looked straight at him. "Logan, it was you who saved me from the demons."

He brushed a strand of hair from her forehead and smiled. "Of course I did. I killed the demons in your apartment."

"No." She shook her head. "In my vision we weren't in my apartment. I was in a cave. It smelled of Sulphur. A demon was trying to kill me. His dagger was coming toward me. I had this vision before. Several times, in fact. The first few times, the demon killed me. But when I had it again, a few days before you came to my shop, the vision had changed. Somebody beheaded the demon before he could kill me. But the demon blood in my eyes blinded me, and I couldn't see my rescuer's face. But just now, when I had the same vision again, I did what Charles said, I went deeper. And I saw your face. Logan, you were the man who rescued me. You came to save me."

He gripped her shoulders. "Where, Winter, where?"

"The Underworld."

Logan let out a shaky breath.

"Charles was right. I can guide my visions. The spell worked. Logan, it worked!" She kissed him exuberantly, and he let it happen.

He couldn't crush her joy. Not when for the first time she was hopeful. Yes, she was now able to control her visions. But maybe it would take a few more tries for her to truly guide them. Because the vision she'd had, the vision of her being in the Underworld could only be half-true. If the demons snatched her, he wouldn't be able to come and rescue her. Not in the Underworld.

Because nobody could enter the Underworld. Nobody other than a demon.

23

Logan had said his goodbyes and left Winter under Gabriel's protection. When he entered the portal hidden away in a tunnel at the 16th Street BART station in San Francisco, he did so with unease. His case wasn't as strong as he'd hoped. Had he had more time, he could have made a better one, but he had to play the cards he was dealt. For once he wished that the trip to the council compound would take longer, but he arrived within seconds.

He took a deep breath and willed the portal's door to open. He stepped out of it and looked around. Everything looked like it always did. Runes were carved into the massive stone walls to ward the building against witchcraft, as well as detection by humans. Cameras were mounted in various locations covering different angles, so guards sitting in a control room could monitor the comings and goings. Several corridors led in different directions, and stairs led to the other levels in the building.

Logan knew the guards would recognize him, but they didn't know why he was here. It was best to make his way to the council chambers as quickly as possible, before some overeager fellow guardian stopped him and asked him about his business.

He navigated through the building swiftly and without losing time. Arriving at the council chamber, he approached the guard standing sentry.

"Evening. Logan Frazer. The council is expecting me," he lied.

While the guard looked at a sheet of paper, presumably the agenda for the day, Logan readied himself for another lie.

"Sorry, Logan, but you're not on the list."

Logan leaned over, glanced at the paper and shook his head. "Yeah, that's because you've got the old agenda.

Happens. Don't worry about it. I won't tell them that you screwed up." He patted him on the shoulder. "But next time make sure you ask if there are any revisions to the schedule before you get it printed." He jerked his thumb toward the chamber. "Or Barclay is gonna be pissed." By referring to Primus by his first name, Logan let the guard assume that he was friends with their leader.

Leaving the confused guard to sputter a few incoherent words, Logan turned to the door, opened it quickly and slipped inside. He closed it silently behind him.

At first the council members didn't notice him. All nine of them were in deep discussion, not sitting around the half-moon shaped table from which they governed, but standing split into different groups behind it.

"Councilmembers," Logan greeted the assembled elders to draw their attention to him.

Several heads turned and with it some of the conversations stopped. The room now quieter, more people turned their heads, until finally, Barclay laid eyes on Logan.

"Logan? What are you doing here?" Barclay took a few steps toward him, then stopped. "We're in the middle of a confidential council session. Where's the guard?"

"I'm afraid I told the guard you were expecting me. A last-minute change to your agenda."

"That's highly irregular," Cinead objected, stepping next to Barclay.

"Indeed," Barclay bit out, just as displeased about the intrusion, while the other members voiced their displeasure with sour looks and narrowed eyes.

Logan lifted a hand in acquiescence. "I understand. But this is a matter of life and death. And it cannot wait."

"Then make it quick," Barclay ordered.

"It's about the psychic, Winter Collins."

"That case is hardly urgent. You executed her, so anything regarding that matter can wait," Barclay said with a dismissive wave toward the door, turning away already.

"She's not dead."

Barclay whipped his head back to him. "Not dead? You had an order!"

"And I can't follow it. This psychic is worth more to us alive than dead. She can help us."

"Help us?" Cinead mocked. "She's a danger. A loose cannon. If the demons get their hands on her, she'll help them destroy us."

"She won't," Logan protested. "She's stronger than you think. Her mind is like a fortress. Nobody can penetrate it. The demons won't be able to influence her, even if they find her. Which they won't."

Barclay took a step closer, narrowing his eyes. "And why is that, Logan?"

Logan squared his stance. "Because she's under my protection."

Gasps rippled through the chamber.

"I have proof that she has visions about the demons, sees things that will give us an edge. And she's getting better at it every minute. She's learning to control the visions, to point them in the direction she wants to go." Not exactly a lie, but he had to give them something. At least so he could buy them some time until Winter had truly mastered her visions.

"Not another word!" Barclay thundered. "How dare you act against the council's vote? Do you have any idea what you've done by refusing an order? Not just refusing it, but doing the exact opposite?"

Barclay didn't have to spell out the crime Logan had committed. Everybody in the room knew what it was.

"She deserves to live! She can help us. She's drawn plans of the Underworld. Plans of a tunnel system."

Barclay scoffed. "And what use would that be to us? We can't enter the Underworld, so a map won't do us any good." He sighed. "We chose you, Logan, because we thought we could trust you with this. We're aware that eliminating a person isn't an easy thing to do. But you've done it before. This is not your first execution order. A mere twenty years ago, you killed a psychic in Detroit without flinching. Why can't you do the same now? Nothing's changed. This one is just as much of a danger as the one in Detroit was."

Logan shook his head, remembering the older woman he'd killed back then. "That case was different. That psychic had already given into the demons. It was only a matter of days until she gave them something they could use to destroy us." He'd had no choice but to kill her to save humankind. But now he had a choice. The choice to save Winter and help her on the right path, while protecting her from the reach of the demons.

"You, Logan?" Cinead shook his head. "I'd never have thought you could be swayed by a pretty face. You of all people. What happened to you? You've never questioned an order before."

"Then maybe it was time I did." Logan tipped his chin up. "Give this woman a chance. She deserves it."

Several council members shook their heads. Murmurs rumbled through their ranks.

Barclay lifted his hand to demand silence. "The council voted. The guards will take you to a lead cell where you will await your trial for treason. We'll find where you're hiding Winter Collins."

"You can't do that!" Logan yelled. He looked at the council members. "Are you all just gonna stand there and allow an innocent to be killed? Are you?"

He caught Virginia's look. There was regret in her eyes. And pain. He knew in that moment how she'd voted. Like Logan, she wanted Winter to live. She was on his side, but five other members weren't. They were the ones he had to convince, and it was certain that Barclay and Cinead were two of them.

"Cinead, please! Have mercy on her," Logan begged.

But the doors were thrown open in that instant, and several guards rushed in.

"Take him to the lead cell!" Barclay ordered.

Two guards grabbed him by the arms, one on each side. Logan tried to shake them off, but it was no use. He'd lost this round. He had to find another way.

24

Winter tossed the uneaten food into the trash can in the twins' kitchen and sighed. She couldn't eat anything. She was too nervous. Her and Logan's fate hung in the balance, and she had no idea in which direction the scales would tip. But of one thing she was certain: the vision she'd had earlier was the same one she'd had previously. Somehow she'd landed in the Underworld, and Logan had come to slay the demons and rescue her. She hoped that if Logan relayed this information to the council, they could be convinced that she was of value to them. But at the same time, the vision worried her, because if she ended up in the Underworld, something would have gone wrong.

"Don't fret," Gabriel said from across the bar that separated the kitchen from the living room. "Logan is a smart man. He knows what he's doing."

She forced herself to smile at him. "It's nothing."

"Clearly it's something."

She sighed. "The vision I had when we got back here after Charles and Wesley did the spell…"

"What about it?"

"If it's true, then the demons will capture me. I don't know when or how, but I'm scared. Not just for me, but for anybody who's protecting me."

Gabriel's forehead furrowed. "Why's that?"

"If the demons catch me and drag me to the Underworld, won't that mean that they'll have killed the person who was protecting me?" She knew it wasn't Logan, because he would come to rescue her. But what if that meant that the demons would manage to kill Gabriel?

"You worry too much." He motioned to one of the barstools.

She walked around the bar and took a seat.

"Let me tell you something about vampires and about demons. They might look ferocious with their green eyes, but vampires are no pussycats. In fact, the demons fear us. You know why?"

She shook her head.

"I don't know whether Logan told you that unlike other preternatural creatures, demons have no aura that identifies them as such. To the naked eye, they look human. So if they disguise their eyes with contact lenses or sunglasses, the Stealth Guardians have no way of spotting them. But the demons can't disguise their scent. And vampires have a superior sense of smell. Once we lock onto them, we're like bloodhounds. We're physically stronger than the demons. That's why they fear us. Though I must say, the Stealth Guardians have a few skills of their own that are nothing to sneeze at."

She had to smile involuntarily. "It's pretty freaky when they walk through walls, isn't it?"

Gabriel chuckled. "Yeah, I'm not ashamed to say that when I first saw that, I freaked out a bit. But they need those skills, because physically they're about equally matched with the demons. Being able to make themselves invisible and walking through walls gives them an edge. Though they do have a disadvantage: their aura identifies them to the demons, so whenever they're not invisible, they're at risk of being spotted."

"Have you known them long, the Stealth Guardians?"

"Only a few years. Not long in the life of an immortal, but long enough to know that I can trust them. They're honorable people, and they want the same thing we want. Peace."

"Peace," she murmured to herself. "I never thought I'd hear that from a vampire, no offense."

Gabriel shrugged. "Just like humans, we have families. We want them to be safe. You've met my children. They're not perfect by any stretch of the imagination. Trust me, they give me enough trouble, but I love them. And I've raised them to be good, to protect the innocent, and to destroy evil. Yes, they have their urges, and there are times when they need to follow them."

"You mean bloodlust?"

"That's a strong word. But yes, when they feel the need to drink blood directly from a human's vein, I don't stop them. But they know the rules. No human may be harmed."

"But doesn't the bite harm them? I mean, it must be painful."

A smirk softened Gabriel's expression. "The bite of a vampire is a very sensual thing. Certainly, there's an initial sting, but it's fleeting and the pleasure that follows makes the human forget it pretty much instantly."

"Oh!" She hadn't expected that. "But in the movies, the bite is always portrayed as violent and bloody. Whole throats being ripped out."

"Propaganda." He shook his head. "It's an amazing pleasure. And if the vampire licks the wound afterwards, there won't even be a scar or any evidence it ever happened."

"Your race is very fascinating."

"Everything new seems fascinating at first. You'll get used to it all very quickly, you'll see. Now that you're part of this world."

She sighed. "I'm not sure I'll ever get used to all this."

Gabriel suddenly jumped from his barstool and spun around.

Winter's heart beat into her throat as she, too whirled around. She hadn't heard anything that would warrant the vampire's reaction, but now she saw what had alerted him.

Two people, a man and a woman, stood in the living room, both armed with daggers and looking dangerous. Winter's gaze flew to the door. It was closed. She quickly reminded herself that these two intruders couldn't be demons, because they couldn't walk through walls, nor could they cast a vortex on the fourth floor of a building. Which meant they had to be Stealth Guardians.

"Hamish? Enya? What the fuck?" Gabriel ground out and immediately put himself as a shield in front of Winter.

Shit! Something had gone wrong at the council, and now they were coming for her!

"Hey, Gabriel," the woman said. She was petite, with long blond braids that wrapped around the back of her head. "Good to see you."

"Yeah, well, I'm not so sure I agree," Gabriel said hesitantly. "What do you want?"

The broad-shouldered man with dark hair and a stubble beard cleared his throat. "We came for the psychic. Let's make this easy, okay?"

"Easy? Easy for whom? You know that I can take both of you and win, or have you forgotten that?"

"We haven't," Enya said with an easy smile. "That's why we're asking nicely."

Gabriel scoffed. "You know I can't give her to you. I've sworn to protect her."

"We know," Hamish said. "And now we're here to take over for you."

"On whose authority?" Gabriel asked.

"A word, Gabriel," Hamish said.

Gabriel glanced back at Winter. "Stay back."

"Gabriel, don't," Winter warned.

"Do as I say." He lowered his voice. "Don't worry, they can't trick me. I'm faster and I'm stronger."

Then he walked toward the two intruders who were still standing casually near the front door.

Winter tensed, expecting the two Stealth Guardians to overpower Gabriel, but nothing happened. With lowered voices, Hamish and Gabriel spoke, but Winter could only make out a few fragments, such as *psychic, council*, and *Logan*.

Her heart was pounding out of control, the seconds ticking by in slow motion. Something was wrong, seriously wrong, because suddenly Gabriel looked over his shoulder and addressed her.

"Hamish and Enya will take you with them. They won't hurt you. You can trust them."

Trust them?

Trust the Stealth Guardians who wanted her dead and Logan tried for treason?

"No!" she screamed. "No!"

25

Flanked by two guards, Logan was walking down the long corridor that led to the lead cells. In less than thirty seconds, he'd be locked in there, and the game would be over. He had to come up with something, and do it fast.

He weighed his options. Option one was to let them lock him up and hope he could sway the council at his trial. But that would leave Winter exposed, and with Manus knowing where he was hiding her, they would find her quickly.

Strike option one.

Option two was to let himself be locked up and hope for a prison break. But who would break him out? By refusing the council's order, he'd most likely also gotten Manus in trouble, since his friend had kept the secret that Winter wasn't dead. For that he would be punished too. Not as severely as Logan, but punished nevertheless. Therefore he couldn't hope for help from Manus or his compound mates.

Scrap option two.

It only left option three. Logan calculated his chances: slightly better than fifty-fifty. Though it was two against one, the two guards weren't out in the field fighting demons on a daily basis. They were most likely rusty, serving at the council compound where nothing ever happened. They wouldn't even see it coming.

When they arrived at the cell, both guards stopped.

"This is the end of the road for you," one said and reached into his pocket for the key.

Logan waited patiently for the guard to retrieve the key and unlock the cell. When he swung it open, stepping aside to do so, Logan gripped the edge of the door and swung it all the way open, hitting the guard with it and slamming him against the wall. While he tumbled to the ground, Logan spun around and swung his fist into the second guard's face.

The guy had already reached for his dagger, but Logan managed to kick it out of his hand. Stunned, the guard took a second too long to throw a punch at Logan. By the time it was meant to connect, Logan had already sidestepped the blow and gotten behind him. Now in the superior position, he kicked him in the back of his knees, sending him to the ground.

From the corner of his eye, Logan saw movement. The guard he'd hit with the door had scrambled to his feet and lunged for Logan, dagger in hand, but Logan dove away, gripped the door and hit the guard with it, this time from behind.

A grunt of pain echoed through the hallway. Soon, somebody would come running and it would all be over. He had to silence the guard now. Logan jumped him from behind and wrestled him to the ground. But the guy was strong, though not as agile as Logan, and managed to land a few hits. Luckily Logan was able to avoid the dagger and roll to the side in time to jump up again.

Just then, the other guard staggered to his feet and Logan saw an opportunity and took it. Gripping the door again, he used it to jump up and kick both legs into the guy's stomach, sending him flying deep into the cell. One down, one to go.

The second guard proved a bit harder to fell. It took several blows and punches and a good number of kicks to drive the guard toward the open door of the cell. Logan felt his strength waning, but he couldn't give up. Winter's life depended on it. That thought charged him with new energy and he kicked the guard as hard as he could until the man tumbled backwards. One more kick, and he was inside the cell, crashing against the other guard, who'd just managed to get up. Perfect timing.

Logan slammed the door to the cell shut and turned the key to lock it. From inside he heard the two guards' screams. Eventually somebody would come to free them, but if he was lucky, he had a few minutes to get out of the council compound.

Not even stopping to catch his breath, Logan raced down the hallway, back to the stairs that would take him down to the level on which the portal was located. He charged around the corner, only to stop dead in his tracks.

"Shit!"

There, casually leaning against the wall, was Manus. Judging by his expression, Manus wasn't surprised to see him.

"So impatient," Manus said calmly. "Couldn't wait for me to break you out, could you? Had to beat up the guards, didn't you?"

"What the—"

"When will you ever learn to trust me?" Manus rolled his eyes. "Did you really think we were gonna let you rot in here?"

Stunned at Manus's words, Logan asked, "How did you know they were gonna lock me up the moment I showed up here?"

"I didn't. But I figured we should be prepared for everything."

"They'll know it was you who helped me escape. You should leave, before somebody sees us together."

Manus smiled. "They don't even know I'm here. Pearce switched off the cameras on the portal level. And he hacked into the surveillance system so we would know if they locked you up." He motioned to the stairs. "Let's go. We don't have much time. Pearce has to switch the cameras back on before the guards in the command room realize that they're not on a live feed and come down here to check what's wrong."

Together they rushed down the stairs, but Manus put a hand on his forearm as soon as they'd reached the lower level. "Easy. Don't run, in case we bump into somebody. We don't want to look suspicious."

"Got it."

It was a long corridor to the portal, and it felt like a walk on a plank, but they encountered nobody on the way.

Logan let out a breath, as Manus placed his hand on the carved dagger that identified the portal. It opened within a second. They both entered, and Manus gripped Logan's arm.

"Hold on," Manus said and everything went dark around them.

"We need to go back to San Francisco," Logan said.

"No," Manus replied.

They were already moving, before Logan could ask his friend where they were headed. For once he didn't protest. Manus wouldn't go through the hassle of saving him only to catapult him into the fire.

After a few seconds, Logan felt his body still and he knew they'd arrived. The portal's door opened and Manus stepped out first, Logan followed. He glanced around.

"You brought me to Baltimore?"

"Safest place right now. Nobody will assume that you're hiding out in your own compound."

"And the others?"

"They're all in agreement. We're a team. We don't leave anybody behind. Even if that person is irrational."

He ignored the jab. "But Winter. She's still in San Francisco. The council will find her." And he wouldn't be there to protect her.

Manus rolled his eyes once more. "I'm not an amateur. Come on."

~ ~ ~

Winter paced in the great room that connected with a modern kitchen. She wasn't alone. Enya, the Stealth Guardian woman who'd whisked her away from San Francisco, was with her—whether as her protector or her prison guard, Winter hadn't yet determined. Nobody had said much to her though they'd treated her kindly, not applying any force on the trip to this compound, as they called it. Nevertheless, she felt like a prisoner.

Frustrated she turned to Enya. "I need to know what's going on. Where is Logan?"

Enya tossed her the kind of look she'd give a child who was asking *Are we there yet?* for the hundredth time. "We're working on that."

"What does that mean?"

Enya's jaw tightened visibly. "It means we're working on it, okay? Now why don't you eat something or watch TV, and stop pestering me with questions I don't have the answers to?"

Before Enya looked away, Winter recognized something in her eyes, something that belied her dismissive words.

"You're worried about him, too, aren't you?"

Enya pivoted and narrowed her eyes. "Well, gee, you *are* a psychic!" Her words dripped with sarcasm.

"Enya, why are you so hostile toward me? I haven't done anything."

"Oh, haven't you?" She braced her hands on her hips. "No, little Miss Innocent didn't do anything other than seduce Logan into betraying his race! And to think I was on your side when I heard the council voted to kill you!" Enya huffed angrily. "Do you have any idea what you've done? Do you? Logan could be executed for this. And it'll all be your fault."

"They'd need to find me first."

Winter's gaze shot to the person who'd spoken. "Logan!" He was entering the kitchen, Manus on his heels.

Logan locked eyes with her, and Winter's heart began to pound. He marched right toward her and pulled her into a tight embrace. "You're safe."

"You're welcome," Enya mumbled behind him.

Releasing Winter from his embrace, but keeping his hand on her lower back, Logan looked at his compound mate. "I owe you one, Enya. I owe all of you."

His words seemed to pacify her somewhat, because she said, "Well, we couldn't let them just take you away from us. Imagine the workload if we had to pick up your share too."

"Truth," Manus added and slapped Enya on the shoulder. "And you know how lazy we are."

The door suddenly opened and more people streamed into the room. She'd met one of them before: Hamish. But the other two men and two women were strangers. As were the two toddlers who ran past the adults and charged into the room, giggling and chasing each other. Children were the last thing she'd expected to see in this place.

Logan looked at Winter and said, "I think it's time for introductions. The important people first." He snatched the toddlers, one with each arm and lifted them up. "What are you two still doing up? It's the middle of the night. Shouldn't you be sleeping?"

The kids only giggled.

"Meet Julia and Xander. They run the show here," Logan said.

One of the women stepped forward and took the girl off Logan's hands. "Don't listen to him. They're not that bad." She smiled. "I'm Leila. And these two belong to me." She looked over her shoulder and pointed at one of the men. "To me and Aiden. And they hate being in bed. They seem to always sense when something exciting is happening in the compound."

Aiden raised his hand in greeting. "Hey."

Logan set the boy back on his feet. "You've met Hamish. Next to him is Tessa, his wife. And that guy is Pearce. He's our computer genius."

Various greetings bounced around the room.

"So, what went down with the council?" Aiden asked.

Logan shrugged. "They didn't give me much of a chance to explain the situation or make a case. I'm afraid your father is pretty hard-nosed."

"Aiden's father?" Winter asked.

Logan nodded. "The head of council is Aiden's father and—"

"But he'll find you." She shot a look at Aiden. If he knew, wouldn't he eventually tell his father?

"Aiden won't tell his father that I'm here, right, Aiden?" Logan asked.

"If I wanted you to rot in that cell, I wouldn't have helped organize your escape," Aiden said.

"They put you in a cell?" Winter asked, frustrated that she was only getting piecemeal information. "And you escaped?"

Pearce suddenly cleared his throat. "May I?"

Logan nodded. "Yeah, I'm kind of curious myself how you guys pulled it off."

Pearce smirked. "Well, we've had our eyes on you ever since Manus found you in San Francisco. When you went to the council to make your case, I'd already prepped everything to watch you there. When the camera caught you being led to the cells, I deactivated the surveillance cameras at the council compound and alerted Manus."

"Nice hacking," Logan commented. "Will they be able to trace you?"

"No chance. The cameras were only out for about three minutes. The guys in the control room probably didn't even realize that I fed them a static image instead of a live feed." He shrugged. "So all Manus had to do was get you out of there once the guards put you in the cell and—"

"Only Logan didn't exactly give me a chance," Manus interrupted. "By the time I got to the cellblock, he'd already overpowered his two guards and locked them in the cell."

"I didn't exactly know that you were coming to get me," Logan said. "If I remember correctly, last time we met you gave me an ultimatum and threatened to bring me in yourself if I didn't comply."

"Yeah, well, I had to try to bring you to your senses." He glanced at Winter and looked her up and down as if assessing her. "But I guess you'd already made your choice."

Winter felt Logan take her hand and squeeze it. "Yes. I made my choice. I'm sorry that you guys have to deal with the fallout from my decision. You know that you don't have to do this. By hiding me and Winter here, you've become accessories. We can leave."

"And go where?" Manus challenged and made a dismissive hand gesture. "You're safest here. Nobody will guess that you're hiding out in your own compound. Nobody would think you'd be that stupid. Now let's regroup and figure out our next steps."

"Next steps?" Winter heard herself ask. "But if Logan wasn't able to convince the council, there's nothing else we can do."

Manus laughed, and several of the others joined in. "You should know something about us, Winter. We don't give up after the first attempt. We've had higher hurdles to climb. We'll figure this one out."

When she met eyes with Logan, he blinked in agreement.

"Manus is right. We won't give up. There's too much at stake." Logan pulled her closer to him and lowered his voice. "I won't give up as long as you're alive."

Tears shot into her eyes, and she had to hold her breath and force them back down to keep from crying in front of everybody. She couldn't show weakness now in front of these strangers who were risking so much for her. She had to prove to them that she was worth their effort.

26

"So we're all in agreement?" Logan asked.

The Stealth Guardians, plus Winter, were assembled in the command center so Pearce could monitor communications in case the council decided to send somebody to the Baltimore compound to look for Logan. They had discovered his escape only twenty minutes after Logan had locked the two guards in the lead cell. Apparently Pearce had covered his electronic tracks well, because so far nobody at the council compound had initiated any action that led Logan to believe they suspected he'd had help escaping.

"If you think it will work," Manus said hesitantly.

For two hours they'd discussed what they needed to do to put together a convincing case the council wouldn't be able to ignore. One that was so strong that even Logan's treason and his compound's complicity in it would be overlooked.

Hamish exchanged a look with Aiden. "If this will cause Winter to have a vision that'll lead to us being able to strike against the demons, I'm all for it. "

"I'm with Hamish," Aiden said. "Of course, it's against all our rules, but we don't have the luxury of waiting for Winter to have a vision out of the blue."

At that, everybody glanced at Winter, who gave an apologetic shrug.

Logan smiled at her reassuringly. "No, we don't have that luxury. I can't let you all take the risk of hiding us here indefinitely. The longer we're here, the riskier it is for all of you. I figure we have three or four days before the council has exhausted all other possibilities. Then even they will figure out that I'm hiding in plain sight."

"You know we won't just kick you out," Pearce said. "But we can always toss you in the lead cell if anybody arrives looking for you. Just to cover our asses. "

"Let's hope it doesn't come to that," Hamish said. Then he motioned to Winter. "You ready for this?"

She nodded.

Logan crossed the distance between him and Winter with three steps and stopped in front of her. "I'll take you to the archive first, then the armory."

"Okay," Winter said.

"Do you need any of us to come with you?" Aiden asked.

Logan looked over his shoulder. "I think you all should rest and be ready if Winter sees something. We have no idea how quickly we'll have something we can act upon. I'm afraid it'll be a waiting game."

He took Winter's hand. "Come, I'll show you my home." Not only that. He would let her touch things, weapons and artefacts, and show her books and pictures, anything that might trigger a vision about his species or the demons.

When they left the command room and stepped into the quiet corridor, Logan turned to Winter. "I'm sorry that we haven't had a minute alone yet. I promise you it won't always be that way. It's just—"

She put her fingers to his lips. "I understand. This is more important right now. I know what's expected of me."

He nodded, and they started walking.

"Your friends are good people." She hesitated. "Even Manus. They all love you. And they trust you. I'll make sure that all they're doing for us isn't in vain."

Logan sighed. "I don't want you to feel under pressure. I know you can't force a vision, and I don't want you to stress out about it. Charles said that you need to let your brain relax."

She cast him a forced smile. "I'm trying to."

"I know."

She let her eyes roam, then pointed to the runes that adorned the walls, ceilings, and floors. "What do they mean? They're runes, right?"

"Yes. They're a sort of warding." He remembered something then. "You drew runes on the door in your shop. You must have seen them in your visions."

"I did. But I didn't know what they meant. Just that I had to draw them." She shrugged. "But I guess they didn't work. The demons came anyway."

"Well, two things you should know about runes. They're not there to ward against demons, not directly anyway. The runes, together with our *virta*, our life force, turn this building invisible. There's powerful magic in these runes. It protects against all other magic. Witches like Charles or Wesley are powerless within these walls."

~ ~ ~

Had she heard right? "This building is invisible?"

Logan nodded.

"But doesn't that mean that people are constantly running into it, like they bumped into us when we were on the train platform?"

He chuckled. "You'd think so, right? But the magic in the runes makes sure that humans automatically turn the other way when they get too close. The building repels them. And they don't even realize it."

They arrived at the stairs. "This way."

Winter walked down the stairs beside him. So many questions were popping into her head. "Your friends seemed a little concerned about you letting me see the archive and armory."

"It's nothing personal, Winter. Giving a stranger access to these things means giving away our secrets. The more you know about us, the more severely you could betray us."

"I would never," she protested and stopped walking.

Logan turned to her and put his hand under her chin. "I know that. I know I can trust you." He pressed a kiss to her lips, and she pressed herself against him in response. It had been too long.

"Mmm," Logan hummed, taking a breath and interrupting the kiss. "I missed that. I missed you. When they marched me down to the lead cell, all I could think of was you and how to get back to you so we could flee."

"I was so scared that you wouldn't come back. When Hamish and Enya came to take me away, I thought... I thought it was over."

Again Logan kissed her, this time deeper and with more fervor. She felt her back connect with the cool stone wall and Logan's chest crushing her breasts. Her breath hitched. Yes, she'd missed him, missed this. Missed his mouth devouring her, his tongue exploring her, his hands caressing her.

She put her arms around him, sliding one hand to his nape to touch his naked skin there and felt him shudder. Encouraged by his passionate reaction, she put her other hand on his backside, gripping him there, feeling his muscles flex under her touch. He ground his groin into her, and the hard ridge of his erection rubbed against her. She let out a moan, and suddenly felt cool air blast against her burning lips.

Logan dipped his mouth to her ear. "Do you have any idea what you're doing to me?" His voice was husky and sent a shiver along her skin.

"I'm beginning to." And she liked the effect she had on him. It gave her an odd sense of power even though she knew Logan was so much stronger, so much more powerful than her. But when she was in his arms, he seemed to yield that power to her.

Logan drew his head back and smiled at her. "We'd better go and do what we came here to do before I forget my good manners and take you against this wall."

When she let out a gasp, he smirked. "As if you wouldn't enjoy me losing control like that."

He was right. She would.

"Later then?" she murmured.

"You can get rid of that question mark right now. 'Cause as soon as we have a few minutes of leisure, I'm going to drag you to my bed."

Anticipation running through her veins made her feel recharged. "I can't wait to see your room."

"Hmm-hmm." Logan hummed and took her hand to usher her down the corridor.

At a door, he stopped and punched a code into the number pad next to it. When a beep sounded, Logan opened the door inwards and stepped aside to let her enter ahead of him. Overhead lights came on automatically, most likely activated by motion sensors.

The room wasn't like anything else Winter had ever seen. It wasn't really a room. It looked more like catacombs, a structure of interconnected caves that held boxes, crates, and shelves. It was dusty here. The shelves held mostly books. The crates were labeled with descriptions, locations, and dates.

"This is our archive," Logan said from behind her. "Every compound in the world has its own. We've been around for centuries, and over time we collected a lot of stuff."

"What kind of stuff?" Winter asked while she walked deeper into the room and let her eyes roam.

"Anything we believe might one day help us in our fight against the demons." He motioned to a row of boxes. "As well as files recording battles and other encounters with the enemy. This is before we started using computers. These days everything gets recorded on our servers. And we're trying to digitize the old files."

"This is huge. I don't even know where to start."

Logan put his hand on her shoulder and made her look at him. "I'll show you where we keep the photographs and paintings. You might recognize something in them. Maybe something you've seen in one of your visions."

She hoped so, because she wanted to be useful, not only because it would save her and Logan's lives, but because she wanted to help destroy the demons. One encounter with those vile creatures, and she knew she would rather die than work for them.

Logan led her to a section of the room, where glass-enclosed cases held old photographs showing different landmarks, people, and objects. She looked at one after another, row after row.

"Anything?" Logan asked.

With a regretful expression, she looked at him. "I'm sorry."

"Don't be. This is just a start. There's lots more to see, and to touch. The armory holds hundreds of weapons, some of them once belonged to the demons."

She nodded. "Maybe I should touch those."

"You will. Let's continue here first." He put his hand on the small of her back. "And I don't want you to fret. It might not work on the first try, okay? Just be patient with yourself."

She turned her face to him. "I wish I could be patient. But so much is at stake. Your life, your friends' lives."

"You shouldn't worry about us. We signed up for this, my friends and I. We've trained for this all our lives. You didn't choose this. You're new to this world. Nobody expects you to work the way we do. You're a civilian."

She shook her head. "Not anymore, Logan. I'm part of this now. And that means I have to do my part."

He stroked his knuckles over her cheek. "So brave."

But she wasn't brave. Deep down she was scared, scared that the demons would snatch her like she'd seen in her vision. And that Logan would have to risk his life again to save her. But she didn't want to tell him about her fear. He already had enough to worry about. She didn't want him to think she was a scared damsel whom he needed to constantly reassure. Even if she needed his strength.

27

Winter had looked at the many pictures they kept in the archive, and touched a great number of the artefacts they'd collected over the years, before they'd moved on to the armory, a large room where they kept weapons of all kinds. She'd touched those too. Still, even after hours of going through the two rooms, their efforts hadn't produced a vision.

"There's not much more we can do right now," Logan said. "It's time you rest."

She looked at him then, disappointment and regret in her eyes. As if she'd failed. He didn't want her to feel like that. She'd done everything he and his colleagues had asked of her.

"It's not working," she murmured.

"Because you're exhausted. We can't force this. Charles said as much. Give it another day. If nothing happens, I'll call Charles and see if he has any other ideas, okay?"

She nodded, but didn't look entirely convinced.

"Come, I'll take you to my quarters."

Winter didn't protest when he guided her through the maze of corridors and up several flights of stairs to where the private living quarters were located. Each guardian had their own suite of rooms they got to furnish and decorate the way they liked. It was their home and would remain their home for as long as they chose to carry out the duties of a guardian.

Logan opened the door to his private domain and let Winter enter ahead of him, then closed the door behind him.

"Make yourself at home."

He watched her acquaint herself with the space. They stood in the living room which featured a large comfortable seating area with a gas fireplace, a small desk in one corner, and bookshelves along one wall. A set of Art Deco pocket doors led into the adjacent bedroom where a king-sized bed dominated the room. Indirect light illuminated the suite and disguised the fact that it had no windows. Fresh air was pumped in through an elaborate air conditioning system, and the temperature was comfortable. An ensuite bathroom with clawfoot tub and an oversized shower completed the suite. This was his home.

"It's beautiful," Winter said and smiled at him. "I never expected something so elegant."

"From a warrior like me, you mean?" He chuckled. "My friends and I spend all our lives in the compound. We all have different tastes, but our private quarters, we get to decorate to our own liking. I love Art Deco, so I chose many pieces reflecting that era."

"I love it."

Logan reached for her and put his arm around her waist. "How about I run you a bath so you can unwind a little, huh?"

She looked up at him from under her dark lashes. "How do you always know what I need?"

"I just know."

She sighed. "You're an amazing man. How will I ever be able to thank you for all you're doing?"

His eyes drifted to the bed, and he noticed her following his look. "I'm sure you'll think of something."

"Hmm." She lifted herself on her toes and kissed him. "Yes, I'm sure."

"I'll run your bath," he said and released her, knowing that if he held her any longer, she wouldn't get to relax. She'd find herself pressed against the nearest flat surface, his cock buried deep inside her.

Logan walked into the bathroom, switched on the lights that provided a soft glow over the tub, and turned on the water. When he heard footsteps behind him, he turned around and watched Winter enter.

She was barefoot and pulling her T-shirt over her head.

"Let me help you," he offered and walked toward her. "I want to undress you. Consider it part of your thanks to me."

She dropped her arms to her sides to give him free rein. "You're easy to please."

"Sometimes the easiest things are the best." He popped the button of her jeans open, then dragged the zipper down. Slowly, he helped her shimmy out of her pants, then dropped them on the hamper.

Winter looked innocent in her white bra and panties. Like forbidden fruit, and just as tantalizing. Her long dark hair fell over her shoulders, a few strands tangling in the straps of her bra. He freed them and brushed his fingers along her skin.

Winter sighed, and the soft sound bounced off the tile walls.

"You're a sight I'll never get tired of."

He ran his hands over her torso, gently stroking over her bra-covered breasts without lingering, before returning to them and rubbing over her nipples. Through the thin fabric he felt them harden to little points. He pinched them lightly, eliciting a moan from their owner. Then he dipped his thumbs beneath the fabric and rubbed over her stiff nipples. Winter's chest rose, and he took her reaction as an invitation and shoved the cups to the side, letting her breasts pop out of their cage. One bra strap slipped from her shoulder, then the other, giving her breasts even more freedom.

He cupped the heavy globes in his palms and squeezed them. He'd always been a breast man, but Winter's breasts were particularly beautiful, perfectly round, perfectly firm, and perfectly delicious.

Logan dipped his head to them and sucked one nipple into his mouth, licking his tongue over it, before showering the other breast with the same attention.

"I thought you wanted to undress me," Winter murmured breathlessly.

"I am, love, I am. I'm just taking my time."

He reached around her, found the clasp of the bra and opened it. He tossed it on the hamper and captured her breasts once more, massaging them with his hands, kneading them, exploring them, while Winter sighed softly.

"See? You need this."

"Yes."

Then he reached for her panties and freed her of them. They landed on top of the hamper, too. His ears picked up the sound of the water running, and he knew it was time to turn it off.

"Don't move," he said and walked to the tub.

He turned off the faucet, testing the water, and realized it was a little too hot. Just as well. He wasn't quite done with Winter. Turning back to her, he pulled his shirt over his head and tossed it aside to join the other clothes.

"Are you joining me in the tub?" Winter asked, watching him.

"No. The tub's too small for it. And the water is still too hot." He was already getting rid of his shoes and socks. His pants followed.

He caught her gaze on him, when he hooked his thumbs into his boxer briefs. "I figured we could kill time until the water is a little cooler."

She smirked. "You mean instead of adding cold water?"

Stripping himself of his underwear, he said, "Where would be the fun in that?" Naked now, he stalked toward her. "Unless you'd prefer to skip this and go straight for the tub?"

Winter slid her hand onto his butt and pulled him to her so his groin connected with her stomach.

"Yeah, didn't think so," he murmured to her and lifted her into his arms.

He carried her to the cushioned bench that stood near one wall and sat down on it, lifting Winter onto his lap so she was straddling him. His cock was hard already. It had taken all of thirty seconds to get him ready. Just looking at her beautiful body and touching her smooth skin, licking her sweet breasts had done that.

"I need to be inside you," he said. "I need to come inside you. To feel that everything is alright."

He lifted her hips to bring his cock to her center, when she suddenly stiffened. His gaze snapped to her face. "Something wrong?"

She hesitated. "I know we talked about this earlier, you know, with you being an immortal."

He wasn't sure what she was talking about.

"But when I saw the twins today, it dawned on me: your race procreates. I mean, you can impregnate a woman. You said back in that motel room that you couldn't."

Logan let out a sigh of relief. "I should have explained things better. I'm sorry. You couldn't know. Yes, we procreate the same way humans do, but there is a small distinction. Stealth Guardian males are born sterile. Only once they go through a bonding ritual with a female, do they become fertile." He brushed his knuckles over her cheek. "I can't get you pregnant, Winter." At least not yet.

"Oh." She stared at him in surprise. Then she seemed to catch herself. "I mean, no offense. I'm not saying that it would be a disaster to get pregnant by you. I mean... you know, but I'm single, and... it's not that I'm religious or anything, but I don't think I have the energy to raise a child on my own, and... anyway, it's not that I don't like children... I do, but—"

"Winter?" he interrupted.

"Hmm?"

"Why are you babbling nervously?"

"I'm not babbling."

He chuckled. She was cute when she was all frazzled. And he could imagine how cute she would look with a child growing in her belly. How sexy she would be. And he could almost feel what it would be like to make love to her knowing she was carrying a child. His child.

Fuck!

Was he going insane? He'd never thought about a woman like this. Never wasted a single thought on bonding with a female, even less on siring a child. But here, with his cock hard and eager to thrust into Winter, he couldn't think of anything he wanted more.

He pulled her head to him. If he were fertile right now, would Winter insist he wear a condom? Would she let him inside her, knowing what could happen? Would she stop him?

But he didn't ask these questions. Instead, Logan captured her lips and kissed her. He gripped her hips, lifted her slightly and adjusted his angle, then dropped her back onto his lap, impaling her on his cock. Winter gasped into his mouth. His own breath caught in his chest. This was better than the times before. Better, because something had changed between them. They were growing closer. The intimacy that was developing between them was palpable now. He could feel it with every movement, every breath.

When Winter began to move up and down on him as if she were a professional rider, he gave into his desire for her and delivered counterthrust after counterthrust. Holding onto her hips, he plunged hard and deep, asserting his claim on her. Her breasts rocked against him with every movement, and he took the opportunity to dip his head to them and press his face into the ample flesh. He kissed a path up between her breasts until he reached the small indentation at the base of her throat.

Winter dropped her head back, while her hips moved more urgently. He could feel her heartbeat pulse against his lips as he kissed her, feel the air pump through her lungs with every labored breath, while together they raced toward orgasm.

Inside her it was like being in an inferno. Flames engulfed him, swallowed him whole, singed him with pleasure, with unspeakable bliss, bliss he believed to be reserved for the bonding ritual. But loving Winter like this, giving himself to her without reservations, without secrets between them, drove him to heights he hadn't known before. He knew it now, knew that now that he'd tasted happiness, he wouldn't be able to give it up again. Whatever happened, he would never be able to be without Winter. She was everything he'd ever craved. The softness to his hardness, the kindness to his gruffness, the light to his dark. The yang to his yin.

He understood his compound mates Hamish and Aiden now. He knew why they'd broken the rules when they'd met the women they were destined to mate with: because there were no rules when it came to love. There would never be any rules. Love transcended them all.

He wanted to tell Winter what he felt, but he knew it was too early. Though she was a preternatural, deep down she still felt human, still acted like a human. And humans needed time before they could declare their love for someone. A preternatural like him didn't need that time. Once he knew, he knew, and all doubts were wiped away. To a preternatural, love could happen like a lightning strike, without warning. In his case, he'd seen the warning signs, but thought the circumstances weren't right. But love didn't care about circumstances, didn't care whether the time was right. As long as the person was right. And Winter was the right one for him.

He could only hope that he was the right one for her.

Winter was panting. Her tempo was increasing, her pussy squeezing him tightly. He could sense how close she was and knew what she needed. He brought his hand between their bodies and found her clit. When he touched it, Winter moaned out loud, and he rubbed over the sensitive organ, while he continued to move his hips back and forth in response to Winter's movements. He was close too, but he was holding on to his control to bring her to a climax first.

"Just relax, love, I've got you," he murmured against her lips, then captured them and kissed her, pouring every ounce of affection he felt for her into the kiss.

He felt her rub herself faster against his finger, up and down, until she suddenly cried out. Her pussy gripped his cock tightly, squeezing and releasing several times in quick succession as her orgasm crashed over her. It was the reward he'd been holding on for: feeling her pleasure ignite his own climax. He gave himself over to it, surrendered to the joy of making love to Winter, and shot his seed deep into her tight channel. He wrapped his arms around her and pressed her to his heaving chest, holding her until they both came down from their high.

Breathing heavily, Winter rested her head on his shoulder, and Logan slowly stood up with her in his arms and carried her to the tub. Gently he lowered her into the warm water.

She hummed contentedly and smiled up at him. "This is perfect."

Logan slid his hands down her body, caressing her breasts, touching her stomach and stroking her legs. "Yes, perfect."

"I wish you could be in the tub with me."

He smiled and kissed her on the lips. "I'd just be trying to get inside you again. Believe me, you'll enjoy your bath much more without me."

She closed her eyes. "Hmm. Handsome, good in bed, and selfless. What did I ever do to deserve this?"

"Plenty." He rose and walked to the shower. After pulling fresh towels from a closet, and placing one next to the tub and hanging one outside the shower stall, he stepped into the shower. While he washed himself, he watched Winter soaking in the tub, her body submerged in the warm water up to her shoulders. The tips of her breasts occasionally peeked through the surface, teasing him.

He wasn't sure whether his constant hard-on would ever go down again. He doubted it. In Winter's presence he seemed to be in a state of constant arousal. Like a stallion in the presence of a mare in heat.

Logan finished his shower quickly and dried off. He found a pair of sweats and put them on. Then he pulled his bathrobe from the closet and hung it near the bathtub.

He leaned over the tub, where Winter looked like she was dozing.

"I'm going to get us something to eat. Are you hungry?"

She lifted her lids only a little bit. "Hmm, yeah, I think I could eat something. What time is it?"

He looked at the digital clock on the marble counter. "It's already mid-morning."

Her eyes widened. "Are you serious? I thought it was still night."

He chuckled. "That's because you haven't slept at all since you left San Francisco. And without windows in the compound it can be easy to lose track of time."

"It's odd that there aren't any windows."

"It's safer that way." He rose. "I'll get us some food. But don't rush. Enjoy your bath. There's a fresh towel for you. And feel free to wear my bathrobe."

He turned and left his private quarters.

28

Only Aiden, Leila, and the twins were in the kitchen when Logan entered. The children were wearing jackets and boots, and Leila had donned a blond wig, a sign that she was leaving the compound. The demons were still after her because of a vaccine she'd created that would be beneficial to the demons' agenda, so she only left the compound heavily disguised. In addition to the blond wig, she also wore broad-rimmed, dark sunglasses. She looked like a movie star.

"Where're you guys going?" Logan asked.

Aiden motioned to the twins who were chasing each other around the kitchen island. "These two need to get out today or somebody is going to strangle them."

"You said it, man, not me."

"Yeah, but you're thinking it, and so is the rest of the compound. You guys are good sports," Aiden said, "but let's face it, kids need to be able to roam outside from time to time."

"As do I," Leila added. "As nice as our extended quarters are, I do get cabin fever on occasion."

Logan grinned. He couldn't blame her. Even though Aiden and Leila had taken over almost the entire top floor of the building with their brood, there was no garden, no terrace, no place where the kids could run wild.

Logan looked at Aiden. "You're taking every precaution, I assume?"

"No worries. I'm going as the Invisible Man so no demon can spot us. They won't recognize Blondie here, nor the kids. We're good," Aiden said.

"Blondie?" Leila chuckled. "So you like my blond hair?"

He put his arms around her. "I like everything about you. I'll show you how much later."

"Guys!" Logan admonished. "Not in front of the kids! They'll be scarred for life!"

Aiden and Leila laughed.

"Come on, Xander, come, Julia," Leila called out to them. "Let's go out!"

The kids charged toward her, almost mowing Logan over on the way.

Ten seconds later, peace and quiet descended on the kitchen. Logan went about pulling together a tray with snacks. Thanks to Leila, there were lots of delicious treats in the refrigerator. While she rarely ever went to the supermarket herself, she wrote out detailed shopping lists, and one of the guardians at the compound did the shopping for her. The choice of food at the compound had definitely improved since Leila had moved in. He couldn't believe that almost four years had passed since that day.

When Logan entered his rooms again, tray in hand, he found Winter lounging on the sofa, dressed in his bathrobe. She'd dried her hair, and her skin looked rosy, her face refreshed.

"You didn't have to rush your bath," he said and set the tray on the coffee table.

"I didn't." She leaned forward to inspect the tray. "Hmm. This looks wonderful. Who does the cooking here?"

"Mostly Leila."

"Remind me to thank her. I'm not much of a cook, you know." She shrugged. "But I like to eat."

"Help yourself. I brought a bit of everything, but if there's something else you want, I'm sure I can find it in the fridge. Just let me know."

"Oh no, this is perfect."

Logan took a seat next to Winter, and they filled their plates and started eating. He hadn't realized how hungry he was.

"So, how come you don't cook?" he asked. "I mean, not that I expect every woman to be able to cook just because she's a woman. But people who like to eat well normally learn how to cook."

Winter gave him a sad smile. "My mom was the one who always cooked for me and dad. She wouldn't let anybody in the kitchen. It was her domain."

"Didn't she want to teach you?"

"She never got a chance. I was only nine, when she and Dad died."

"I'm sorry, I should have realized that when you mentioned it the other day. I shouldn't have asked."

"That's okay."

"What happened to you after your parents' death?"

"My grandmother raised me."

"I'm glad you had family to take care of you." He couldn't imagine what it would have been like for a nine-year-old to go into the foster care system.

"Yeah, I had Grandma." Despite the positive words, there was a sadness in her voice that made Logan look at her. "But then she died, too. I was fourteen."

"Only fourteen?" Logan put his hand on her arm and squeezed it. "I'm so sorry."

"She wasn't that old, you know, for a grandmother."

"Cancer?" he guessed.

To his surprise, Winter shook her head. "Something with the heart, they think. After her death, I went to a foster family. When my foster father got transferred to Wilmington, they petitioned the court to let me move out of state with them. So I left Detroit behind. Never went back."

"So you're originally from Detroit? Wasn't it hard to leave everything behind, your friends, the memories of your family?"

The smile she gave him was bittersweet. "Not really. The earlier memories, those were good ones. But the time with my grandmother…"

"Didn't you like her?"

"I loved her. But things were difficult. She was sick. Or at least the doctors thought she was sick. They diagnosed her with some mental illness that has a Latin name I can't pronounce. But after everything that happened in the last few days, I don't believe anymore that she was mentally ill. I think she was a psychic, too. I think I inherited my gift from her."

Logan's heartbeat accelerated. "What makes you think she was a psychic?"

"She was always talking about seeing things that weren't there. The doctors thought she was having hallucinations. I mean after what Wesley and Charles said, I think "psychic" would fit the bill, don't you?"

He nodded slowly. Unfortunately, Winter's grandmother also fit the description of somebody he knew. "How long ago did your grandmother die?"

"It'll be twenty years this December."

Logan swallowed away the lump that was rising in his throat. Twenty years. "And she lived in her home in Detroit at the time?"

Winter shook her head. "She wasn't at home anymore. They'd put her in a mental hospital. They thought she'd get better…"

Logan didn't hear the rest of the sentence, because his heart was thundering in his ears. The psychic he'd killed was Winter's grandmother. Because of him, because of what he'd done, Winter had ended up in foster care. Without family.

Guilt barreled into him. Pain slammed on top of it, suffocating him.

What had he done?

He'd killed the grandmother of the woman he loved. Winter would never forgive him for this. Still, he had to tell her. He had to confess what he'd done. He couldn't let her sit next to her grandmother's murderer without her knowledge.

"Winter…" His voice trailed off.

"Oh, what's that?" She suddenly bent down to pick something up from underneath the coffee table.

He recognized the stuffed toy in her hand. "Oh, one of Julia's toys," he said automatically.

"Oh God, no!" Clutching the toy, Winter shot up.

Alarmed, Logan jumped up and gripped her shoulders. "What's wrong?"

But Winter wasn't looking at him. She was looking through him. He knew instantly what it meant. She was having a vision.

Her face distorted in horror, her eyes widening, tears brimming in them, while her lips quivered. "No," she murmured. "No, please, no!"

Whatever she saw had to be horrible, but Logan didn't dare shake her out of it. She had to go through this, had to see everything the vision could reveal. All he could do was hold her, let her know he was there, even though he didn't dare speak in case he broke her concentration.

Winter's head moved from side to side, as if she was searching for something, while her arms twitched, one arm reaching out, trying to grab something, but only gripping air, while in her other hand she held on to the toy.

All of a sudden, Winter dropped the toy and wailed, tears streaming down her face.

His heart broke for her. He hated seeing her in pain like this and wished he could take the pain upon himself. He felt her hands on his bare chest and realized that her eyes were focusing again.

"You have to save them, Logan," she begged, choking the words out amidst tears. "The twins, you have to save them."

Logan's heart stopped. "Aiden's and Leila's twins?" He involuntarily gripped her shoulders tighter as panic charged through his body. "What did you see?"

"The demons, they're attacking them. Aiden, and a blond woman. She looked familiar. And the kids they're right there, crying, screaming, scared."

"A blond woman? With dark sun glasses?"

She nodded. "How do you know?"

"It's Leila. She disguises herself when she leaves the compound. I saw them earlier in the kitchen, getting ready to leave with the twins."

"You have to call them back, now! Or the demons will get them."

Logan rushed to the nightstand and picked up the receiver, hit the pre-programmed number for Aiden's cell phone and let it ring. Once, twice, three times.

"Damn it, pick up!"

"It's Aiden. Leave me a message," the pre-recorded voice said.

"Fuck!" Logan cursed. "Aiden, you've gotta get back to the compound with Leila and the kids. The demons are going to attack you. Winter had a vision. You hear me? Come back immediately!"

He disconnected the call and pressed the button for the intercom next to his bed that connected to the command center. "Pearce, you there?"

"Yo, what's up?" Pearce replied through the crackling line.

"Track Aiden's cell phone. I need to know where he is."

"What's wrong?"

"Winter had a vision of him, Leila, and the kids being attacked. I saw them leave the compound less than an hour ago."

"Shit! I'm on it." There was more crackling on the line.

Meanwhile Logan rushed to his closet, pulled out a pair of pants and a fresh shirt, and started dressing. "Winter, get dressed."

He didn't have to tell her, because she was already rushing into the bathroom to grab her clothes.

"Shit!" Pearce's voice came through the intercom again.

Logan pressed the button. "Where is he?"

"I don't know. But his phone is in the compound."

"Fuck!" Logan grabbed socks and slipped them on, then reached for his shoes. "Alert everybody, get them to suit up. We have to find them. I'll be down in the command center in a minute."

"Got it."

As he laced his boots, he looked at Winter, who was almost ready too.

"In your vision, did you see where they were?" he asked.

"It looked like a store, maybe a shopping mall. I couldn't read the name of the shop." She slipped into her shoes. "But I'll recognize it when I see it. We just have to get in the general vicinity."

"We?" He shook his head. "You're not coming with us. There's no way I'm putting you in the path of the demons."

"You have no choice, Logan! I saw where they were. You need me."

"Then describe to me what the place looks like. You don't need to come."

"I can't possibly describe everything I saw. Do you really want to risk the twins' lives? Damn it, Logan, I'm coming with you. I can find them."

He grumbled to himself, but he knew she was right. Without the name of the store where Aiden had taken his family, they had nothing to go on. They had to rely on the fragments Winter had seen in her vision and hope she would recognize them when she was confronted with them again. Whether he liked it or not, she had to come with them.

"You won't leave my side. Is that clear?"

"Crystal," she said.

He handed her a jacket. "Put this on and let's go."

29

By the time Logan and Winter reached the command center, Hamish and Manus had already joined Pearce.

"Where's Enya?" Logan asked.

"She got called in as a second for an injured guardian in Seattle for the day," Pearce informed him.

"Damn! What did you find on Aiden?"

"Aiden's cell phone is charging in the kitchen. He must have forgotten it," Hamish said.

"I tried Leila's phone," Pearce said, "but it's not switched on. She probably left it upstairs in their quarters."

"Fuck," Logan cursed once again. Then he motioned to the computer. "Can you pull up every major shopping center within forty-five minutes of here?"

Pearce looked at him. "Can you narrow that down a bit? There's gotta be hundreds of shops within those parameters."

Winter approached the console. "I saw clothes. For kids."

Pearce nodded and started typing something on his keyboard. "Okay, kids' clothing stores. That helps a bit." He pointed to the screen where a map had appeared. A cluster of red dots was strewn haphazardly over the map as if somebody had tossed a sack of marbles on it.

"Too many," Winter murmured.

Pearce punched another command on his keyboard, and several blue lines appeared going outward from the location of the compound, stopping at various distances from it. "Taking into account traffic conditions, these lines represent the maximum distance you could travel from the compound by car within the last forty-five minutes."

"Okay, that's better," Logan said. "Can you hide the shops that he couldn't have reached?"

Pearce tapped on his keyboard, and a large number of the dots disappeared. At the same time, he made the map larger, providing a closer view of the different locations.

"Can you do a satellite view of that?" Winter asked.

"Sure." Pearce clicked the mouse, and the streets disappeared. The red dots and blue lines were now superimposed over satellite imagery of buildings, green spaces, and other terrain.

"It wasn't a strip mall," Winter said. "When I looked out of the store's window, there were no cars."

"Okay, an indoor mall," Logan suggested and pointed to two spots on the map. "Pearce, are these the only two indoor malls within range?"

"Yeah, pretty sure."

"Zoom in on this one," Logan ordered, then turned to Winter. "Anything familiar about the structure?"

She shook her head. "Sorry. From above they all look the same."

"Hold on," Pearce said and switched to another window. "I can pull up the website for the mall, see if they have pictures you can look at."

Within a few seconds, Pearce had pulled up the website and navigated to the gallery. He scrolled through the images slowly, while Winter perused them. She kept shaking her head.

"None of this looks familiar." She looked up. "How about the other mall?"

Pearce searched for the second mall on the browser, but a 404 Error came up. "Something is wrong with their website."

"Shit!" Logan cursed. He locked eyes with Winter. "Are you sure that you recognize nothing in the first mall?"

She nodded. "Absolutely. It has to be the other one."

Logan exchanged looks with his friends. Hamish nodded, as did Manus.

"Let's do it," Logan said. He turned to Pearce. "You stay here. Keep trying Leila's phone in case she has it with her and she switches it on. The rest of you, let's go." He opened a wall cupboard where several daggers were stored. He took two for himself, then handed one to Winter. "For self-defense only. Don't attack the demons. Stay back. Only use this if they charge at you."

She took the dagger and put it in the pocket of her jacket.

The drive to the shopping mall took too long, even with Hamish breaking every traffic law. Unfortunately there were no lost portals close to the shopping mall that they could have used instead. And Winter hadn't seen anything that gave her an indication of the time when the attack was supposed to occur. For all Logan knew, they could already be too late. His heart clenched. He prayed that they would reach Aiden and his family in time.

When Hamish pulled the car into the large parking lot and drove up to the side entrance, Logan said, "We'll go in invisibly. We don't want the demons to latch onto us, or scare any bystanders. Make sure Winter can see you though."

Hamish and Manus nodded.

"It's up to Winter now to help us find the shop as quickly as possible."

Hamish switched off the engine, and everybody jumped out.

At the door, his friends cloaked themselves, while Logan cloaked both Winter and himself. Then they marched into the indoor mall. As Logan had already seen on the map and during the drive, the place was about four city blocks long and one block wide, with additional wings toward the middle of the structure. Pop music droned from speakers in the walls and ceiling.

Winter immediately rushed to the information board and perused it quickly. She ran her finger over the list of stores under the heading apparel.

"Too many," she murmured. "And the kids' stores are all over the place. Shit!" She looked over her shoulder at him, looking stressed.

"Breathe, Winter. Concentrate and think back to the vision. Did you see any colors? Any columns, maybe the escalators? Or one of the stalls that line the middle of the walkway?"

He watched her close her eyes. Her chest rose and fell. "Something yellow, just outside the store window. It's moving. An elephant." She opened her eyes. "It doesn't make sense."

But Logan was already addressing Hamish and Manus. "Keep your eyes open for anything yellow. Possibly a kids' ride that looks like an elephant." Then he took Winter's hand, and together they rushed down one side of the mall, while Manus and Hamish ran along the other side, parallel to them.

At each kids' clothing store, they stopped briefly and looked inside, before continuing on. With every yard they covered, Logan's heart pounded more frantically.

They reached one of the wings, and Logan looked down the length of it. There was only one stall in the middle of the wide walkway, as well as a board with rotating electronic advertising, but no kids' ride shaped like an elephant.

"Nothing down there," Logan said to Winter and motioned for them to continue.

"Wait!"

Winter's voice jolted him and made him look over his shoulder.

~ ~ ~

Winter had already started following Logan, when something yellow caught her eye. She whipped her head in the direction: the advertising board. It had just turned to a yellow background, advertising a travel site. She stopped and pointed to it. "Yellow!"

"But there's no kids ride down there."

He was right, but something made her wait as she continued to stare at the board. Finally it changed screens again, and there it was: an ad featuring an elephant moving across the African plains.

"This is the elephant. It's there. It's down there," she said excitedly, her pulse pounding wildly.

In a few moments, she'd have another encounter with the demons, and she was scared. But the lives of two children were on the line, and she couldn't just stand by without acting. She rushed down the side wing toward the advertising board.

"Winter! Damn it!" Logan ran after her, catching up with her. He grabbed her arm, then put a finger to the communications device in his ear. "Hamish, Manus, down the east wing, toward the end. Opposite an advertising board."

She couldn't hear their response, but assumed they were coming, and continued walking. A few more steps and she and Logan could see the shop opposite the sign. It was indeed a children's clothing store. Colorful decorations hung in the large store window and obstructed the view into the shop, forcing them to approach the door to look inside.

Winter slammed her hand over her mouth to smother her gasp. There, near the cash register lay a blond woman in a pool of her own blood. She lay on her front, obscuring a clear view of her face.

Please, don't let it be Leila!

Winter's eyes traveled past the dead woman toward the back of the shop, and she saw them: demons. Three of them from what she could tell. Aiden was fighting them off as well as he could, but he was injured. The kids were nowhere to be seen.

Logan stormed past her into the store and jumped one of the demons, ripping him off Aiden and slicing his throat. A second demon turned and aimed his dagger at him.

Winter rushed into the store, desperately looking for the twins so she could get them out. She peered past the cash register, bending over the low counter to see if they were hiding behind it, but the space was empty. Then a movement caught her eye and she whipped her head toward the door. Hamish and Manus stormed in.

Winter spun her head back to Logan and the demons. Logan was battling one demon, while Aiden was having trouble fighting the other, one of his arms hanging limply by his side. With horror, she saw the demon plunge his dagger toward the injured guardian. He stopped in mid-motion. Hamish had snatched him from behind, dragged him back, and was now slicing his throat from ear to ear.

Her stomach lurched as she saw the green blood ooze from the dead creature. She looked away, her gaze now landing on Logan, who'd finished the third demon.

"Didn't leave me any," Manus complained, waving his unused dagger.

Hamish rushed to Aiden and put his arm around his waist to prevent him from collapsing. "Leila, the kids?"

Aiden motioned to the back of the store, where only now, Winter saw a door. "Storeroom," Aiden pressed out. Then he looked at the spot where the blond woman lay. "I couldn't save the store owner."

Manus opened the door to the store room. "Leila, Xander, Julia, it's all clear."

Leila popped her head out, her children clinging to her legs. When her eyes fell on her husband, she let out a sigh of relief. "Oh, God."

Manus pulled Julia into his arms, and Xander ran to his father. Leila, tears in her eyes, put her arms around her husband.

Aiden looked at his compound mates. "How did you guys know we were in trouble?"

Three sets of eyes—Hamish's, Manus's, and Logan's—landed on Winter.

"Winter had a vision," Logan said.

Aiden looked at her, locking eyes. "I owe you my family's lives."

Winter sighed, tears stinging her eyes. "It's all good now. It's over." But her heart was still pounding, and she hadn't been able to prevent the death of the store owner. She glanced at the dead woman again and shuddered, when she felt Logan's hand on her arm.

"We need to clean up here, but we'll be as quick as we can," he said. Then he leaned in. "You did good, real good. You just saved the lives of Barclay's family. He'll change his vote."

"His vote?" Aiden said from behind them.

Winter looked at him, as did Logan.

"My father voted to let Winter live."

"You spoke to him about Winter?"

Aiden shook his head and winced from the pain of his injuries. "It's not what you think. He calls me sometimes, talks to me about difficult decisions. When they voted on Winter's fate, he called me without telling me any names or saying what the vote was about. But he was troubled by it. He said that he'd voted with the minority, but as the head of the council, he had to assure that the decision the council made was executed. I'm sorry. But he's not the one you need to convince." He smiled at Winter. "He already knows how valuable you are. But don't despair. This incident might still convince another council member to change his or her vote. I'll be your star witness."

"Thank you, Aiden," Winter said, forcing a smile.

"No. Thank you."

While Hamish and Manus went about wrapping up the dead demons, using large black trash bags from the store room, Leila took care of Aiden's injuries. The kids sat on the floor, playing with toys from the store.

"There's a surveillance camera," Logan said. "We need to find the recording."

"I saw some electronic equipment in the storeroom," Leila said.

"Thanks." Logan marched into the storeroom.

Winter walked to the shop door and turned the sign in it to "We're closed", then closed the door. She was about to turn away from it to attend to the children, when a wheelchair entered her peripheral vision. She glanced down the walkway. An older woman in an electric wheelchair slowly drove by the store, her eyes looking forward, a colorful knitted bag on her lap. Winter stared at the bag. Her grandmother had had the same one: blue and orange with streaks of green and brown. It had been en vogue in the seventies, but it stuck out like a sore thumb now.

She shrugged and tried to turn away, but something stopped her. She stared at the bag again, but now the bag wasn't sitting in the lap of the woman in the wheelchair. It was sitting on a chair next to a hospital bed. Her grandmother's hospital bed. And there, in the bed, lay her grandmother. The medical staff had restrained her for fear she'd go into one of her fits and hurt herself.

Winter's throat constricted. She looked so vulnerable.

A heart rate monitor beeped steadily.

A sound at the door made Winter turn her head. The door opened, and involuntarily, she stepped back into the shadows of the room. A man entered. He was tall and athletic and dressed in street clothes. Not one of the doctors or nurses that attended to Winter's grandmother. He stepped closer to the bed and pulled something from his pocket.

Winter stared at it. It was a syringe. Gasping, she walked to the other side of the bed until she stood almost opposite him and could see his face. She froze, as did every drop of her blood. The man in her grandmother's room, the man holding a syringe in his hand, was Logan.

She tried to scream, but no sound issued from her throat. All she could do was watch helplessly as Logan inserted the syringe into her grandmother's arm and emptied it into her.

Her grandmother's chest suddenly heaved, and a choking sound came from her throat. A second later, she collapsed back into the bed. The heart rate monitor started issuing one continuous sound. Flatline. Logan had killed her grandmother. Killed a helpless woman in her sleep.

Suddenly the room was gone. Winter spun around. She was back in the shop.

Logan came out of the storeroom. "I deleted the recording."

"We're almost done here, too," Manus said.

Winter continued staring at Logan, who finally looked at her. A quizzical look on his face, he walked toward her. "Everything okay, love?"

How dare he call her love? Oh God, she'd made love to her grandmother's killer. To the man who'd robbed her of the last member of her family.

"You killed her."

"What?" He looked confused.

"I saw you. I saw you in her room. You injected her with poison. You killed her."

An expression of dread crossed Logan's face. She knew it then. He knew it too. It was true.

"You killed my grandmother."

Tears now blurred her vision.

"Winter, I can explain."

"Explain? You killed her! You killed an innocent woman! I hate you!" she screamed and pivoted.

She ripped the door open. She had to get out of here. She couldn't be in the same space as Logan. She was suffocating.

"Winter, please!"

She ran outside into the hallway and turned toward the exit. She didn't get far. She felt a hand on her arm.

"Let go, Logan!" she yelled and spun her head to him.

But it wasn't Logan. Green demon eyes stared back at her. "Gotcha!"

The demon made a movement with his arm, and suddenly a swirling mass of fog and wind appeared out of nowhere. A vortex.

"Noooooo!"

It wasn't Winter who screamed, but somebody else. It was Logan's voice.

But the demon was already dragging her into the vortex, and she lost all sense of orientation. Panic overtook her body. Another one of her visions was coming true: the demon was taking her into the Underworld.

30

Logan raced toward the vortex, ready to jump inside. He lunged for it, felt the cold fog at his fingertips, catapulted himself forward—and landed on the stone floor. The vortex had closed and disappeared. And with it, Winter. Taken by the demons. Gone.

"Fuck!"

"Shit!" Manus echoed behind him. "They must have had a lookout."

Logan turned around. "We have to get her back. I have to get her back."

"Impossible," Manus said, regret coloring his voice. "We're fucked."

"I'm not giving up. I'm going to get her back."

"From the Underworld?" Manus shook his head. "It's over, Logan. We screwed up."

"*We?*" Logan shook his head. "You didn't do anything wrong. *I* screwed up. I screwed everything up. If I'd told her immediately, she would have never been out here."

"So it's true what she said, that you killed her grandmother?"

Logan dropped his head. "She was a psychic too. The demons had gotten their hooks into her. I did what I was ordered to do. She was beyond saving. I just didn't know that she was Winter's grandmother. I only found out a few hours ago."

"Oh fuck!"

"Yeah, fuck!" And he had to make it right. He couldn't let Winter suffer in the Underworld. He had to save her. "I have to find a way to get to the Underworld."

"There's no way to get in. "

"There has to be. Winter had a vision. She saw me coming to her rescue in the Underworld. So there has to be a way in."

Vehemently, Manus shook his head. "That's suicide. Even if you found a way in—and there's none—no Stealth Guardian has ever been in the Underworld."

Logan suddenly stiffened. "You're wrong. Virginia. She and Wesley. They got in. And they got out again."

Manus's eyes widened. "That was an accident. And nobody has ever tried to replicate it."

"Then somebody has to try now."

"You're crazy."

No, he wasn't crazy. He was scared for Winter, worried about what the demons would do to her. He had to get her out of there as quickly as possible. "I'm going to San Francisco."

He didn't wait for a response, but charged out the side entrance and headed for the car.

Despite using the compound's portal to San Francisco, it took almost two hours to reach Wesley's house. He'd called ahead, advising Wesley that he was on his way and that he should make sure that Virginia was home, but not tell her that Logan was coming. He didn't want her to alert the council. After telling Wesley it was a matter of life and death, the witch didn't ask any more questions.

When he entered Wesley's house and marched into the living room, not having used the door bell or the door, Virginia stared at him in disbelief.

"What the fuck, Logan?" Her hand went to the dagger that was sheathed at her hip. As so often, she wore the black uniform of the enforcers, the elite policing force of the Stealth Guardians she'd once been part of.

"Easy, babe," Wes said, and put his hand on her arm. "I have a feeling Logan needs our help."

She shot him a suspicious look. "You knew he was coming? That's why you wanted me to be here?"

Wes shrugged. "Hear him out first before you strangle me or him."

Logan could see that Virginia was fuming, but she seemed to get herself under control and said tightly, "Fine."

She tipped her chin in Logan's direction. "Talk, and make it quick. You're still a fugitive, and I intend to bring you in."

"I'm aware of that. But I hope I can change your mind."

Virginia sat down on the couch and motioned to an armchair. Logan sat down opposite her, while Wesley dropped onto the armrest of the sofa and rested his arm casually on the backrest behind Virginia.

Logan took a deep breath. "The psychic I was supposed to kill was taken by the demons about two hours ago."

Virginia leaned forward. "Goddamn it! This is exactly why the council wanted her dead. Fuck!"

"But *you* didn't, did you? You voted to let her live."

She narrowed her eyes. "How do you know that? The council's votes are secret."

"I could sense it when I made my case in front of the council. That's why I've come to you. Because I know you'll give me a chance."

Virginia scoffed. "A chance? Logan, the demons have her! You know what that means?"

He was fully aware of it. But he couldn't allow himself to dwell on it. He had to keep a clear head so he could rescue her. "I intend to get her back."

"From the Underworld?" Virginia stared at him as if he had grown horns and a tail.

"And you and Wesley will help me. You're the only two people who've ever been in the Underworld. With your help, I'm going to go down there and get her out."

Virginia gasped.

"You're fucking nuts!" Wesley exclaimed. "We barely made it out of there alive. And you want to go down there voluntarily? Have you lost your fucking mind?"

"No, I haven't. But I know I'm meant to save Winter. She saw it."

"In her visions? So the spell is working?" Wes asked excitedly.

Virginia snapped her head to her husband. "Spell? You did a spell for her? Behind my back?"

"Oops."

"Goddamn it, Wes! You should have told me!"

"If I'd told you, you would have had to report it to the council. Think about it, babe, I was trying to keep you out of it."

"We'll talk about this later."

She directed her gaze back to Logan, and Wes took the opportunity to wink at him. He didn't seem to be too concerned that he couldn't talk Virginia out of punishing him too harshly.

"I'm sorry," Logan said quickly, "it wasn't my intention to stir up trouble between you two. But I didn't know where else to go."

"Hmm," Virginia muttered. "So what do you want?"

"I need to know how you got into the Underworld."

"But you know that already. It was an accident," Virginia said.

"That's what you think. But you must have done something to get down there. Even if you didn't do it consciously. Something sent you down to Zoltan's lair. And I need to know what it was. I need to get to Winter. I need to get her out of there."

Virginia gave him a strange look. "This is not just about her being a psychic and you trying to correct your mistake, is it?"

He shook his head.

"You're in love with her," Wes stated.

Logan looked at his hosts. He didn't have to nod or say anything, because he knew they could see it in his eyes. "Will you help me?"

"Okay." Virginia exchanged a look with Wesley. "When the council compound was attacked by the demons, I was furious. I suspected Wes of somehow having given our location away to the demons—"

"—which was later proven incorrect," Wes interrupted quickly.

"Yes," Virginia conceded. "But at the time, I was furious. At him, at the demons. I wanted to kill Wes, so I raced to his cell and opened it. I made the mistake of stepping inside the lead cell..."

Logan nodded. "It diminished your powers, sucked out your strength."

"That was my luck," Wes said, "or I would be dead now."

"Anyway," Virginia continued, "a demon attacked us while we were in the cell. I wasn't strong enough, but Wes saved me in the end. He proved to me that he wasn't with the demons." A tender look passed between them. "When the self-destruct alarm sounded, we raced to the portal. We were the last two people in the building. We managed to get in, but it seemed to take forever for the portal to close. The countdown had already started."

"What did you concentrate on when you were in the portal? What location?" Logan asked eagerly.

Virginia shrugged. "I don't know. I just wanted to get out of there before the whole place blew. I was angry at the demons. I wanted to kick their asses."

"Yeah, we all did when we heard about it."

"That's all I was thinking about, and then suddenly the portal shook, and we got tossed around. At first I thought we'd been blown up with the portal and were buried in its rubble, but we realized pretty quickly that the portal had transported us to the Underworld."

"It was a pretty big explosion," Wes added.

"Tell me again exactly what you were thinking when the portal blew up," Logan demanded.

Virginia sighed. "I already told you. I wanted to kick the demons' asses. I wanted to go down there and beat the shit out of them."

Logan jumped up. "That's it!"

Virginia stared at him, saying nothing.

Wesley asked, "What?"

"Virginia said she was thinking of going down there to beat the shit out of them. She was furious, full of anger and hate, and then the portal blew."

Wes rose. "I think I know where you're going with this." Excited, he continued, "The reason we landed in the Underworld were three things: the explosion, Virginia's anger coupled with the thought of wanting to go into the Underworld to beat their asses, and voila: you're in the Underworld."

Logan nodded. "A strong emotion, a release of massive energy, and concentrating on the location while in the portal. Put these three things together, and you can enter the Underworld." He looked at Virginia, who hadn't said a word since Wesley and he had started making their assumptions. "Don't you think it will work, Virginia?"

"You mean sticking you in a portal and blowing it up?" she asked with a raised eyebrow.

"Exactly."

"It won't," she claimed.

"But it worked for you and Wes," Logan protested. "We just need to try. It has to be it. It has to work."

"You'll end up dead," she said.

"You can't know that."

Virginia shot up from the couch. "I do know."

Her words made him pause for a second. "What? What are you saying?"

Virginia huffed.

"What are you not telling us, babe?" Wes asked, walking toward his wife.

Virginia looked at Wes then back at Logan. "Goddamn it! We tried, okay? The council figured it out after we got back from the Underworld. When I was debriefed, I met with the brightest minds of our species and we dissected what had happened to me and Wes. And we figured it out. But it didn't work."

"How can you know it didn't?" Logan asked.

A sad look appeared in Virginia's face. "We had a volunteer, a guardian who was willing to be our guinea pig. He did exactly what you're suggesting now. He walked into a portal, concentrated on his hate for the demons, and we blew him up." She blinked as if the memory was too horrific to bear. "We found his body blown to bits within the rubble of the portal. He didn't make it, Logan, it didn't work."

Logan sighed and dropped his head. "And he did everything you did at the time?" He lifted his head and saw Virginia nod.

"I'm sorry, Logan. But I can't allow you to risk your life so recklessly."

"Why didn't you tell me about that, babe?" Wes asked.

Virginia looked at her husband. "The council wanted to keep this under wraps. A failure like that would have had demoralizing effects."

Logan squeezed his eyes shut. "But Winter, she saw that I was coming. She saw that I would rescue her."

"Her vision must be wrong," Virginia said.

Logan turned away, fearing that his emotions would overwhelm him. How could he give up now, when Winter meant everything to him? She owned his heart. She *was* his heart. The love he felt for her...

He spun around. "Love," he murmured, then stared at Virginia and Wesley, suddenly remembering something. "Drake said that love is the strongest emotion, that it can move mountains because of its infinite energy. Your volunteer... all he had was hate, and it wasn't in a situation of life and death. It was an experiment. Do you think he could really put himself into a state where he had sufficient hate to make the portal respond? I bet that was the problem. But when you and Wes escaped the compromised compound, it was a life and death situation. Your emotions were running high. Your hate was at a fever pitch."

"This is nuts," Virginia said.

Logan shook his head. "Maybe, but it'll work. I love Winter. And love is stronger than hate. Love is more powerful. It will send me to the Underworld. Because it has to. Winter needs me. She's waiting for me."

"You're absolutely fucking crazy," Virginia said. "Hell, even if it works, there's no guarantee that you'll ever make it out of the Underworld alive."

"You made it out. Winter and I will, too."

Or they'd die together.

31

The small cave-like cell was dimly lit. It wasn't cold, but Winter shivered nevertheless. Her jacket was gone, and with it the dagger in its pocket. The floor beneath her feet was rough, the ceiling jagged. The shape of the cell wasn't symmetrical, but created by nature, by the shifting of tectonic plates. There was oxygen down here, but it was cut with the intense stink of Sulphur and other gases that were released by the active earth underneath through crevices in the rock. Geothermal energy heated this place, and most likely provided it with energy to use for whatever purposes the inhabitants of this underground maze deemed necessary. She knew where she was. She'd seen it in her visions many times. Feared it. This was the Underworld, the place the green-eyed demons called home.

Everything she'd seen in her visions was coming true. Only it was worse. In her visions, she'd seen Logan slay the demons for her. But she knew now that he wouldn't come. Not now that she'd found out that he'd killed her grandmother. He had no reason to come for her now. He wouldn't risk his life for a woman who hated him. His betrayal hurt more than anything she'd ever felt. He'd lied to her, lied all this time to hide his cruel act.

The sound of heavy boots hitting the stone floor made her snap her head to the thick wooden door that looked like it belonged in a medieval castle. A key was turned in the lock, and a moment later the door swung outward and a demon appeared, filling almost the entire frame. He wasn't the same demon who'd dragged her into the vortex.

"You! Come!"

The words weren't an invitation. She had no choice but to do what he said. He let her exit the cell then motioned her down a corridor, sticking to her heels like pesky toilet paper to a wet shoe. Every so often, his hand shot forward to direct her toward another corridor, grunting his displeasure when she didn't react quickly enough. She'd seen the corridors before. In her visions. This was the vast tunnel system of the Underworld. She'd drawn it.

"Stop!" The command was like a slap in the face.

Her heart began to thunder.

The demon squeezed past her, his vile body rubbing against her and making her want to gag. He knocked at a door that she would have missed. A voice from inside invited them in, and the demon opened the door wide, but Winter couldn't see past him into the interior.

"The psychic, oh Great One."

"Send her in."

The brutish demon stepped aside and grabbed her upper arm, shoving her into the room not too gently, almost as if he had to prove to his superior that he hadn't treated her with any kindness or consideration. Not that he had. But now, he made this fact abundantly clear.

"Dismissed," the demon behind the massive desk said.

Winter barely heard the door close behind her, because her focus was on the demon the other one had called *Great One*. He had to be their leader. She perused him carefully. Just like the other demons she'd encountered previously, his eyes were poison-green. He was a large man, broad-shouldered, muscular, strong. His dark hair was short, his face clean-shaven, though a dark shadow around his chin and mouth indicated that if he wanted to grow a beard, it would be just as dark and thick.

He was dressed in the clothing of a guerilla fighter, reminding her of Fidel Castro in his younger years. He exuded confidence and power. But there was something else about him that she hadn't expected to see in a demon. He was handsome. Movie-star handsome.

She tried to shake off the notion. It couldn't be that she found this vile creature attractive. Was she hallucinating?

He rose now and walked toward her, an easy smile forming on his lips. "Miss Collins, I apologize for your rough treatment at the hands of my subjects," he said with a deep, soothing voice that would make any radio personality jealous. "I've tried to teach them manners, but alas, it's useless. I'm having more luxurious quarters readied for you as we speak."

He reached for her hand, and she was too paralyzed to refuse it. His touch was warm and gentle. With it, she realized that this demon was more dangerous than any of his underlings. This demon had charisma and knew how to use it. Just like so many serial killers who'd lured their unsuspecting victims into a trap. But she wouldn't fall for it. She knew better. She knew what the demons were capable of.

"It's a pleasure to finally make your acquaintance," he said, squeezing her hand before releasing it again. "You may call me Zoltan. May I call you Winter? Such a pretty name. So unusual, yet so fitting for a special woman like you."

Oh God! Was he flirting with her? Did he think this was a date rather than a kidnapping? This was sick! Absolutely sick!

"You kidnapped me!" she ground out with a clenched jaw.

Another charming smile, but behind it she saw his barely leashed anger. "Now, now, Winter, let's not start our new friendship with accusations."

"I'm not your friend! I'm your prisoner."

His eyes narrowed a fraction, but then he seemed to relax again. She'd never seen a man who had such iron control over himself, when she knew he wanted to crush her resistance with brute force. But this demon, this Zoltan as he called himself, was smart. He had a plan.

"I'm going to rectify that. As I said before, my subjects are a little on the rough side and don't know how to deal with honored guests." He motioned to the door. "But it's time to eat. I'm sure you're hungry. I've brought in a chef specially for you."

"You shouldn't have bothered," she sniped. "I'm not intending to stay long."

A belly laugh suddenly filled the room, bouncing off the uneven rock walls.

There was even a sparkle of mischief glimmering in Zoltan's eyes. "And I, my dear Winter, intend to change your mind." He stepped a little closer, his face serious now, his eyes cold and hard. "I always get what I want."

There was an underlying growl in his voice that sent a chill through her bones. Yes, Zoltan was dangerous, because he knew how to manipulate others. But she was prepared for it. She wasn't stupid and wouldn't fall for his tricks. Instead, she would try to learn as much as she could about him. And somehow, she would make it out of here. Or she would die trying.

"I believe dinner is served. Shall we?"

She swallowed her disgust and gave a tight nod. She had no choice but to obey.

It took several minutes walking through the maze of interconnected tunnels to reach another cave. This one had several access points, though there were no doors. A chandelier with at least two dozen candles hung from the ceiling, where a long table served as the centerpiece of the room. At least ten chairs surrounded the stone table, but only two places were set at one end of it. Like a gentleman, Zoltan pulled back the chair for her and motioned her to sit. But she wasn't fooled. This was all part of him playing the civilized man so he could seduce her to his side.

Winter sat in the proffered chair and watched Zoltan take the seat at the head of the table.

"So, this is all yours," she said. "Your kingdom. What do they call you? The devil? Lord of the Underworld?"

He gave a half-hearted smile and unfolded the napkin, laying it across his lap. "They call me the Great One. And no, I'm not the devil. But I am Lord of the Underworld." He made an all-encompassing motion with his hand. "It might not look like much to you, but this is a vast empire, one I'm expanding with each day."

Clearly, Zoltan liked to talk about his accomplishments, just like any despot did. Good. She would keep him talking. "How vast? Are we talking a few acres? Like a small European principality?"

He cast her an assessing look. "Nothing about me or my empire is small. You'd do well to remember that."

She didn't miss the sexual innuendo in his words. She lifted her chin in disdain, ready to come back with a retort, but footsteps coming from one of the entrances distracted her and made her turn her head.

"Ah, dinner," Zoltan said.

Two demons carried trays, looking entirely uncomfortable, as if they'd never done this before. They placed the trays awkwardly on the table, lifting the covers from the various bowls and plates. Delicious smells drifted to her. And not only that. The presentation of the dishes was something she would only expect in a fancy restaurant.

"The chef has a Michelin star," Zoltan explained.

She snapped her head to him, annoyed that he'd noticed her appreciation. It had been a reflex, and it would have no bearing on how she felt about the Underworld or the demons.

"I didn't know the Underworld gave out Michelin stars."

"We don't," Zoltan said. "But I wanted only the best for you. So I convinced this chef to work for me."

"Convinced?" She could imagine what that had looked like.

A chuckle came from Zoltan. "Don't worry, I made him an offer he couldn't refuse."

"How original. So your favorite movie is *The Godfather*?"

"You're very witty. I'm glad. It will make for many animated dinner conversations. I've lacked good company down here." He motioned to the two demons who still stood near the table, waiting. "What do you still want?" he growled, his voice like that of an angry dictator. "Get lost!"

The two demons replied, "Yes, oh Great One!" then hurried out of the dining room.

"Apologies," Zoltan said. "It's hard to train them." When she didn't answer, he pointed to the plates. "Please, help yourself."

They began eating. Winter wasn't particularly hungry, but forced herself to take a little bit from each plate so as not to anger her host. Zoltan on the other hand had a healthy appetite and devoured large amounts of food.

"My subjects tell me that the Stealth Guardians were trying to turn you against us with their fake news about us."

"Fake news?" Was he serious?

"It's not all black and white like the guardians would have you believe. The demons aren't all bad, nor are the guardians all good. Even they kill when it's in their interest."

"You mean they kill people like you. Demons. Monsters."

"Oh, they do that, yes. But they kill others too. Innocents. People that might expose them. People that they deem a danger to them. They claim it's for the greater good. But who decides what the greater good is?"

He looked at her as if he really sought an answer from her, as if it wasn't a rhetorical question. She took the bait. "The victors write the history books."

"Exactly. The war isn't over, so who knows what the greater good is? Who says the way of life the guardians are trying to protect is the right way? One species' terrorist is another species' freedom fighter. We're the freedom fighters. We fight for the right of every human to choose their destiny, not be dictated by morals and conventions or told what is right and what is wrong."

"That's your opinion. You support death and destruction. You feed off fear and evil. And you want to make me believe that your way will give humans a true choice? I don't have to be a psychic to know that you're wrong. You instigate evil in the world."

"And the guardians are choir boys?" he shot back.

Winter hesitated. She knew they weren't. Logan had committed an evil act. Killed an innocent, her grandmother. And he'd lied about it. Had kept the truth from her.

"See," Zoltan said, leaning in, his voice soothing again, "they're not all good either. They act in their self-interest too. And they do hurt people. Everybody does. There's nobody truly good in this world. Everybody has a dark side. And everybody tries to hide it. My subjects and I are different. We have evolved. We are free because we don't suppress our dark side. We don't lie about what we are. We just are. Everybody else is just lying to themselves."

She shook her head. She couldn't accept that. He was trying to manipulate her. She couldn't allow it. She had to push back. "You have a very skewed view of the world and the humans who inhabit it. There is good in this world. I've seen good. And I've seen evil. And I know the difference."

"Do you? You're not the only one who thought so at first. But everybody changes their mind in the long run. Even those people you think are good through and through. All you need to do is give them a good reason to change their mind." He put his napkin on the table. "Shall I tell you a story?"

Winter looked at him and knew that she wouldn't like whatever he was about to tell her.

32

Virginia had found a lost portal a little over one hour north of San Francisco that was remote enough that an explosion wouldn't attract undue attention. Blowing up the portal located inside the BART station in the middle of the Mission district wasn't an option. It would destroy the station and kill innocents. Logan understood and accepted that. It didn't make the drive up north and his impatience any easier to bear.

He was in the car with Wesley driving, Virginia riding shotgun. A second car was following them: Quinn and Ryder, both well-versed in explosives, had packed the trunk of their car with everything they could possibly need to literally send Logan to hell.

Logan knew what he was doing was madness, but he couldn't give up. He had to get to Winter. Whether that meant his certain death, he didn't know nor care. He needed to see Winter. He couldn't let her believe for one hour longer that he'd betrayed her. Her words still echoed in his mind.

I hate you.

They had sliced through his heart and shredded it. He couldn't let her believe that he'd callously killed her grandmother. He needed to explain to her that he'd had no choice. But first and foremost, he had to snatch Winter from Zoltan's claws, no matter the cost.

The portal was located in the woods of Sonoma. Wesley had used it once, and it was too far away from any homes or other structures for an explosion to be seen, though the sound would travel. But with some luck anybody who heard the explosion would attribute the sound to a supersonic plane passing or a car backfiring.

The hut in the middle of the woods was really a lean-to. There were only three wooden walls and a roof; the forth wall was a massive boulder into which a Stealth Guardian dagger was carved. This was the portal.

Quinn and Ryder unpacked the heavy bags they'd carried the two miles from where they'd parked the cars, and started setting up their equipment.

"Can I help with anything?" Logan asked, hoping to speed up the process.

Quinn looked up. "I know you're impatient. I get it. But working with explosives is an art. It'll take the time it takes."

"Don't worry, we're good," Ryder assured him. "We'll make sure this explosion releases the energy you need. The rest is up to you."

Logan sighed and ran a hand through his hair. "Thanks, guys. I appreciate all you're doing."

"Hey, Logan," Wes called out to him.

Logan pivoted and walked to where he and Virginia were standing, a safe distance away from the explosives.

"So, this is it," Wes said.

"You sure about this?" Virginia asked. "You can still change your mind."

He gave her a regretful smile. "There's no going back. I have to go get her. It's my mess. I have to clean it up." But it was more than that. He loved Winter, and he'd rather die saving her life than not try at all.

"Okay, then." Wes dug into his backpack and pulled a rectangular item from it that was no larger than his palm. "Thomas gave me this from our vault at Scanguards. It's the strongest GPS transmitter on the market. We figured if you actually do manage to land in the Underworld, we might as well test this thing and see if we can track you. Might give us an indication as to where Zoltan's lair is located."

Logan reached for it. "Okay. Though I doubt that it'll work down there."

"So do I," Virginia admitted, "but we might as well try. Got nothing to lose, right?"

"Right."

"In any case," Wes added, "If and when you make it back, it'll help us find you and pick you up wherever you land."

"Sounds good."

"Best put it in your boot, in case you get captured and they search you," Wesley suggested.

Logan crouched down and stashed the slim device in his boot, then rose.

"How many weapons do you have?" Virginia asked, looking concerned.

Logan opened his jacket. His inside pockets were loaded with daggers, two on each side. "One strapped to each ankle, one on my hip. I think I'm good."

Virginia nodded, satisfied. "And the map?"

He patted his pocket. "Right here." He'd had the foresight to bring the tunnel map Winter had drawn from the compound. He didn't know how accurate or how useful it would be, but maybe it would help.

Wes and Virginia exchanged a look. Then Wes shrugged. "It's more than what you and I had when we were down there. And we got out."

"Pure luck," Virginia claimed.

"Maybe I'll be lucky too," Logan said.

Wes reached into his other pocket and pulled out a vial. "Here's some luck in a bottle. You know what to do with it?"

Logan took it and stashed it in a padded inside pocket of his jacket. "If it survives the trip. You sure it works?"

Wes shrugged. "Didn't exactly have time to test it."

"Hope the potion won't kill me," Logan said.

Wes grimaced. "Doubt it."

Logan looked over his shoulder, where Quinn and Ryder were still busy setting up the explosive charges. For a few minutes, he fell silent. This was either the most brilliant or the most stupid idea he'd ever had. He hoped the former was the case.

"Almost ready," Quinn called out. "We're just setting up the detonator."

A few minutes later, they were ready.

"What do you want me to tell your parents?" Virginia asked.

Logan took a deep breath. "My parents know that being a warrior comes with risks. They'll understand."

"I wish you luck," Virginia said.

Wes slapped him on the shoulder. "Kick their asses for me, will you?"

If Winter's vision was accurate then he would do more than just that. He'd behead the fuckers.

Without another word, he walked to the hut, where Quinn and Ryder were waiting for him.

Quinn nodded at him. "I've set it up so the countdown is loud enough for you to hear inside the portal. I'm giving you ten seconds. Enough time for us to get far enough away, and for you to do whatever you need to do."

"Got it."

"One other thing: once I start the countdown, I can't abort. This is a simple one-way setup. We didn't have time to—"

Logan lifted his hand to stop him. "It's good. Let's do this." He looked at Ryder, then back at Quinn. "Thank you both."

He walked inside the hut and laid his palm over the dagger that was engraved in the rock. Warmth built beneath it and within a second or two the portal was open. He stepped inside and pivoted, looking out at his friends. With a last nod, he willed the portal to close.

It took a few seconds, before he heard the countdown start. Concentrating on his mission, he focused on his hate for the demons, and on his need to save Winter.

Three.

On his love for her and the knowledge that he couldn't live without her.

Two.

On the promise he'd made to her. *You're safe with me. I'll protect you. Always.*

One.

And on his anger toward himself for having failed her. *I'm going to make it right. I'm coming for you, Winter. I'm coming to rescue you. And I'm going to slay the demons for you.*

The explosion rocked the portal, flinging him in the air, slamming him against the rock. He tumbled in weightlessness, losing his sense of up and down.

Fucking demons!

Again he smashed against the rock. This time head first. Then nothing. Only darkness as his body dropped limply.

33

Zoltan brought the glass to his lips and drank from his wine. Winter ignored hers. She didn't want to drink, because she needed all her wits about her, couldn't afford to get tipsy, let alone drunk. She knew that Zoltan noticed that she wasn't drinking, but he didn't say anything. Instead, he cast her one of those superior looks that he was so good at. As if he knew something she didn't. Or simply, because he knew he was stronger than her, and that she would ultimately lose whatever battle they were waging.

"Everybody has their breaking point," Zoltan said. "In the end, everybody gives in."

"Yeah, you said that before. Get to the point," she said. Where she got the courage that allowed her to talk to him like that, she didn't know. Maybe it was because she had nothing to lose, nothing but her dignity. Her life was already forfeit. She was living on borrowed time. They both knew it. Maybe that was the reason he didn't lash out at her now, despite her disrespectful tone.

"Well, then let me get to the story." He set down the glass and leaned back in his chair. "I wasn't the Great One back then. I was just a grunt, just another demon eager to please his master. You see, I was more ambitious than my brethren, more eager to make it to the top. I took greater risks and reaped greater rewards."

"Is this why you had me kidnapped? So you could boast to me about your successes?"

He *tsked*. "So impatient. I was like that once too. But I learned patience, just like you will. I learned to wait for the right time, the right opportunity. It paid off. I got wind of a psychic. I watched her. I found out everything there was to find out about her. You see, if you want to truly bring somebody onto your side, you have to know their pressure points." He tipped his finger to his temple. "You have to know what makes them tick." He chuckled. "With most people it's money, power, or sex. But this woman, she was different. She wasn't interested in money or power. And frankly, she was a little too old to care about sex." He shrugged. "But you know what she cared about?"

He leaned forward, staring at her.

Winter held her breath. She already suspected who he was talking about. But she wasn't going to give anything away, just in case she was wrong.

"You. She cared about you."

Her grandmother. He was talking about her grandmother.

Zoltan smile was self-congratulatory. "Yes, she was an interesting woman, your grandmother. But she had a weakness. She loved you, and wanted to protect you at all costs. She fought against me for a long time. But in the end, she decided you were worth her sacrifice. We had a deal. I would leave you in peace to live your life as you chose, and she would come with me and serve me and my master."

Winter shook her head. "No, never! My grandmother was good. She would never have worked for you! Never!"

Zoltan tilted his head to the side and studied her. "You're cut from the same cloth as she. We didn't know at the time that you would inherit her gift. But that's beside the point. The point is, she gave in because she knew it was best for everybody." Suddenly his expression darkened and he slammed his fist on the table.

Winter shuddered at the sudden outburst.

"But those damn Stealth Guardians! They had to interfere, didn't they?"

She didn't dare answer, not when Zoltan looked like he was ready to kill somebody.

"My apologies," he pressed out through clenched teeth. "But what they did was unconscionable. They killed your grandmother. Killed her before I could get her to safety. They're cold-blooded killers. A life means nothing to them. Your grandmother would have lived with us here, but the Stealth Guardians killed her. They took her from you. They don't care about you. They never did. As soon as you become a liability, they'll kill you. You'll never be safe with them."

Winter jumped up and kicked her chair back. "And I'll be safe with you? How gullible do you think I am? You were able to manipulate my grandmother because she wanted to protect me. But you have nothing on me! I'll never agree to work for you. I'd rather die!"

"How dramatic. I love a passionate woman. You know why you were safe all those years after your grandmother's death? It wasn't my doing. The Great One punished me for my failure in bringing him a psychic. For nearly ten years I rotted in a cell down here. Meanwhile none of his nitwit subjects kept track of you. They lost you. By the time I was free again, nobody could find you. Until last week." He laughed triumphantly and rose. "Imagine how elated I was, when I realized you'd inherited your grandmother's gift. Still, I was willing to go easy on you, despite what I had to endure because of you. I wanted to give you a choice and make you a partner in this."

"Partner? To a demon? Never!" She glared at him defiantly.

He narrowed his eyes. "Very well. There are other ways to gain your compliance."

Inside she shuddered at the thought of torture, but she lifted her chin nevertheless. "Go ahead, hurt me. But it won't change anything. I'll never give in. You don't have a bargaining chip like you had with my grandmother." And she didn't blame her grandmother for giving in. She understood now. Just as she understood why Logan had to kill her grandmother. But it didn't matter anymore, because she'd never have the opportunity to tell him that she was wrong.

Zoltan raised his hand and she flinched, expecting a blow. Instead, he stroked his hand over her cheek. Winter recoiled at the touch.

"I wouldn't hurt a pretty face like yours." He lifted his finger to her temple. "But I will get in here. And you will give in."

"No!"

"Is that your final answer?"

She spat in his face.

He didn't bother wiping the spit off his cheek. His demon-green eyes flashed, then locked with hers and she was unable to look away. At the same time, she felt a tightness in her chest and her heart began to pound furiously.

You are mine now. I'm your master.

She heard his words, but his lips didn't move.

Surrender!

The demand was accompanied by a wave of pain washing over her head, penetrating her skull.

"Noooo!" she screamed.

She couldn't allow him in, couldn't give in. This invasion was different from the one she'd experienced with Gabriel, but her mind's reaction was the same. She pushed against it, fought with every cell of her body against the foreign power wanting to invade her mind and focused only on one thing: survival. She felt electricity spark around her, saw blue light appearing at the edge of her vision, sensed her hair standing up in all directions. At the same time, she felt a supernatural strength inside her, her psychic power defending itself.

She held on for dear life, fought against Zoltan's invading thoughts, trying to get her to surrender to his power. But with every new command that he sent into her mind, her psychic power seemed to grow stronger.

Zoltan screamed and slammed his hands against his temples, stumbling backwards. Still, Winter continued to fight, continued to bombard him with her power.

Suddenly strong arms ripped her backwards and tackled her to the floor. She lost her concentration. Simultaneously, Zoltan's invasion ceased. She struggled against the two demons who'd come to their master's aid, but they were too strong. Her own power seemed to be zapped. She had nothing left.

She heard Zoltan's angry growls before he entered her field of vision. He glared down at her.

"Get her up," he ordered his two subjects.

They followed his command and jerked her to her feet.

"I'll teach you to defy me, you bitch!" he yelled.

She only saw his fist when it was already too late. Even if she'd seen it earlier, she wouldn't have had any defense against it. It hit the side of her head, snapping it in the opposite direction. The force of the blow was so violent that it flung her against the nearest wall. Pain seared through her entire body. She tried to hold on to her consciousness, tried to grasp at something, clawing at the wall behind her, but it was no use.

She opened her eyes, trying to focus, but everything around her was gone. The demons, Zoltan, the dining room. Gone. In its stead was a pleasant room with a large window, a soft rug beneath her feet. The furniture was old fashioned, antique even. Outside it was dark.

The crying of a baby made her spin around. It came from a wooden crib. It was just as old as the rest of the furniture in the room. It reminded her of the kind of furniture that belonged in a palace in the 1800s. Next to the crib, a single candle was lit.

The baby kept crying. She approached the crib and looked in. The child, a boy, was naked and had thrown off his blanket. She reached into the crib, but realized then that she couldn't cover the child, because she wasn't really there.

A sound across the room made her shift her gaze away from the child. Her heart stopped. Poison-green eyes blinked at her from the door. The demon wore a long cloak with a hood. The darkness in the room did the rest to obscure his face. Frightened for the child, Winter tried to scream, but no sound left her throat. Unimpeded, the demon approached. He reached into the crib. Oh God, he would kill the baby! But the demon lifted the boy into his arms, holding him to his chest as if he were a treasure. Winter stared at the demon, then at the naked baby. The candlelight suddenly spotlighted a curious looking birthmark on the baby's bottom.

Then there was another movement. The demon reached in his pocket. He pulled out a small metal flask, opened it and poured the liquid into the crib. Red blood stained the sheets. The flask empty now, the demon put it back in his pocket and turned, leaving the room with the child in his arms.

Winter ran after him, following him down the stairs of the big mansion. But she couldn't stop him. The moment he reached the first floor, he made a movement with his free hand and conjured a vortex. A second later, he jumped in and disappeared.

Oh God, no!

Tears streamed down her face. The vortex vanished, and suddenly she was staring at a portrait of a man and a woman, a baby in her arms. They both wore clothes that would have been fashionable in the Regency period, but something else drew her attention. On the man's hip sat a dagger. The same kind of dagger she'd seen Logan and his friends wield. The man was a Stealth Guardian, of that she was certain. And a demon had kidnapped his child.

34

Winter heard something rattle in the distance, then the echo of footsteps in a cavernous space. Her head was spinning, and she took a breath. Her lungs filled with a vile stench and jolted her back to consciousness. Her eyes flew open.

Fuck! This couldn't be good.

The smell came from a pit filled with hot, bubbling lava. It was only about as large as a jacuzzi. And dipping into it would be instantly fatal. She shuddered at the thought of somebody slipping and accidentally falling in, and wondered why nobody had bothered covering it. A moment later, she realized why. Her gaze fell on metal implements laid out on a table nearby, implements that could inflict pain. This was a torture chamber, and the lava pit was its ultimate threat.

Shit! She had to get out of here before somebody came and tried any of the instruments on her. She managed to take two steps, before she was jerked back to the wall, a short, sharp pain ripping through her ankle.

"What the—"

Chains bound both her ankles. They assured that she couldn't move farther than two feet away from the wall. Apparently the demons weren't quite stupid enough to leave her in this cave without restricting her movements. She tried to reach her feet to see if she could get out of the chains, but realized she had chains around her wrists too.

The footfalls she'd heard earlier became louder now, and a few moments later she saw a demon march into the cave from the entrance to her right. There were two more entrances, one straight ahead of her and one to her left, but the one to her left was hard to access, because the lava pit was right in front of it, leaving only a slim ledge to walk past it. It wouldn't be her first choice to try to escape the cave via that route. Not that it looked like she was going to be escaping any time soon.

The demon stopped in front of her. His size alone was intimidating, as were his glaring green eyes and his grim look. But what made it worse was that she knew what he was sent to do: torture her until she succumbed to Zoltan's demands.

Manus had warned her, and he'd been right. While she had successfully defended herself against Zoltan's mental invasion, she had no defenses against physical torture. And after injuring Zoltan he would have no mercy on her until she gave in. What surprised her, however, was why he hadn't come himself and had instead sent one of his demons to hurt her. She could have sworn that he would want to be witness to her pain. Had she maybe injured him so badly that he didn't feel up to the task right now?

Not that it mattered much. She was sure the demon who glared at her would be just as cruel as Zoltan himself.

He lifted his hand now, and she saw the dagger he was holding. Instinctively she raised her arms to shield her face, and the chains rattled again.

She recognized the demon now. He was the one who in an earlier vision had killed her, but in a later one had lost his head to Logan's dagger. But everything had changed since then.

"Go ahead," she spat with a braveness she didn't possess. "You might as well save yourself the time and kill me now, because I won't give in to Zoltan. You can tell him that."

He slapped her face with the back of his hand, knocking her head sideways. Pain seared through her and radiated down her neck and spine. She felt something wet trickle down inside her nose and knew it was blood.

"Bastard!" she ground out, refusing to give in to the urge to cry. She wouldn't give the monster the satisfaction.

The demon brought his knife closer and leaned in. He opened his mouth, but nothing came out, no word, no insult. Instead his face suddenly contorted. Then a growl rolled over his lips, but before it could turn into a scream, a hand clamped over his mouth from behind and jerked him back.

The demon struggled, but the person behind him had the upper hand and wrangled him to the ground, face down. Now Winter could see why he was so easily felled. A dagger was stuck in his back, and green blood was oozing from the mortal wound. The person who'd killed the demon now twisted the dagger some more, making sure the demon was dead, then pulled it from the wound and carefully wiped the green blood off the blade using his victim's clothing. Only then did he look at her, but she'd already recognized him when he'd yanked the demon to the ground.

"Logan..."

Their eyes connected. He'd come. After everything, he'd come to rescue her.

"I was scared I'd be too late," Logan said.

She stared down at the demon again. "In my vision, it was different. You beheaded him."

He nodded. "I know. You told me, and you were covered in his blood because of it. I can't have that, or I can't make you invisible."

She understood immediately. By telling him about her vision, she'd given him the opportunity to change the outcome and thus the future.

"We've gotta get out of here," he said.

She raised her hands, showing him the chains. "Same on my ankles."

He pulled something from his inside pocket and went to work on the shackles around her feet. They clicked open faster than she'd expected. Her feet were free, but then suddenly Logan whipped his head toward one of the entrances.

"Wh—"

He pressed his hand over her lips, preventing her from speaking, and leaned in. "Demons. Drop your arms all the way so the shackles look as if they're hanging there."

Panicked she stared at him. It took her brain a second or two to realize what Logan was planning. With some luck, the approaching demons would only see their dead comrade on the floor and assume she'd fled. She dropped her arms and crouched down a bit, so the chains were hanging loosely from the wall, so the demons wouldn't notice that they were still holding their prisoner. Because the prisoner and her rescuer were now invisible.

Two demons entered the cave. She recognized one of them immediately. Zoltan. He'd come to watch her be tortured.

His eyes immediately went to where Winter was standing. Her heart pounded so loud that she thought the sound would echo in the cave.

"Where the fuck is she?" Zoltan yelled. Then his eyes shifted and fell on the dead demon who lay not even a yard away from Logan.

He charged toward his dead subject, his companion on his heels, and kicked him with his foot. But the demon didn't move. Zoltan cursed, his head raised to the ceiling. "The fucking idiot! Gets himself killed by a woman!"

He spun around, looked at the chains again, and for a heart-stopping moment Winter wondered if he'd step closer. Already, he was close enough to touch Logan if he stretched out his hand. Would Logan be fast enough to spin around and drive his dagger into the leader of the Underworld, or would Zoltan be stronger? And the second demon, would he kill Winter while Logan and Zoltan fought?

Her lungs felt like they were exploding and she wanted to gasp for air, but she didn't dare, because the slightest sound, the smallest movement might alert Zoltan to their presence. She felt perspiration run down from her forehead along the side of her nose. Oh God, no, it was tickling her. A few more seconds, and she would have to sneeze.

Suddenly Zoltan turned to his underling. "Find the bitch! If she thinks she can play her little mind tricks on me, I'm gonna play, but according to my rules."

The demon nodded. "May I suggest something, oh Great One?"

"What is it, Vintoq?"

"Have the guards at the vortex circles tripled, in case she tries to escape by forcing one of our own."

Zoltan let out a laugh. "Forcing? With what? She's unarmed, and she's a sprite of a thing."

"But her mental powers, oh Great One. She injured you. And I'd venture a guess that if she set her mind to it, she could force a demon to transport her out of here by using those powers on him."

Winter exchanged a look with Logan. Was she really capable of that? Or was it merely an unsubstantiated fear the underling was expressing?

Zoltan seemed to contemplate it. "Do it. Hurry!"

Vintoq rushed out of the cave, while Zoltan headed to the other exit. Just as he reached it, he braced himself against the rock wall and groaned in pain.

"Fuck!"

Then he stumbled along, hurrying out of Winter's field of vision.

Logan finally took his hand off her mouth. "We have to hurry or we won't get out of here alive."

35

Logan finally removed the shackles around Winter's wrists and rose. As much as he needed to take her into his arms and explain to her why he'd had to kill her grandmother, there was no time for it. They had to make it to one of the vortex circles before they were swarming with demon guards. If that happened, his escape plan would be dead on arrival.

"This way," he said and pointed to the exit Zoltan's underling had used.

Winter shook her head. "More demons will come from there. I know it."

He stared at her for a second, then nodded. "Your vision." He pointed to the tunnel Zoltan had used. "How about that one?"

"Same." She motioned to the opening at the other side of the cave. "Nobody came from there."

Logan realized immediately why. "The lava pit." He exchanged a look with Winter, then took her hand. "We'll have to be careful." But they had no choice. It was either navigating their way around the lava pit, or running straight into the arms of more demons.

They walked toward the pit, and Logan could already hear sounds coming from one of the other tunnels. He quickly assessed the ledge around the pit and tested it with one foot. A piece of stone broke off and fell into the bubbling pool of lava, where it instantly turned into liquid.

Winter gasped.

"We'll make it," he assured her. "I'll go first. We'll walk as closely to the wall as possible. Stay behind me."

She nodded, but he could see the fear in her eyes.

Taking a deep breath, he walked forward, one hand gripping the indentations along the wall, the other clasped in

Winter's. Beneath him, he could feel the stone start to give. Eventually the hot lava from beneath it would erode the stone, liquefying it, and making this tunnel inaccessible. But he hoped that day wasn't today.

Slowly they inched forward toward the tunnel entrance. Four more yards, then three. The ledge got slimmer here, and Logan knew he had to change his approach. He stopped, calculated the risk, and made his decision. He turned his head to look at Winter.

"Do you trust me?"

"Yes."

"Here's what I'll have to do." Logan pointed to the ledge. "That won't support the two of us at the same time. I'll have to go ahead. You need to stay here, hold on to the rock wall for balance. As soon as I'm on the other side, I'm going to help you over."

He saw her swallow hard. "Oh God."

"I won't let you die."

Winter nodded, her body shaking.

He let go of her hand and moved forward, gingerly setting one foot in front of the other, while trying to take some of his weight off the ledge by holding onto the jagged rock to his left. Two more yards. Three more steps. He set his right foot on the solid surface at the entrance to the tunnel and pushed off. His left leg jerked downward, and he lurched forward, falling into the tunnel. He rolled around and looked back. A piece of the ledge he'd stepped on had fallen into the pit.

His eyes shot to Winter, who clung to the rock wall, her feet still on the ledge, but between them there was now a gap of two yards, a gap too risky for her to jump over. Winter looked at him in utter horror.

"I'm going to get you. Hold on." He removed his backpack and pulled out a rope with a hook on one end. Quickly, he looked for a solid object to anchor the hook to and found a large boulder only a few yards into the tunnel. He tested the rope, making sure it wouldn't slip, then returned to the opening of the tunnel, measured the distance between him and Winter with his eyes, and tied the rope around his waist, leaving sufficient length so he could move as much as he needed to.

He stepped to the very edge of the pit and felt the rope behind him tighten, while he leaned forward, his feet braced on the edge of the pit, his body held by the rope. This was as far as he could go.

His gaze connected with Winter's. "I'm halfway there. It's only a yard now, Winter. Just reach your arms out and reach for me. I'll catch you. And I'll pull us back."

Cold fear shone from her eyes. Tears brimmed at their rim. "Logan, it won't hold us both."

"It will." It had to. "Trust me, Winter. I'm not going to leave you here. We're getting out of this place." He reached out his arms toward her. "Do it."

He watched as she hesitantly let go of the rock wall and took one more step toward him. She stood at the very edge now.

"Reach your arms out."

He could see she was shaking, but finally Winter reached her arms out, bridging the distance between them, and he grabbed her and pulled her toward him, just as beneath Winter's feet more of the ledge crumbled.

He twisted to the side and swung his precious cargo toward the tunnel, releasing her there. Winter rolled onto the ground. With a sigh of relief, Logan pulled himself in along the rope until he had found his balance again. He looked back at the pit, and beyond it, in the cave where Winter had been imprisoned, he saw several demons.

He untied himself from the rope and helped Winter up. "You hurt?" he whispered.

She shook her head.

He snatched his backpack, took Winter's hand and started running down the tunnel. After about a hundred yards, there was an intersection. Logan pulled out the map Winter had drawn and looked at it, holding it closer to one of the flames shooting out through the crevices in the rock.

"This way," he said.

Winter put her hand on his arm and pointed to the map. "No. Those vortex circles are too close to the tunnels Zoltan and the other demons used. They'll already have too many guards there." She pointed to another circle where several tunnels converged. "This one is farther away. Chances are they haven't reached it yet to add more guards."

"You're right. Let's go that way then."

They ran most of the way, hurrying as much as they could without making too much noise. On occasion, they had to consult the map. Logan was surprised at how accurate it was, and glad for it. By his estimate, it took them about ten minutes to get close to the vortex circle. Logan could see it at the end of the tunnel.

He stopped and pulled Winter close to him, so he could explain the next step.

"We have to get to the vortex circle and get a demon to open a vortex for us so we can travel to the human world."

"Are you saying that I should try to influence a demon? I don't know how to do that. I've never tried it. What if it doesn't work?"

Logan shook his head. "I have a better plan." He reached into his inside pocket and pulled out a vial. "Wesley gave me this. It'll temporarily turn my eyes demon-green, and remove my aura, so the demons won't realize that I'm a Stealth Guardian."

"You mean, you'll be able to cast a vortex to get us out of here?"

He shook his head. "Alas, no. But don't worry. I have a plan. Do you trust me?"

She nodded.

"Then do exactly what I tell you to do once we reach the vortex circle." He opened the vial and downed the liquid in it. "This had better work." The potion tasted disgusting. He almost gagged.

"Oh my God," Winter whispered.

"What?"

She pointed to his eyes. "Demon eyes."

"Good. Let's go. We'll be visible now." He paused for a second. "And sorry about this."

Before she could protest, he grabbed her by her bicep and led her toward the circle. In the distance he could hear shouting and footsteps approaching. Reinforcements. He had to act quickly.

"Hey, you!" Logan addressed the guard who stood at the edge of the circle holding a clipboard.

Almost bored, the demon said, "State your business."

"Orders from the Great One," Logan said and dragged Winter closer. "He needs you to take her up top now. There's a mutiny afoot." He motioned to the tunnel from which sounds could be heard. "They want to kill her. It's of the utmost importance to the Great One to hide this woman. Go! Take her up top."

"Why don't you do it? I've got guard duties."

Logan went right up in his face and growled, "Because the Great One gave me explicit orders! That's why! Or would you rather feel his wrath? Shall I tell him you questioned his orders?"

The demon suddenly shrank away. "No, no. I'll do it. Of course. Where does he want me to take her?"

"To San Francisco. Once you're there, hide her, stay with her. The Great One will find you when it's safe."

The demon nodded dutifully and Logan released Winter's arm. She stared at him, frightened and shocked. But it was good this way. She looked genuinely scared. The demon wouldn't suspect a thing.

"Go!"

The demon snatched Winter by the arm and cast a vortex in the middle of the circle, then jumped in with her.

Not losing any time, Logan made himself invisible and lunged after them. Inside the swirling mass of fog and mist it was dark, but his eyes could make out Winter's form, and he snatched her hand and held on to it.

Transporting through a demon's vortex felt the same as transporting through a Stealth Guardian's portal, with one difference. Logan could hear the demon's thoughts.

Goddamn it, why is it always me who has to follow orders?

Not much longer, Logan thought to himself.

Suddenly he felt Winter and the demon move, and realized they'd arrived and were stepping out of the vortex. Logan, still invisible, followed them, holding Winter's hand. The vortex closed behind them and Logan saw where they'd landed: in a warehouse district close to the water.

Not wanting to take any chances, Logan let go of Winter's hand and pulled out his dagger. Without making a sound, he approached the demon and stabbed the dagger into his heart. There was a gurgling sound, then the demon's dead body fell to the ground, making a satisfying thump.

Finally able to breathe, Logan turned to Winter and made himself visible. She threw herself into his arms without hesitation.

"Oh God," she said tearfully. "I was so scared. I thought you were going to stay down there. I thought you wouldn't make it."

He rubbed his hands over her back. "And leave you in the hands of a demon? Not a chance."

"You came. After everything that happened, you came to save me." She sniffled.

He drew back a little. This was the moment he'd dreaded most. Because despite having saved Winter from the demons, he'd done something that he wasn't sure she could ever forgive.

Logan wiped a tear from her cheek. "Winter, I need to tell you something. The way we left things…" He dropped his arms to release her. "Your grandmother. I did kill her. I'm sorry. I wish I could say that it wasn't me. That I didn't do it. But I did. I had to. Not because I was ordered to, but because she was already gone. They already had her. She'd succumbed to them."

He dropped his head so he didn't have to look at her anymore. Didn't have to see the hatred in her eyes.

A soft hand suddenly caressed his cheek and he snapped his head back up to stare at Winter.

"I already know. Zoltan told me. I think he wanted to prove to me that everybody eventually submits, even a woman as good as my grandmother." She paused. "He also told me that he used me as the bargaining chip. It was my fault, Logan, my fault that my grandmother succumbed to them. Zoltan threatened her with hurting me if she didn't give in. She did it for me, you see." She shook her head. "It wasn't your fault. You did what you had to do. And knowing what I know now, I would have done it myself, as much as it would have hurt me." Tears streamed down her face now.

Logan pulled her into his arms. "I'm so sorry, Winter, I'm so sorry you had to find out and go through all this. I wish I could have spared you this pain."

She sobbed against his chest. "I'm so sorry I didn't trust you enough."

"It's all good now, love, it's all good. You're safe now, and I'm going to keep it that way."

She lifted her head and smiled at him through her tears. "You still have green eyes."

"Sorry about that. Wes didn't say how long the potion would last." He brought one hand to her face. "Do you mind if I kiss you anyway, even though I look like a demon?"

He'd barely finished his sentence, when Winter's lips were on his and she was kissing him. He responded to her immediately, pulling her even tighter into his embrace, not wanting to ever let her go again.

"Well, looks like it all went well then," a familiar male voice suddenly said from a few feet away.

Reluctantly, Logan severed the kiss and turned his head to see Wesley and Virginia approaching.

"Your timing sucks, Wes," Logan said with a smirk.

"I can see that," Wes replied and exchanged a look with his wife.

Virginia stared right into Logan's eyes. "Still green like those of a demon. If I didn't know you were one of us, I'd be stabbing you with my dagger right now."

Logan smiled at her. "You do have a very talented husband."

Virginia glanced at Wes. "Oh, I know."

Wes grinned. "I am. But the GPS device didn't hold up. It went dead the moment the portal exploded. We had no idea if you made it or not. Until a few minutes ago, when the GPS kicked into high gear right here in San Francisco."

"Guess it doesn't work in the Underworld," Logan said.

"Would have been too good to be true," Virginia added, then nodded at Winter. "I'm glad you made it. But you know this isn't the end."

Winter sucked in a deep breath. "Will they let me live?"

Virginia gave her a reassuring smile. "It's up to you now to convince the council members. You already have my vote."

Logan sought Winter's gaze. "We can do this." Because failing wasn't an option.

36

All members of the Council of Nine were assembled, seven men and two women including Virginia, when Winter entered the chamber accompanied by Logan. Virginia had gone ahead and informed the council in broad strokes about what had happened after Logan had escaped the lead cell at the council compound. Aiden had joined her to directly appeal to his father for leniency, given that Winter's and Logan's actions had saved Barclay's family from certain death.

Now they were finally ready to hear Winter and Logan speak in their own defense, and decide their fate.

Winter didn't let her gaze linger too long on any individual council member, feeling intimidated in their presence. Instead she looked forward, fixing her eyes on the gavel in Barclay's hand. Logan had instructed her beforehand only to speak to the council once spoken to and show the utmost respect.

"Well, Logan," Barclay started, "it seems we all underestimated you."

Winter took a breath of relief. This sounded like good news.

"Not only did you act against the council's orders and subsequently lose your charge to the demons, no, you were also reckless enough to let your friends from Scanguards blow up one of our portals with you inside. Have you completely lost your mind? What if it had killed you instead of sending you into Zoltan's Underworld?"

"It worked, as you well know," Logan said.

Barclay growled. "Yes, it worked. That doesn't mean the council approves of your actions. What if you hadn't been able to come back? Then not only would the demons have a psychic at their mercy, but also a Stealth Guardian warrior.

Or did you not even consider this possibility before making such a foolhardy choice?"

Several councilmembers grumbled in agreement with their leader.

"I take full responsibility for my actions," Logan said. "However, I didn't go into this without a plan. I knew it would work, and I knew how to escape the Underworld. With Winter. I'd planned for every eventuality."

Winter dropped her lids, not wanting to catch anybody's eye, so they wouldn't see the doubt in them, because even she had wondered whether they'd make it out of the Underworld. She doubted that escaping a torture chamber by bridging a bubbling lava pit had been part of Logan's plan. There'd been plenty of improvising involved in her rescue.

"Then maybe you also planned for the psychic to be captured by the demons after you rescued Aiden and his family?" another councilmember chimed in, his words dripping with sarcasm.

"Since you mention the successful rescue of Aiden and his family, Councilmember Ian," Logan pivoted like a skillful politician, "that rescue would not have been possible without the help of said psychic." He motioned to Winter. "Winter saw the attack in her vision and—"

"Yes, yes, we're already aware of this," Ian said impatiently, "but what I'm trying to point out is that a psychic under your protection was snatched by the demons. It's the very reason the majority of this council voted to eliminate her."

At that Winter shivered. She hated that word. It sounded so clinical, yet it was cruel.

"With all due respect, councilmember," Logan said, his voice sounding even tighter, "Winter has proven to all of you that she can be of use to us. That her visions can save lives."

"Nobody is disputing that fact," Barclay calmly interjected.

Winter lifted her eyes and looked at Barclay, who sat in the middle of the crescent-shaped table. He did his best to look impartial, but she knew from Aiden that he was on her side. He was willing to let her live. But five others on the council weren't.

"Maybe it's time to let Winter speak for herself," Barclay said kindly.

A few councilmembers uttered their displeasure, but Barclay made a motion with his hand. "Any questions for the psychic?"

A woman raised her hand.

"Riona, go ahead."

The woman looked straight at her, and Winter had to meet her gaze in order not to appear rude. "When you were captured, what secrets did you divulge to the demons?"

"None!" Winter said immediately.

Riona raised her eyebrows. "Come, come, Miss Collins, according to the reports we received, you were a prisoner for over six hours, and you expect us to believe that in that time the demons weren't able to influence you in any way, be it by using their mental powers or by means of physical torture?" She let out a laugh. "I wasn't born yesterday, neither were my colleagues."

Winter felt her shoulders stiffen. This woman wouldn't be easily convinced. "Zoltan tried it with charm at first. He told me that your race isn't any better than his. That you kill just as indiscriminately as he does."

Gasps went through the assembly.

"His words, not mine," she said quickly. "But his charm didn't work on me. I wasn't fooled by his propaganda. So he tried to get into my mind."

"So you gave him information," Riona coaxed, and exchanged glances with her colleagues.

Winter shook her head. "I injured him."

Riona snapped her gaze back to Winter. "You did what?"

"I injured Zoltan, their leader. When he tried to get into my head, I fought back. My psychic powers pushed him out. My mind isn't like that of an ordinary human. I didn't know that until I met Gabriel, a vampire who works for Scanguards…"

"We know him," Barclay interjected. "Continue."

"Gabriel tried to help me with my visions, so I could learn to guide them, but the process failed. However, during that attempt, we learned that my mind is like a fortress. It won't allow any invasion. My mind will fight back and injure whomever is trying to invade it." She looked at Logan.

He nodded. They had discussed earlier what she would have to tell the council to win them over. He seemed pleased now.

"I burned Gabriel's face and hands. I injured a powerful vampire, and I injured Zoltan, the leader of the demons. I may not look like it, I may look physically weak, but I'm stronger than Zoltan. I'll never give in to him or his demons."

Murmurs went through the chamber.

"Barclay?" another councilmember asked.

"Go ahead, Cinead."

"Miss Collins, that may be the case. But would you have withstood physical torture?" Cinead asked.

"It never came to that," Winter said.

She pushed her chin up and looked at the man who'd spoken, hoping to dispel his doubts. He was about Barclay's age, a man who in human years looked like he was in his late forties, early fifties, but considering Logan was already two hundred years old, this councilmember was probably at least double Logan's age. However, it wasn't his age that made her look at him closer. His face looked familiar. As if they'd met before.

But before she could place him, Cinead continued, "But it will come to that if you fall into their hands again. What then?"

"That's an unfair question," Logan interrupted.

Cinead shot a displeased look at Logan. "It's a valid one. I want her to answer."

Cinead stared right at her, looking dominant and regal. She'd seen that look before. She knew where. She was certain of it. The man on the painting. The man with his wife and infant son.

"The child," Winter murmured, recalling her vision. "It was your son."

"Answer Cinead's question!" Riona interrupted.

Cinead put his hand on her forearm, stopping her, his eyes still pinned on Winter. "What child?" His voice was different now, colored with emotions that hadn't been present earlier.

"The baby in the crib. The one the demon stole."

Cinead shook his head. "Stole? No. My son... You're just making this up. You heard something. Somebody told you about my son... About his death..." His voice faltered.

"He had a birthmark on his butt cheek."

Cinead glared at Logan. "Did you put her up to this? I swear I'll challenge you to a fight if you did!"

"I never mentioned your son to Winter, I swear. Damn it, I never even mentioned you to Winter," Logan said.

Cinead's eyes landed back on Winter. "Let's get to the bottom of your tarot card mumbo-jumbo. What kind of birthmark?"

"It was odd, hard to describe."

"Just as I thought, you're lying. You had no vision about my son. You—"

"An axe. It looked like an axe."

Cinead gasped. His expression changed. Pain darkened his features. "You saw the demons kill my son?"

"No. Not kill. A demon came and took him out of the crib. Carefully, actually, as if he didn't want to hurt him."

"That's a lie! There was blood. They didn't even leave me his body to bury," Cinead cried out. "Goddamn it! Get her out of my sight! My vote stands! Eliminate her!"

"That wasn't your son's blood. The demon had a flask with blood. Red. Like a human's or an animal's, but it was blood. And he spilled it over the mattress and the sheets in the crib. He didn't harm the baby. He cradled your son to his chest as if he was precious. I followed him."

"Followed him?" Cinead echoed.

"In my vision. I followed him down the stairs, and there in the hallway of this mansion, your home, he conjured up a vortex and disappeared with the child. And I was left looking at a portrait of you with your wife and an infant in her arms. I swear it's what I saw. The baby was alive when the demon disappeared in the vortex."

"But..." Cinead exchanged looks with his colleagues, confusion and something else spreading on his face: hope.

Hope that his son was alive. "Are you aware how long ago this happened, Winter?"

She shook her head. "I can only guess from the type of furniture and the clothing you and your wife wore in the painting. Sometime in the Regency period."

Cinead nodded. "Over two hundred years ago my son was taken from me. I buried an empty coffin, and I grieved for him." Tears were welling up in his eyes. "Can I really believe that there's hope? That my son is alive?"

Winter stepped closer to the table, and nobody stopped her. Right in front of Cinead, she halted. "He was alive when the demon took him. If he wanted to kill your son, why not kill him right there and then? Wouldn't it have been worse having to see your son's mutilated body, knowing the pain he had suffered?" Winter shook her head and reached her hand across the table to clasp Cinead's. "I don't believe they killed him. They just wanted to make sure you thought he was dead so you would never come looking for him."

Cinead locked eyes with her. "Angus, his name was Angus." Then he looked toward the center of the table, where Barclay sat. "I would like to change my vote. I want Winter protected at all times."

Winter squeezed Cinead's hand.

"Will you help me find Angus?" he asked.

She nodded, tears now streaming down her face. Moments later, she felt Logan put his arms around her and pull her into an embrace.

Suddenly everybody was speaking at the same time, until Barclay's gavel sounded to call for order in the chamber.

"The vote has been changed. Winter Collins, you'll be assigned a permanent guardian for your protection. We will discuss everything further in another session. Now for Logan's punishment. Logan, considering the unusual events that have taken place, the council will reconvene at another time to discuss appropriate action, however, in the meantime the council will reduce the charge of treason to the lesser charge of insubordination. This meeting is adjourned." Barclay hit the gavel on the table once more.

"Thank you, Primus," Logan said and bowed.

Immediately the noise level escalated, while councilmembers rose from their seats, the doors opened, and Logan's friends, who'd been waiting outside, entered.

"You did it," Logan said to her. "You changed their minds."

"With your help."

He shook his head. "You didn't need my help." He smiled. "Why didn't you tell me about your vision earlier?"

"There was no time." She looked at Cinead, who'd now rounded the table and was heading their way. "I had the vision just after Zoltan tried to invade my mind, before he knocked me unconscious. I'd forgotten about it with everything else that happened in the last twenty-four hours." She smiled at Cinead. "But when I recognized you from the painting, it all came back."

"Was Zoltan the demon who kidnapped my son and staged his death?"

Winter shook her head. "I don't know. It was too dark in the room. And he wore a cloak and a hood. I only saw his green eyes for a moment, but I couldn't really see his face." She sighed. "I'm sorry. But I'll do everything I can to help you find Angus."

"If he's still alive," Cinead said, though he smiled with hope in his eyes.

"If he's not, I'll find out what happened to him. So you can have closure."

Cinead nodded and took her hands. "I misjudged you. Many of us did. I'm sorry for what we did to your grandmother. When we voted on you, we didn't know you were her granddaughter. Different last name, different cities, you know, there wasn't much time to look into your background. We were afraid that the demons would get to you."

"Like they'd gotten to my grandmother," Winter said. "I don't blame you or the council. Now that I've met Zoltan and know what he and his demons are capable of, I understand that you had to do what you did. My grandmother had a weakness, me." She glanced at Logan. "I'll never succumb to Zoltan. Because all I feel around me is strength. I can be strong for you, for all of you. I will be your eyes and ears."

Cinead squeezed her hands and released them. "You take good care of her, Logan. Winter is part of our family now. And we protect what's ours."

Part of our family. The words echoed in Winter's head and made her heart swell with joy.

She was part of something now.

She wasn't alone anymore.

37

Logan closed the door to his private quarters behind him. One week had passed since the council had revoked Winter's execution order. The council had been lenient with him, too, and had only issued a warning with regard to his insubordination.

"Winter?" he called out.

He heard sounds from the ensuite bathroom and walked toward the door just as Winter came out, dressed in a short bathrobe, her hair damp, her cheeks rosy.

God, how he loved this woman. He hadn't told her yet, not in those words. He didn't want to pressure her, didn't want her to think that because he'd saved her life, she owed him anything in return. But it hadn't stopped him from showering her with affection, or showing her with his body how much he desired her, adored her, loved her.

Looking at her now though, he knew he couldn't hold it in any longer. He had to confess what he wanted. And hope that she was ready.

"Logan," she murmured in that seductive way that always led to the same thing, him tearing her clothes off and burying his cock deep inside her. "You're back earlier than I expected."

With a smile, he walked toward her. "I hope that doesn't bother you."

She reached for his arm and pulled him closer. "I was thinking…"

"Yes?" He untied her robe's belt and slid his hands inside. Her skin was warm and soft.

"Oh," she sighed.

"You said you were thinking?" He caressed her hips before moving his hands up to her breasts.

"I can't remember now."

He squeezed her breasts gently, loving the feel of her firm flesh filling his palms. "Can't have been that important then." He dipped his head to brush a soft kiss to her lips, while he guided her back a step so her back connected with the wall. "You smell good. I bet you taste even better." He dropped down to his knees in front of her.

"Logan…"

But whatever else she wanted to say didn't leave her lips, because Logan was already pressing a kiss into her damp pubic hair. "Mmm." Then he gripped her leg and lifted it over his shoulder, so her thigh came to rest on it.

"You're crazy," she murmured on a panted breath.

"Yes, crazy about you." He brought his mouth to her nether lips and licked over them.

He'd done this a lot in the last week, pleasured her with his mouth before he'd rutted on her like an animal. She'd never once complained about being taken like that. Every single time she'd welcomed him with open arms and demanded he fuck her harder. They'd spent entire nights making love, and even when they'd fallen asleep, he hadn't severed contact with her. Many times he'd awoken in the middle of the night, more randy than a sailor on shore leave. At those times he'd woken her by driving his cock into her, and she'd moaned in pleasure and surrendered her body to him. But was she ready to surrender her heart to him, too?

Beneath his lips he felt Winter's flesh quiver. Her irregular breaths and her soft moans confirmed what he already knew. She was close to her climax. And at his mercy, because he'd learned how to draw out her orgasm, and how to bring it on. He'd learned that a long, slow lick of his tongue would tamp down her arousal, and that sucking her clit between his lips and pressing down could bring on an orgasm in an instant. Winter knew it, too.

"Logan, please!"

He heard her urgent plea and followed it. While he slid his middle finger into her succulent pussy, he drew her clit into his mouth.

A shaky breath burst from Winter's throat.

He pressed his lips together and thrust his finger into her to the hilt.

Winter's pussy spasmed around his finger and under his lips. He felt her knee buckle and steadied her with his free hand, until her orgasm ebbed.

Then without haste, he withdrew his finger from her, set her leg back on the floor and rose. He wrapped his arms around her inside her robe and held her tight.

"I love it when you come. It makes me so hard."

"How hard?"

He pressed his groin to her so she could feel him.

"I could do with that," she said with a suggestive look.

He chuckled. "Hold that thought. There's something else I want to do first."

"But you already—"

He silenced her with a kiss, then drew his head back. He took a deep breath. "I need to tell you something."

She hesitated. "About?"

"About our situation here."

"At the compound?"

He nodded. "I spoke to the council today."

"About my living here?"

"Yes. They've given me two choices. Since you're now allied with us and working for us as a psychic, the council has offered to set you up in your own secure compound, complete with 24/7 protection."

"But I already have 24/7 protection with you," she protested, a frown building on her forehead.

"I'm getting to that. I need to lay out all your options, so you know that whatever option you choose, you'll be safe from the demons. And you'll have everything you'll ever need. The council will take care of all your needs, your living expenses, everything."

She nodded. "You said options, plural. What's the other option?"

"The other option depends on how you feel about me."

"You know how I feel about you."

He sighed. "Actually, I don't. Not really. I know you're grateful that I saved your life, and I know you enjoy having sex with me. Just like I enjoy having sex with you."

"Is this where you tell me you enjoy the sex, but..." She pulled out of his arms. "Well, I guess it was too good to be true. I should have known. I mean, you never said the L-word. I just assumed that because you risked your life by coming to the Underworld to rescue me that it wasn't out of duty. It's okay."

He gripped her chin and made her look at him. Now he saw everything he needed to know. "No, it's not okay. And the reason I never said the L-word is because I didn't want you to say it back because you were grateful."

He pulled her back into his arms. "Winter, I love you. I know now that I should have told you how I felt the moment we were back from the Underworld. But I didn't want to push my luck. You'd only just forgiven me for what I'd done in the past and—"

She put a finger over his lips. "I love you, Logan. I wanted to tell you, but... I guess I didn't want to push my luck either."

Logan let out a relieved chuckle. "Look at us. Brave in so many ways, yet scared when it comes to love."

"Not anymore," she said and smiled. Then she lowered her hand to his crotch and pressed it against his erection. "Now were you gonna take me to bed and use this gorgeous cock to drive me wild?"

"Yeah, about that..."

She raised her eyebrows. "What now?"

"About that other option the council offered..."

"Yeah?"

"You have the option of living here, at the Baltimore compound, with me. Under one condition."

"Which is?"

"You would have to bond with me. To become my eternal mate."

"Is this a proposal?"

"What if it is?"

"Then you should probably get down on your knees," she suggested with a smirk.

"I believe I was just on my knees a minute ago."

"Yeah, but that was for something else."

"You're a very demanding woman."

"Is that a problem?"

He released her. "No. I like a challenge." He went down on one knee and looked up at her, serious now. "Winter, will you be my wife, my eternal mate, my forever?"

Tears brimmed at her eyes and she sniffled. "Yes, yes, of course. Oh Logan!"

He jumped up and kissed her. He lifted her into his arms and carried her to the bed, where he laid her on the sheets. She looked up at him, love and affection shining in her eyes. How had he ever been so blind not to see she loved him as much as he loved her? What had taken him so long?

"Can we have a short engagement?" she asked breathlessly.

"The shortest engagement you can think of." He began to get undressed. "This will be our wedding night." There was no need to wait, nor to explain to her that the bonding ritual would kill them both if their love wasn't true. He had no such fear, because their love for each other was real, true, and deep.

~ ~ ~

"Tonight?" Winter stared at him, trying to digest his words. Did he mean to say that they wouldn't have to waste time waiting for arrangements to be made, for a wedding to be planned, and all that useless stuff that went with it? "But we need a minister or some sort of government official, don't we?"

Undeterred, Logan continued shedding his clothes. "Stealth Guardians don't get married in the traditional way. We don't need a minister or a justice of the peace. There will be no witnesses."

"And it is legal?"

He rid himself of his last piece of clothing and slid one knee on the mattress beside her. "Oh, my love, it will not only be legal, it will be the strongest bond anybody can form. It will give you immortality and tie us together for eternity."

Immortality, eternity. Those words hummed in her body like a second heartbeat. "You mean I'll become like you? A Stealth Guardian?"

He rolled over her, pushing her legs apart to settle at her center, his cock poised at her pussy. "No. You'll still be a psychic, but you won't age, you'll remain young with me by your side. Because what we'll share tonight will tie our hearts together. Do you want this?"

Winter slid her hand to his nape and felt him shiver at the touch. "Yes, Logan, I want you, I want everything so we can be together forever. I love you."

She suddenly felt his cock jerk, and shifted to get closer, when Logan thrust forward and drove into her. "I love you, Winter, with all my heart." Seated deep inside her, he stilled and caressed her cheek. "Making love tonight will be different. It'll be the Stealth Guardian way. You'll feel things you've never felt until now. And through it, we'll bond."

"How?"

"Just follow my lead. I'll guide you."

She pulled his head to her and kissed him, showing him that she trusted him. Logan began to move inside her, his cock filling her, stretching her, so familiar, yet so exciting. They'd made love every night since they'd returned to the compound. And every night she'd felt as if it couldn't possibly get any better—and then it did. Logan was a passionate lover, a man with a healthy appetite and immense stamina.

She loved the way he looked at her when he made love to her, just like he did now. It made her feel like she was the only person in the world. And to know that he loved her, truly loved her without reservations was more than she'd ever hoped for.

She felt her heartbeat accelerate every time their bodies came together with one long thrust, connecting not just on a physical level, but on a spiritual one, too. Everything seemed to disappear, to blur, as if her vision was swimming. She blinked, wondering if she was crying with joy, but when she opened her eyes again, her vision was even blurrier than before. Around them, a mass of fog was swirling, and she felt as if they were floating.

"Wh—?"

"Don't be afraid, my love. I'm doing this," Logan said softly, and kissed her.

Then she felt it, felt an energy surge inside her, fill her, strengthen her. Every cell of her body seemed to rejuvenate. Her heart beat excitedly, her pulse drummed in her veins, and farther below, where Logan's cock drove into her, her muscles pulsed with renewed vigor. Her clit was close to exploding. The approach of an orgasm had never felt so intense.

Logan severed the kiss and pulled his head back. "I've given you my *virta*, my life force. Look at your arms."

She snapped her head to the side, lifted one arm closer to her face. "Oh my God!" Her skin shimmered golden. "What's happening to me?"

Logan slowed his thrusts. "I'm sharing myself with you."

Astonishment and wonder spread in her. "It's beautiful." Everything inside her felt free and strong.

"Now you have to send it back to me, to complete the circle." He looked at her hand. "Lay your hand over my heart."

Winter placed her hand over Logan's heart and watched in fascination. Her own heart seemed to suddenly be on fire—not in a destructive kind of way, but like a soothing flame. She felt that heat travel through her now, upward to her shoulder, then down along her arm. She could see the flames now, watched them travel to her hand and into her fingers. From there, tiny little sparks seemed to explode and pierce Logan's skin.

Logan threw his head back and groaned, but he didn't pull back, and she continued sending more of his virta back to him. She understood now, because she was connected to him. She saw his heart. Saw it beat for her, saw his love for her and knew it was true and strong. She saw his honor, his goodness, saw everything she loved about him. And she saw something else. She saw a vision of herself in the future. Herself and Logan, and the life they would create together. One day.

"Logan," she murmured, "oh, my love." Tears blurred her vision now and she allowed them to come. They were tears of joy and relief.

They would both live and love. They would be together. Happy.

She locked eyes with him. "You're mine now. My guardian. My hero. My love."

A soft smile played on his lips. "Nobody will ever take you away from me again. I promise." He brushed his lips to her. "And now it's time I pleasure my wife so she won't have any complaints about her new husband's performance in bed."

And Logan did just that. Indeed, she had no complaints, because it turned out that the golden shimmer his virta had left on her skin, was still there. And as long as she shimmered golden, every touch from Logan sent another wave of pleasure through her body, making her climax again and again.

38

Zoltan closed the vortex behind him with an angry flick of his head. Nothing was going his way. His idiot subjects had allowed a Stealth Guardian to steal his psychic from right under their noses. Imbeciles! Had those idiots not gotten themselves killed, Zoltan would have done it himself. But now there was nobody appropriate to punish. So he'd made his way to the human world. He needed to feed. Maybe that would tamp down the fury coursing through his veins.

He charged into the next alley. He knew his way around this area very well. This was drug central. He loved this neighborhood. On every corner there was a human who not only deserved to die, but was practically asking for it. And tonight he was in the mood for killing.

The dealer, who thought he was well-hidden in the entrance to a closed repair shop, was easy to spot. Zoltan marched toward him and cornered him in the entryway.

"What the fuck?" the jerk hissed and pulled a knife. "Get out of my fucking face."

Undeterred by the weak threat, Zoltan pressed the dealer against the door and snatched him by the throat. "No, I'm gonna get right in your face." He chuckled to himself. Did these stupid humans really think that a few strong words and a little blade of stainless steel would scare him? "I'm your master now. And I'm gonna suck the life out of you."

Normally, he would glare at him with his green eyes now, but Zoltan had donned his special colored contact lenses since feeding wasn't his only purpose for coming to the human world. He couldn't risk being recognized. Unable to frighten the drug dealer with his green eyes, Zoltan simply squeezed his throat tighter and concentrated on his mind.

"I'm taking your life force. I'm going to enjoy every last ounce of you before you die."

Finally the dealer seemed to realize that Zoltan meant business, but his struggles were fruitless. Fear rose in him. Zoltan could feel it call to him.

"I love the smell of your fear. Yes, give it to me." He leaned in closer and saw a white mist ooze from his victim's nostrils and mouth. "Yes, come to papa."

Zoltan sucked in the fear that streamed from his victim. With every breath, it nourished him, made him stronger, and displaced his fury and the disappointment he'd experienced yet again as a result of his subjects' incompetence.

He could feel the dealer's life force slowly extinguishing. He could stop feeding now if he wanted to, and leave the man alive, but tonight he felt no mercy. Tonight, he wanted to bring death. So he sucked harder and took more, took all of it, until all that was left of the drug dealer was a lifeless shell.

Zoltan let go of his neck and tossed him in the garbage where he belonged. He felt better now.

Strengthened, he marched out of the alley and made his way to a better area, one where fancy high-rises and classy restaurants had sprung up in the last years.

He reached into the pocket of his long coat and pulled out a key fob, swiped it on a pad at one of the high-rises and gained entry. The foyer was empty. He walked to the elevators and pressed the button. Moments later, a ping sounded. Zoltan waited for the doors to open. He was about to rush in, when he stopped, narrowly preventing himself from crashing into the woman coming out of it.

"Oh, excuse me," she said and looked him up and down.

"My apologies," Zoltan said quickly, and slid into the elevator, eager to get to his condo, already pressing the button for his floor.

"Mr. Vaughn, isn't it?"

He snapped his head to her, forcing a smile. "Evening, ma'am."

He pressed the button to close the door, hoping to avoid a conversation with the woman who inexplicably knew his assumed name, a name he'd taken a few years earlier together with the condo that belonged to the real Mr. Vaughn.

He'd tried to remain under the radar, sneaking in and out of the building at times when he was least likely to encounter the other residents. It appeared that despite being careful, somebody had taken notice of him. For a moment he wondered whether he should take care of her, make sure she wouldn't snoop around. But a person from his building disappearing might draw more attention to him than he wanted to deal with. It was best to instead keep an eye on her for now. He could always kill her later if necessary.

Zoltan slid his hand between the closing doors.

"Mrs. . . . ?" he asked.

"Rollins, my mailbox is next to yours."

"Ah!" he said with another forced smile. "So nice to finally meet you."

Now that he knew who she was, he allowed the doors to slowly close. "Have a good evening, Mrs. Rollins."

"Miss," she corrected him, just before the doors closed and the elevator started ascending.

Miss? Even better. At least there would be no pesky husband to get rid of if Miss Rollins turned into a problem.

When moments later Zoltan entered his condo, he let out a deep breath. He liked coming here. The luxurious place was a far cry from his lair in the Underworld. The view was breathtaking, and not having to deal with his stupid subjects for a few hours helped him recharge his batteries, particularly after the debilitating, migraine-like attacks that had been plaguing him for many years and were getting worse. Hiding those attacks from his underlings had become increasingly difficult.

But here, in his refuge, he could let himself go and be himself, or at least a version of himself, the version that now called itself Eric Vaughn.

It would only be for a few hours before he would have to return and be Zoltan, the Great One, again.

ABOUT THE AUTHOR

Tina Folsom was born in Germany and has been living in English speaking countries for over 25 years, since 2001 in San Francisco, where she's married to an American.

Tina has always been a bit of a globe trotter: after living in Lausanne, Switzerland, she briefly worked on a cruise ship in the Mediterranean, then lived a year in Munich, before moving to London. There, she became an accountant. But after 8 years she decided to move overseas.

In New York she studied drama at the American Academy of Dramatic Arts, then moved to Los Angeles a year later to pursue studies in screenwriting. This is also where she met her husband, who she followed to San Francisco three months after first meeting him.

In San Francisco, Tina worked as a tax accountant and even opened her own firm, then went into real estate, however, she missed writing. In 2008 she wrote her first romance and never looked back.

She's always loved vampires and decided that vampire and paranormal romance was her calling. She now has over 36 novels in English and dozens in other languages (Spanish, German, and French) and continues to write, as well as have her existing novels translated.

For more about Tina Folsom:

www.tinawritesromance.com
http://www.facebook.com/TinaFolsomFans
Twitter: @Tina_Folsom
Email: tina@tinawritesromance.com

Made in the USA
Las Vegas, NV
15 October 2021